Ren and Rory

Ren and Rory

Molly Ferguson

Pittington, Craig

Molly Ferguson

I would love to thank the people who helped me with this project, the people who read it and gave me feedback, who provided me with a few quotes to use, who designed the original book cover for it, and who were just generally encouraging to me about it: Priscilla Pittington, Danielle Craig, Kristin Ferguson, and Mel M.

To my talented friend Molly. It was an honor to not only read your book, but gain a connection with these characters and their world. I hope everyone enjoys the story of Ren and Rory as much as I did.— Priscilla Pittington

CONTENTS

Chapter 1: RENEE—New Beginnings (Saturday, December 14, 1996)

Everybody looked at me like a smaller version of Jenny. They said we had the same eyes, bone structure, and smile. But Jenny was a much harder worker than me—she took homework very seriously, worked extra hours babysitting loud, messy children for free sometimes, and did extra credit when she already had a hundred in the class. One time, her percent in English class was one-hundred ten percent. No one believed me, but it was true.

We were traveling down to a town called Friendly, Texas, from Maryland. I was feeling anything but friendly right now. Jenny was on her way back to college, still her first year. She'd taken a full load of classes during the summer, even more than the usual load for people, and had the Fall semester off. Even though it was still a long way off before starting Spring classes, she preferred coming back and getting settled.

Jenny graduated top of her class and obtained a huge scholarship, not that she needed it. During the ceremony, people kept asking me if we were sisters. *"No,"* I'd say through gritted teeth. *"We're cousins."* It didn't matter to me that Jenny was a high-ranking, gifted learner in advanced sciences, or that she might be the first to discover a cure for aids. She didn't care when my mother was destroyed five years back. When my mom had gone into a coma after a horrible motorcycle accident. When she wasn't strong enough to pull through, and my aunt thought it best to pull the cord. I didn't speak for a week. My mother had been traveling down south for a weekend vacation, and decided to hang out with some of her old high school buddies, most of which were guys, all with similar interests to her.

My aunt Sheila was ashamed of her younger sister. "Rowdy and rough sports are for *men*," she spat every night at dinner, reprimanding my mom as though she'd committed a felony. "It's despicable how you walk around with your head in the clouds and your need for adventure, and your, your..." she cringed, "your lack of proper manners!" They were polar opposites. When you looked at them, my mom had wild waves for hair that she dyed frequently, spoke in quick, broken sentences when she was excited, and wore nothing short of comfy t-shirts, old jeans, and worn sneakers. The only kind of movies she'd watch were action flicks. Sheila was the orderly, organized, clean-cut one from head to toe. Stick-straight hair parted down the middle with freshly-trimmed ends, dressed formally, and a crisp, articulate tongue. She watched heartstring-pulling romances with a box of tissues.

And that's who came to be my new guardian the weekend my mother never came home. Jenny cried that night, and Sheila remained at her side, patting little thirteen-year old Jenny on the back. "Jenny, your aunt just didn't know when to quit. She was reckless and rash. She'd been driving herself down this road for years now." Speaking as if my mother had a drug addiction, rather than a like for athletics.

Never again did Jenny cry about mom or speak of her existence. When I'd mention her name, she'd only stare at me blankly. I hated Sheila. She wasn't the least bit sad about my mother. And I hated

Jenny for being weak and asking my aunt 'how high' whenever asked to jump. But Sheila knew she couldn't do the same to me. I loved my mom dearly, and nothing would change that. And Sheila didn't like it when people didn't jump.

I'd been in that backseat for hours and fell asleep. I was almost in touch with a sweet dream when I heard a rough muffling sound. "Ren!" someone whispered and was shaking me. "Hey Ren, c'mon, get up!" It was Aunt Sheila. I glanced through the window. Jenny was already walking up the steps to the two fancy red doors of the hotel, with her bags in hand. "Grab a bag," Sheila said tiredly.

"Don't call me that," I hissed. My mom had named me *Renee.* Not *Ren.*

"I'll call you whatever I want," she snapped, patience all run out.

"Sheila..." I provoked. If she wasn't going to respect my birth name, why should I call her 'aunt'?

Sheila sucked in her breath and continued on.

I slowly got up and reached for the first item I saw. I noticed the nameplate on it in fancy writing: *Jenny.* Disgusted, I forced my-self to carry its heavy weight over my own small backpack over my shoulders. *What* could she possibly have in here? I'd thought she just packed clothes and bathroom necessities...

My eyes were clouded up with darkness. I had a sick feeling we were going to have to do more than one trip. As I got out of the car, I could feel the warm and humid air of a Southern night hit me like a door slammed in my face. It was December, but that didn't mean the south didn't still have humidity. I couldn't *wait* to get back home.

Sheila checked us in and snatched the key from the front desk with a tight-smile indicating how sullen she had grown waiting. "Goodnight!" the lady said, cheerfully waving as we headed up the velvety stairs with red rose patterns, my fingers running against the cold, shiny wooden railing. "Sleep well!"

There was a bathroom on the second floor that Jenny insisted on going to, because she couldn't make it to our room on time. Really, she only wanted to leave me alone with Sheila. Because whenever Sheila and I were alone, we almost always got into a huge argument.

So the two of us walked down the never-ending hallway in screaming silence, neither one turning her head or even acknowledging the other's presence. We arrived safely at the door, both of us unscathed.

My dad opened it before Sheila stuck the key in. He looked paler than usual, being the only full white person next to a Native American woman, and his mixed daughter with not a hint of white in her. "Hi," he said, looking tired. He'd traveled from Washington to meet us here, though Sheila had to pay for it. My dad had been unemployed for some time now. He'd already been falling down even before my mom had died. Then he fell into an even deeper depression afterwards, and even with the little money he'd gotten from checks or unemployment, he spent it unwisely. Tonight, Sheila thought that, even with his irresponsibility, I'd feel a little bit better with him here. I could see the red veins surrounding his green irises.

I may have also forgotten to mention that I was born out of wedlock. My parents had never married, but they both loved and were there for me. It was why Sheila was the one to get full custody of me rather than my dad. I had the feeling though, that even if he and my mom had been married, she still would've won. He had enough trouble supporting himself, let alone a teenager. And people always looked at the woman as the more qualified one anyhow.

But I was still bitter, and I was bitter about the fact that I seemed to be the only one who was bitter with Sheila. I wished she hadn't pulled the cord. I remembered how I unspeakably despised her for so many years after that, and probably still do. If it had been a volcanic eruption before, it was still a forest fire now. It hadn't died down that much. *"Why'd you do it?"* I had asked in a low, angry monotone, not really sounding like a question.

"She's not going to wake up," he'd responded. I guessed it was like severing her life from Earth would at least make something certain for us. Make something definite. Instead of waiting, waiting, and waiting to see if she'd come out of it. When the truth was, and we both knew it, she wasn't going to.

For a long time after that, all he did was apologize to me, and I acted like a spoiled brat. He tried unsuccessfully to set up nights where we could go out to dinner, just the two of us, father and daughter. The more time passed, the softer I grew toward him. Until I finally couldn't stay mad at him any longer. And I couldn't deny that he was all I had left.

"Dad!" I said. I sounded like a little girl and walked into his arms. I buried my face in his neck-length blonde hair. He looked younger than thirty-eight.

"Hey there, Renee," he said laughing. "How are you dear?"

"Great."

"You've finally grown! Why don't you all settle in and relax? You must be exhausted."

"Are we ever!" Sheila replied, flinging her bags on the bed. "I'm just about ready to hit the mattress."

"I think that lady did something wrong," Jenny scoffed, walking through the door after us. "It smells like smoke in here. She guaranteed us a 'no-smoking' room."

Actually she had just said "Sleep well."

"She probably made a mistake," my father said.

Sheila's nostril flared. "Hm. It does smell a bit stuffy in here. I'll just open the window a little."

"This world is full of mistakes," Jenny muttered under her breath while glancing in my direction.

I poured my belongings on the ground next to my bed. Sheila turned on the TV and she and my dad got into a conversation about how some politicians were full of shit. Jenny went to the bathroom to shower. I pulled out my notepad and started sketching a party dress with a short denim jacket and matching hat. If I just got into a decent college (which I should have no problem with), I could get away from Sheila and Jenny and work to get an acceptable career. But if I got accepted to design school...that would be wonderful. It had always been my dream to create clothes for different people, *ordinary* people. Not elaborate costumes you *ooh* and *ahh* at on runways in Paris and New York, but no one ever actually wore them.

Sheila got up and clapped her hands. "Okay everybody, time for bed. Ren, you start school on Monday."

I dropped my pen. There were a couple seconds of silence. "Huh? No I don't..." I said. "You said we don't get back to Maryland until Wednesday of next week."

"I lied," she said bluntly. "We're staying here. I sold our house, and the rest of our belongings are soon to come by shipment. And I enrolled you at a new high school here."

"What?!" I screamed. "You—but—I—"

"Well, I just couldn't resist the offer I got here at the sleek new salon a few blocks away. Your father is here, and this way, Jenny won't be all alone. She can come home instead of sleeping in a dorm. Less money for all of us. You *do* want to save money, especially in the hopes of going to design school, right Ren?"

So that's how it was going to be. Manipulation.

"I bought a brand new house. The cost of living is so much cheaper than in Maryland. You'll love it. Two separate bathrooms, a shaded deck, and a basement."

"I liked our old house," I mumbled. It was a lame response, but I couldn't help it. I would not let her weasel out of this. "And what about your old salon?" Now it was my turn.

"*That* shack?" she asked, dripping with sarcasm. "Oh yes, that was an awfully beautiful place to work. Cockroaches in every room, a fan that didn't work, chair cushions older than me..."

I gritted my teeth. "How long have you been planning this?"

"For a while now."

"*What?*" I shrieked.

My dad grabbed my arm and shushed me. "Renee, please, there are people sleeping next door!" he hissed.

I lowered my voice. "How could you *do* this to me?" I didn't feel sleepy anymore. I felt like going for a run, race against the adrenaline, the harm that had just been done. I would never see my best friend, Jasmine, again. Did she know about this? I had to call her immediately.

"There will be no calls to her," Sheila said, grabbing the phone from me and placing it firmly back on the hook. "We all need our sleep. It's well past midnight."

"You lying, vindictive, BITCH!"

Sheila gasped, every remnant of calmness drained from her face. "Your behavior is an outrage! Do you have any idea how much trouble I go through just to take care of you? Do you know how ungrateful you are? This may not be what you like, but get used to it, because I'm not your mother."

"SHEILA!" my dad yelled. So much for the people next door.

Sheila, eyes wide, held out her hands, as though she had no choice for what she was doing. My dad exhaled slowly, trying to keep his temper under control. "Now you know. I'm sorry I didn't tell you. I didn't know it was official until Sheila here announced she bought the place."

That was all there was to it. Arguing wouldn't get our house back nor would it enroll me back into the same high school of people I grew up loving and loving to hate; the same neighborhood I first learned to walk, ride a bike, climb the monkey bars; the same place I went trick-or-treating for the first time, went to my first Homecoming, and *was* going to go to junior Prom this year. I had laughed and joked around and acted like a dork with my friends. I'd had fun.

***

It was now one-thirty. I was exhausted, and thankful the next day wasn't Monday. What would Monday be like? I wasn't good with new schools. I'd had only two experiences, and each sent me happily back to my original, which had been in the same town. This was across the country.

As soon as everyone else went to bed, I laid my head down, crying softly into the pillow and the dark. The darkness didn't wipe my tears away or change time. But there was something about it that was comforting. It embraced me. It made everything invisible. It blanketed me against the cold, confusing, and unknown world.

Chapter 2: RENEE—Anger Is Just One Letter Short Of Danger... (Sunday, December 15, 1996)

"Hi...Jasmine?"

She gasped. "Ren!"

"Did I wake you?"

"No, no, I just didn't expect to hear from you so soon. How's the trip been?" she asked excitedly.

"Well...um...not good." I paused. "It's not just a trip. We're staying."

There was a long pause. "Staying?"

What an evil word 'staying' had become. "Yes," I said slowly, not even looking at the phone, as if not wanting to look in a person's eyes when you had bad news. "Sheila is making me."

"Ren, I...I don't know what to say." She was never the type to say 'I'm so sorry for your predicament', which I appreciated. It sounded too close to pity when people said that, which I hated.

"I know," I said. "Sheila can rot in hell."

"Hm. She could've told you much sooner. Jesus."

"I'll keep calling you. I'll keep writing to you."

"I know," she said. "And I enjoy hearing from you. But don't pressure yourself, Renee."

I sighed. I was still so tired and in shock that I literally didn't have the energy to cry.

"But Ren, I have some spectacular news, and I hope it cheers you up at a little."

My curiosity peaked. What could possibly cheer me up when I couldn't even see my best friend anymore?

"Next summer, my family's traveling to Europe. To the U.K. specifically, but probably other parts as well. And—mom and dad said I could bring at least one friend!"

I gasped. "No..."

"Yes. Say YES, Renee. You'll get to see a fashion show maybe, get some inspiration. I know it might not be your taste of clothes of course, but—and we'll get to see Big Ben! And ride on the other side of cars. And maybe go to a Europop concert!"

Her bubbly excitement was contagious to me, and for just a moment, I forgot about my troubles. "I'll do everything I can to help make it happen, Jasmine."

Unfortunately, as soon as I hung up the phone, I returned to reality and remembered that there were obstacles in the way. Human obstacles.

"Why are you smiling?" Sheila asked suspiciously. It would suit her to be annoyed at the fact that I still even had the ability to smile.

"Oh, um, I just got an invitation from Jasmine. To go to Europe."

Sheila's eyebrows rose in astonishment. "Oh," she breathed. She'd always wanted to go to Europe too. "And just when might this be?"

"Next summer."

"You can't go."

Repressing the urge to scream again, I took a deep breath and asked, "Why?"

"Next summer will be one of your final summers. You have to get a job and work very hard at it. You think those college books are going to pay for themselves?"

"Dad," I asked calmly when he entered the room, "can I go to Europe next summer?"

He almost choked on his coffee. "Why?"

"Jasmine invited me."

"We'll think about it, honey."

"Can I go visit some friends up in North Carolina Sunday?" Jenny called from the bathroom.

"Sure," Sheila replied without hesitation.

"Why does she get to visit friends? Mine would be in the summer. She's just returning from break to *college,* Sheila. She'll have a lot of work to do," I stated very truthfully.

"Because I can trust her."

"You can trust me too," I said through clenched teeth.

Jenny came out of the bathroom in a tube top, a jean mini skirt, and a pair of knee-high, chunky-heeled, platform boots.

"You trust her in *that* when it's December?"

"First off, we're inside. Secondly, it seems like you're just mad you've yet to grow into a body like mine," Jenny said to me, smirking.

"Well, I guess it's good you have it, since you're the one aiming to make a career out of it."

To be honest, I never had evidence of Jenny doing anything remotely sexual. But when curvy girls who showed lots of skin made fun of my flat-chested figure, I had to strike somewhere.

Jenny's mouth hung open, about to let loose an equally inappropriate insult or a string of swear words when my dad intervened.

"Enough!" We both fell silent. "How about you two girls go out for breakfast somewhere? It will give Sheila and I time to move our belongings into the new house." In other words, *We need you out of the way. Shoo.*

We both grimaced as we got ready. I wrote a note reminding myself to write a letter to Jasmine as soon as possible, and left it on my bed. Jenny combed through her hair and put on some lip gloss.

My dad caught my arm before we left. "Renee." He had a worried look on his face and then smiled awkwardly. "Uh...please remember to eat plenty."

"Dad, stop it," I said sharply.

"I'm just worried," he said, sounding hurt. "You're very thin—"

No, I just don't have the physique of a grown woman. "I'm fine," I responded. "Just leave me alone." I unintentionally slammed the door.

***

There was a breakfast restaurant within walking distance from the hotel. While we walked down the sidewalk, Jenny and I kept our distance from each other as much as possible, trying to act like strangers. We could've passed for it too.

I saw a boy leaning against a brick building. He was slender with skin so pale, it was almost *literally* white. Black hair fell all around his prominent face. He leaned against the brick wall, a dazed, confused expression on his face. He just stared off into the distance, eyebrows arched, the occasional breeze blowing at his hair.

"What are you looking at? Come *on!*" Jenny said, snapping me out of my trance. She grabbed my arm and kept me moving forward. I glanced back, but he was gone.

***

Jenny and I got a table for two and sat there for about five minutes until a tall Asian boy came over with a pen and notepad in hand and took our orders. I tried to avoid gazing at my reflection in the metal napkin holder—braces and thick-rimmed glasses. My eyes followed him after he took our order. Sheila would gag if she saw him. Part of his hair was dyed bright purple, with side-swept bangs, and he had a lip piercing. Off-limits, as far as Sheila was concerned.

Jenny got up to go to the bathroom. A minute after she left, the boy came back. He couldn't have gotten our food that quickly. "Hi," he said. "Um...mind if I sit down?"

I was surprised, but then, there weren't many people in here. I guessed the place wasn't that busy today.

"Go ahead," I replied.

He slid into the booth next to me. "I um..." He glanced around awkwardly before settling his eyes back on me. "Well, I heard your sister when she was coming out of the bathroom, talking to mine." He nodded his head over in the direction towards the entrance. Sure enough, Jenny was talking to some brunette who looked to be a couple years older. I noticed she was wearing a college shirt, with the same logo as the one on Jenny's hat. "And I heard her say she didn't really have anything important to do, and that she was 'finished' with her meal. Sounds like she was going to ditch you and leave you to pay the bill." He looked down, blushing.

"She's my cousin, actually. And she's really a bitch."

He smiled. "I can still get you some breakfast. For free, if you'd like."

"Actually, no. That's alright."

"What's your name?"

"Renee. Renee Brenner."

"Hey Renee, I'm Jeremiah Martin. Nice to meet you. Are you new here?"

"Yeah, I just got here last night, actually."

"Then I guess you want to meet new people, don't you." I nodded. "Want to meet my girlfriend over there? It won't take long."

I smiled and got up, following him. He led me toward the back corner of the restaurant. A young black girl, shorter than me, sat fiddling around with the jukebox at her table. She was very pretty. Long black hair dyed hot pink on the ends, a small pink and black jacket, a choker around her neck, and dark-red painted nails.

"Hey Sidney, this is Renee," Jeremiah said.

The girl turned to me and smiled. Her white teeth contrasted her dark skin. "Hi. I'm Sidney Wilcox." We shook hands. "I've never seen you around before. Friendly is a pretty small town."

"She just moved here," Jeremiah said.

"Oh, where from? Are you going to our high school?"

"Maryland," I replied. "And yeah, probably. Wilcox High?"

"Yep, that's the one," Sidney laughed. "Me and my brother Sonny get teased about that all the time." She glanced at her watch. "Oh crap. I've got to go meet my boss—or hopefully future boss. I'm applying for a job, and I have an interview set up in about two hours. Maybe we can hang out later."

"Yeah, that'd be nice."

"Well, you want to meet somewhere at around three? You know where...the Robertson movie theater is? On Main Street? They show older films."

I remembered passing it on my way here with Jenny. "Yeah."

"Jeremiah and I were planning to see *The Lost Boys.*"

"Again?" Jeremiah moaned. "We saw it during Halloween, we saw it during the summer..."

"Want to join us?" Sidney asked me, ignoring him. "Don't worry," she added quickly when I started to say I had no money, "On me."

"Really? That's neat!"

"Great! So we'll meet you in the front at around three? It starts at three-ten. That sound good?"

"Yeah," I said returning the smile. "That's sounds good."

Jeremiah playfully knuckled Sidney's head as I waved goodbye and walked out in higher spirits.

***

I was delighted. I didn't have to be back at my new house until dark. Funny how Sheila used various excuses to keep me away from my friends, yet she let me roam about by myself whenever and wherever I wanted. Maybe I should just sneak out to go with Jasmine next summer. Yeah. Sneak off to Europe.

When I met up with Sidney and Jeremiah at the theater later, it turned out that it was closed because of a sudden water leak and damage. "That just figures!" Sidney scolded, kicking the ground. "Well, come on. Want to go to the ice cream parlor down the road? My treat."

When we arrived, I was impressed by how cozy the parlor looked. Instead of just being a small place with plastic tables and chairs, there were stools, booths, and even a floral couch on the far side of the room. The small television in the ceiling corner was running an ad for a movie this Friday, though I wasn't sure how anyone was supposed to hear it with the metal song playing from the speakers. Sidney pointed to the TV. "I want to see that." It was a slasher flick that would feature a new masked assailant that got off on murdering teenagers. Couldn't tell whether it was supposed to be strictly horror or also a dark comedy.

Jeremiah and I each got a chocolate milkshake while Sidney got two scoops of mint chocolate chip. As soon as we sat down, Jeremiah said, "Just heading to the bathroom," nuzzling Sidney's neck.

"Oh, you're here too," came a deep voice. A shorter but more muscular guy, wearing a flannel hoodie and a backwards baseball cap was sitting a few tables down.

"Hey Sonny!" Sidney waved at him. "What are you doing here?"

Sonny also shared Sidney's bone structure and wide round eyes. I could instantly tell they were brother and sister.

"What do you mean 'What are you doing here'?" he asked in mock outrage. "It's ice cream."

"This is Renee."

"Hi Renee, nice to meet you," he said, shaking my hand. "You've now met the better sibling."

He dodged a slap from Sidney. "Sonny's the older one," she said to me. "I know, hard to believe."

"Only because I'm the fun one," Sonny retorted.

"Shouldn't you be at home working on your science project?" She put her hand to her chin and glanced over to the bathroom. "Come to think of it, it's also Jeremiah's project."

"We're getting our energy," Sonny said, gesturing to his Hershey-drizzled sundae.

"Sonny!" Jeremiah said, arriving back. "Perfect timing."

The TV now played a music video, matching the song on the speakers. It featured people forming a circle around the artist. It was too fascinating to take my eyes away from it. Then a new song came on, very much the opposite of what had just played. It was a slow and sad love song, something about walking out of someone's life.

"Awww...you two should slow dance to this," Sonny said. "Or maybe one of you can lip sync it outside the other's window when you have a fight."

"As if," Sidney said, making a face.

When we all finished our treats, Sidney turned to me and said, "You want to come to our place for a little while?"

"Sure."

Sidney lived down the block. She had a fancy room to match her bubbly personality. Black curtains, maroon velvet pillows, a blood-red lava lamp on her black wooden desk. Posters of Tim Burton,

Punk bands, and Japanese rock musicians lay across her black walls. She also had a volleyball trophy sitting atop her bureau. She talked about how her family went on vacation most summers, and that one year, they actually went out of the country—to Japan. I'd wondered how she knew so much about it. She'd even made a friend there who gradually was learning English, and they wrote back and forth to each other from across the world. "I'm going to tell her we should start emailing," Sidney said. "It'll be easier. The electronic age is upon us."

We sat on her bed and she showed me old horror movie tapes she owned, old monster comic books, and old kids' TV shows and movies we'd both watched when we were little. "Hey, maybe on Friday we can check out that new slasher flick coming out."

"Erm…" I said. Truthfully I was a complete chicken when it came to horror movies. I eyed one of the cartoons she had laid out on the bed.

Sidney laughed. "It's okay if you don't want to."

Suddenly Jeremiah walked in wearing black jeans but no shirt.

"Jerry!" Sidney laughed. "Put a shirt on, you pervert," she joked.

"Why? It's hot as hell in here."

"Not hot, humid." Understandable, since I began to hear thunder outside.

"Besides," Jeremiah continued, "I feel more comfortable without a shirt. I don't really like clothes that much."

"That's nice."

"What was it like where you're from, Renee?" Sidney asked, turning to me.

"Much cooler. Maryland is probably freezing right about now."

I heard Sonny call from outside the room, "I wonder if we'll ever get a White Christmas."

"We won't," Sidney said sadly.

"You never know," I said. "I've heard there's even been times when Florida's gotten snow."

Sidney snorted. "Only a light dusting, and even that happens once in a blue moon."

"There's been reports of snowfall there before. In fact, one city had its first White Christmas just back in '89. Hey Jerry," Sonny asked. "Are we going to do it or not?"

"Yeah, in a sec." Jerry pulled on a shirt. "Well, you two girls have fun. We have science to do."

***

On my way home, I headed toward the bookstore, next to the theater. I decided to make a pitstop, taking a look inside.

He was standing right near the posters. The same boy that caught my eye earlier. "See you, Rory," someone said, patting him on the back as they walked by. He flinched a little, but just nodded.

The old man from behind the counter got a bad vibe from him. I couldn't see why until I saw the boy—Rory—over at the revolving display of bookmarks. He walked over to the magazine stand and picked one up.

He held it closely, eyeing it like prey, flipping through it. His face was all the way relaxed, completely emotionless. Then it turned to disgust as he flipped back to the cover. He promptly ripped it into shreds, and the floor was covered with little scraps of paper.

The cashier's eyes practically bulged out of his head. "You'll—you'll have to pay for that, young man."

Rory just glared back. He dug in his pocket and slammed down a couple dollars on the register desk.

"Good. Now you can just leave. And never come again," the cashier scolded.

Rory turned on his heel, his jaw clenched.

It wasn't until then I realized I'd been holding my breath. I went on looking through the shelves of books, acting like I hadn't noticed, but wondering what the hell just happened.

As I passed the magazine rack, I saw one of the pieces of shreds. Picking it up, I briefly read a quote saying, *"Child abuse is a boy-who-cried-wolf phenomenon—kids who get bad grades or speak out of turn, deserve a whooping. Discipline is no longer accepted as it once was.*

Chapter 3: RORY- Good Morning (Monday, December 16, 1996)

I jumped at the sudden sound of my alarm clock. It sounded like the screaming I had heard hours earlier, except not as bad. At two a.m., I'd tried to block out the sound with my headphones blasting as loud as possible. What a good thing it was we didn't live in condominiums.

My sore arms were under my pillow, because I had been lying on my stomach. I slowly reached out and turned it off. I slipped out of bed and reached for the first item I could pull out of my closet.

I threw all articles of clothing on as fast as possible in a quick rush to escape the chill of the house. I still felt the goosebumps erupt on my arms underneath. We couldn't afford heat for the cold mornings, due to the low wages my mom made. At least she worked. More than I could say for my dad.

After I dressed, I made my way across the pint-sized room, only to slip and go straight for the cold hard wooden floor. Lying in pain for a couple seconds, I sat up to realize the object was the mirror I shattered the night before. My hand was bleeding. I sat there fuming for a few seconds and jerked my head to the side to get my hair out of my eyes.

It was only six and I was already angry. I hated mirrors. When I looked at myself, deeper beyond my own individual features, I saw something cold, mean, and hard. It made me wonder at times if I was slowly transforming into my own horror. A horror I didn't know how my mom could've married.

I stomped into the bathroom, slamming the door so hard it shook the whole room. The cobwebs in the corner of the ceiling shook.

It wasn't difficult to trigger my temper these days. Things that didn't matter all that much back then irritated me now. Habit picked up from my father.

Immediately, I turned on the faucet and ran my bloody hand under the warm running water, hanging my head low to avoid looking in the mirror. After a few seconds, I grabbed the towel, and looked up at my reflection. Even if you tried your hardest, if it was there in front of you, you will look no matter what. I was surprised it didn't crack, as I stared myself down like a cat ready to pounce on its prey. There were dark bags under my eyes. I'd probably start aging once I was in my twenties while everyone else wouldn't start until their forties or fifties. And when was the last time I smiled?

As soon as I bandaged the wound up, I passed by my room again and saw the broken glass. I'd be lying if I said I wasn't scared. This one little sear in the skin would be nothing compared to what's to come. *Would he be mad I broke the mirror?*

I stomped downstairs and entered the kitchen to get some toast. My mom's new co-worker was already down there talking to my mom. *Great.* Why had my mom invited her here? This was no place for guests.

The woman glanced at me, frowned, and whispered something into my mom's ear. A look of annoyance spread over my mom's face.

When she heard a yawn from the next room over, a brief flash of fear crossed her face before she fixed it back to normal again.

"Okay, well I've got to go finish running a few errands before work." The woman seemed like she was from the opposite world from us. Dressed up, clean and crisp, with long perfectly straight hair that made it unsurprising that she worked in a salon. My mother had barely combed hers yet. "Are you sure you don't want a ride to the salon?" her coworker asked.

"Uh—no hun, that's fine. I'll be right over." My mom sure was good at putting on an act.

My mom's expression, however, went back to fearful once her co-worker left the house. I wondered if our guest could smell the beer...or if she noticed how messy some parts of the house were. She was the kind of person who would comment on it too.

"What was *she* doing here?" I asked, sharper than I intended.

"Oh Rory, she was only here for a few seconds. Calm down." My mother brushed tiny strands of brown hair out of her eyes.

I realized that I was standing there staring at her right arm. It was badly damaged, not the color it should've been. "Wh-what... did..."

"I—well—you see, I shouldn't have...it's just a little burn mark." she stammered.

"Oh yeah, it's a burn mark alright." I said, appalled. It wasn't little though.

"Look, it was my own fault. I shouldn't have—"

"Mom. Please."

She didn't say anything else for a couple minutes until finally, "Your father would like to see you." Not *Darryl*. Not *My husband*. 'Your father'.

I entered the living room. It used to be colorful with toys and stuffed animals back twelve years ago when things were a bit jollier. Now it was dark, grey, and dusty. More like an attic than a room for families. And the only little bit of light that shown were the rays slipping through the small and cracked window. How the crack got there was a forgotten tale.

He sat there on the couch. Hands in a steeple together in front of his face. His eyes were purple and sunken. He was dazing off into the distance, perhaps reaching for something outside. I didn't understand why he was like this, especially towards me. If he didn't want me, he could've just dumped what he had into a garbage can around an alley corner way back when.

His eyes moved up toward me and nothing else. "Did you break my mirror?" he asked behind his hands, a little muffled. Everything in the house was his.

"Yes," I said looking at my feet, "b-but—"

"B-b-b-but..." he said, mocking me. He stood up and walked over, towering over me. He swayed a little. His words slurred a little, but he was still in control. He was always in control. You couldn't overpower him and you couldn't stop him either.

"I'll replace it," I stuttered, silently berating myself for sounding so pitiful. "It's just a mirror. I'll pay for it."

"OH, you sure will..." and he whirled around and slapped me across the face so hard I thought he left a print there. The sound of it hurt my ears. I bet it could've been heard from outside. I had twirled around and banged against the wall like a horrible bird who couldn't fly. Then he used one big, saucer-like hand to grab a handful of my hair and the other to hold me up and pin me against the wall. My face was pressed against the rough, hard, chipped wall. His mouth was so close to my ear, I could smell his nauseating breath, and almost feel his teeth.

"You will...NEVER touch anything in this house again. Got it? You have anger like me? Deal with it. I have my way...you get yours. Destruction of items will not be tolerated."

But destruction of people apparently is, I didn't say.

He wasn't mad because of the value of the mirror. He was mad because that was one less thing now he could destroy.

He sucked in a breath. "You're just like your mother," he growled in disgust. "Weak, pathetic, and *worthless.*"

After he released my scalp I returned to the kitchen, just in time to catch my mom slipping from the wet counter and using her wrist to break the fall. Her injured wrist.

She yelped out in pain. I bent down to help her up. She was so skinny and so frail. She was in so much excruciating pain that she was only seconds away from tears. "Mom—"

She yanked away from me and a slow sobbing sound began to erupt from her, growing faster by the minute. She grasped a chair and pulled herself up. She sat at the table and hid her face.

"Mom..." I began. "There's nothing I could've done."

"I know."

"If you want me to, I can get a nurse to look at it."

"No, Rory. Look, why do you always get him so ANGRY?"

My mouth dropped. I just stood there staring back at her. Then I lowered my eyes. "Go to work mom," I said abruptly.

"I can't. I feel sick."

"Then don't go."

"*Rory!* How're we going to eat then?"

"I don't know, why do I have to make the goddamn decisions around here?" I shouted.

She started sobbing all over again. I sighed and ran my fingers through my hair, trying my best not to yank the strands out by the root.

Suddenly I felt something big and strong grip the back of my shirt and pull me off my feet like a tornado. I spun around.

"Wash the dishes," he said in a low voice.

I walked over to the sink, fuming, and started the dishes. It was hard when you had to be the parent.

"Why are you still here?" he snarled at my mom. "Go to work, damn it! Do you think our food is just going to grow off the trees?" I watched him shove my mother, a woman who was a third of his size and strength and one that was already hurt for that matter, up against the wall.

I turned around, my fist shaking and sweating, trying to keep control of the plate I was holding.

Not enough control. My dad whirled around again and whipped the plate right out of my hand. It crashed to the floor loudly and shattered into a million pieces.

His face blazed at me now with eyes on fire. He pointed to the floor. "Pick it up."

"You pick it up."

I felt a sharp pain drive up my knee and then another one in my neck. I gasped and felt the hard floor meet my forehead instantly.

I sat up seeing lights dancing around my eyes, wondering what the hell had just happened. I heard loud steps that became louder and louder. I turned my head about an inch toward the sound and it froze involuntarily in place.

My heart was in my stomach and in my throat at once. He had his hand wrapped around my neck. It didn't hurt because he wasn't actually pressing down or anything, but I knew it was like a viper ready to strike at any minute. "Don't challenge me." His breath washed over me and I almost fainted. "Understand?"

He didn't wait for an answer. He just got up, releasing his hand. Even though it hadn't squeezed, I felt like I could breathe again. I noticed mom was no longer around. The front door was wide open and her shoes were gone. She must've fled to work after all. Just like she did every morning. So much for going out of my way to try to save her ass every so often. She couldn't even try the same for me.

My mom used to be completely different. She'd cook fancy meals from recipes in her cookbook, knit mittens for us in the wintertime, and take me and my brother, as little children, to the pond in the park to feed the ducks. Back then, she used to be healthier too. More color to her face, happier eyes, and more meat on her bones.

I lay there panting for a few seconds. I worked on steadying my breath and trying not to hyperventilate. I had a big heavy lump in my throat. *Calm down*, I told myself. *It'll be fine.*

Deep inside, I never truly meant it. But I learned to get through the day—and be focused on the fact that I could wake to see a new one. I couldn't let anyone, including myself, believe that I was weak—it would kill me. So I just had to let it slip by and avoid it as much as possible. Lie. *Everything's okay.*

When I had the chance, I got everything I needed and walked out. Usually I would slip out the back door, but something told me he was lurking out there, on the porch, with more beer. I couldn't risk it or I'd be late for school. As I walked by the coat rack, I saw some dents in the wall. I shuddered and walked past.

It wasn't always this bad. Not before my brother left. Even though there was still the anger, still the occasional bruises, and still worried questions and glances from teachers who had no business, it didn't happen quite as often. I spent the entire second grade making up excuse after excuse. *"I fell off my bike,"* or *"I slipped. I tripped over some rocks."* These were so obviously overused that I got even stranger looks. But back then, it only happened about once or twice a year. Now it happened every week.

Lately, it had gotten more severe. My dad had taken it to a new level. Burn marks from curling irons, threats with knives, even forcing me to sleep outside at one point by locking me out. In the chilly weather.

As I stumbled down the steps, I had a strange feeling someone was watching me.

4

Chapter 4: RENEE-A Torn Piece of Memory (Monday, December 16, 1996)

The next morning was full of disaster. I was already tired as it was from not being able to sleep all night. We'd just started moving into the house, and I was exhausted from not only all the things I'd helped carry in, but also the thought of a lot MORE we'd have to do later. The movers at least got our beds, couches, and furniture in. We still didn't have air-conditioning or heat, and while it may be cold in the morning and at night, it was still humid later.

It all started when Jenny came running into my room, whining. I could've cared if it was something serious. But no. Apparently, someone had moved her clothes out of place. And her comb. *A comb.* But the thing was, her clothes were never in place. They were scattered all over the place as if she was the only one who lived here. I couldn't even walk through the bathroom (which we had to share since there was only one) without tripping on something of hers. So sometimes I'd moved them out of my way. Simple as that.

Finally she calmed down and went back to doing the one thing she did best aside from schoolwork—making a mess. I got a good glimpse of her room. The only organization was in her numerous Shakespeare and science books lined up on the top shelf. I never understood how she and Sheila got along so well, being complete opposites when it came to mess, Sheila being a clean and pristine freak.

"Renee, where did you put my comb?" Jenny asked.

"On the sink, out of my way."

Jenny's fists shook and then she yelled something to me in French. I didn't know what it was, but I was willing to bet it had a bunch of swearing in it. How could someone so stuck up and stupid be so smart? She read Shakespeare, was practically fluent in French, and actually found math and science to be fun. *Fun.* Maybe that's where all her organizational skills went. There weren't any left for her regular life.

I came downstairs where Sheila was spraying air freshener and organizing magazines. She had brought with her and set up a few pictures last night. I stared at a photo framed in silver that showed the whole family. Me, Jenny, Sheila, mom, dad, and Jenny's dad, who died when we were both little. He'd been French and that's where Jenny learned it.

"*Renee*...you should wear something a little nicer!" Sheila complained. "Do you just throw stuff on in the morning? It's sloppy." She went back to cleaning and inspecting her newly manicured nails.

I was wearing a sweatshirt, maybe a size or two big for me, and some subtly flared jeans with a belt. As usual, my dad got all concerned at the fact that they were loose. He claimed I used to fit into them both perfectly. Which wasn't true.

Jenny came downstairs, still combing her hair, and said, "Ironic that you want to be a fashion designer when you don't even know how to dress yourself. And you claim you want to design women's clothes...you should design for MEN'S clothes. You sound like one yourself."

I cringed. She always made fun of my deep voice and the fact that some people mistook me for a boy if they only heard me and had not seen me. A young boy, but a boy no less.

Sheila clapped her hands. "Let's go! Renee, you don't want to be late for your first day at school."

I really didn't know what the point was since I was going to be on winter break in a week from now. I also didn't know what the point was of my aunt clapping and telling me to hurry up when she took her time putting in her onyx earrings in front of the oval mirror near our door, trying on different pairs of heels, and deciding which of five coats to wear.

***

Sidney called and offered me a ride, which I graciously accepted. Sheila wanted to argue about it, but she eventually gave in and just drove Jenny. I sat in the back of Sidney's convertible with Sonny, while Jeremiah sat up front in the passenger's seat. We passed a sight of younger kids, probably pre-teens, busy throwing rocks at someone's car. "Look at those monsters," Sidney scoffed loudly, hands gripping the steering wheel.

The radio played a mix of holiday songs along with songs that had been hits throughout the year. Sonny kept singing along to the lyrics all wrong, and the rest of us were practically in tears of laughter. Jeremiah messed around and turned the volume all the way up whenever a boyband or girl group came on, prompting Sidney to swear at him and turn it back down, glancing around anxiously to see if anyone else in public heard it. "Shhh," Sonny said at one point. "Don't speak. I can barely breathe."

"It's 'Barely Breathing'," Sidney said, rolling her eyes. "If you're going to make terrible puns."

Go figure that my favorite artist and holiday tune would come on just as we parked.

So Sonny decided to sing that for me too. He made a parody of it by referencing some girl at the school named June, who apparently was in a few of his classes. She was across the schoolyard when we arrived, talking to a few people, out of ear reach of Sonny's rendition.

"All I want for Christmas is June..." he sang.

"Christmas in June?" Jeremiah asked.

"This is so embarrassing," Sidney muttered, leading me by the arm away from them, a smile playing around on her lips.

Sonny and I had English first. Sonny, I quickly discovered, was the class clown, and pretty good at it. He was always the center of attention, the life of the party, making people laugh.

A boy walked in the room, with wispy black hair. Everything was black actually, from his clothes, to his nails, to his shoes, to even a little bit of eyeliner I thought. Or maybe he just had thick eyelashes. It was an interesting style that I hadn't considered attractive before, but it suited him just fine. Perhaps it wasn't conventionally attractive, but it had a different quality of attraction to it. After he handed the teacher his pass, Rory, I recognized, walked toward his desk, which was a couple desks behind me. "What are you looking at?" he asked me. I flinched.

The teacher gave us an assignment and stepped out of the room temporarily to talk to an administrator. Which is of course the universal cue for the class to erupt in chatter.

"And so," Sonny laughed, "here's how Sidney spilled the beans about how we were the ones who broke the lamp. She was all like, 'Dad, we're sorry this happened.' And then, 'We didn't mean to—' And then she stops short, realizing what she just said. I could've strangled her.'" There were giggles from people grouped around him, which was at least a good half of the class. "Did she have a mouth on her back then," he said. "Those were the days. We would've gotten away with so much more, if only Sidney had used her brain as much as she does now."

"At least she has a brain." That came from Rory's quiet voice.

"Excuse me?" Sonny responded, turning his head almost completely around. "Did I just hear a buzzing sound?"

"Yeah. Your own voice."

"Really? Your ex really likes my voice. She laughs at it all the time."

The class erupted in a chorus of "Oooooh!" I could tell Rory was starting to lose his cool. It didn't seem like this was a difficult person to aggravate. His lips pressed together into a straight line and his eyes became tiny slits.

"Plus, I've still got my sibling. She didn't have to run away from me, because I treat her nicely."

Whatever he was talking about, that did it. If Sonny had wanted to continue, he never got a chance. Rory got up so quickly, the chair almost fell over. He went straight toward Sonny at full speed. He was only about three inches away from Sonny when a couple people got up and pulled him back before anything could happen. Rory's hands were shaking and his face was turning a pinkish color. "Don't talk about my brother, asshole!" he practically screamed just as Ms. Johnston walked back into the room in shock.

"What is going on here?" Her voice echoed against the walls now that it was silent.

Nobody answered.

"Rory?"

Rory pulled away from the people gripping his arms and sat back down. "Nothing." He crumbled up a piece of paper.

"Hey...that's mine," Sonny said, trying with all his might to not let his voice crack with laughter.

Rory tossed the paper over behind him. "Sit there and keep testing me. You'll be eating it for lunch."

Sonny shrugged when the teacher looked at him, playing clueless.

As we headed out of the class into the busy hallways, I noticed Ms. Johnston grab Rory by the arm and pulled him back in.

Sonny caught up with Sidney. "That little prick has been giving me trouble again."

Sidney sighed. "What has he done now?"

"Bitch came up in my face and nearly lost me in his breath," Sonny replied.

Jeremiah came walking our way with a deck of cards in hand. He held them out to Sidney. "Choose a card and memorize it."

She took one and showed it to Sonny and I. "Nine of hearts," she said.

"No, actually, that's a six of hearts," Sonny said.

"No, I'm pretty sure it's a nine...oh wait, it only has six hearts on it."

"Because you're looking at it UPSIDE DOWN, genius!"

Then Rory walked out of the classroom. Some people scattered along the halls immediately, as if it were a warning signal. The horsing around between Sonny and Sidney ceased gradually as Rory approached them.

"Thanks bastard, I almost got detention."

Sonny beamed. "Then you should get some temper control, kid."

"Oh Rory, chill," Sidney said, rolling her eyes. "Fighting is meaningless."

Rory turned to her. Jeremiah walked over and glared down at him. "Get lost."

Rory's gaze shifted up to Jeremiah, a sly smile starting to form along his lips. "And what now?" He let out a hoarse laugh. "Is Sidney's big bad boyfriend going to hurt me?"

Jeremiah continued to glare. He was visibly seething. I thought he might actually hit Rory for a second.

Rory turned to Sonny, his smile wiping off as fast as a crumb. His voice was low and threatening. "I don't give a damn what you think. I don't even give a damn what you say about me anymore. But don't you go talking smack about him."

"Who—"

"You *know* who." Someone grabbed his shoulder, turned him around, and dragged him away, shooting a glare in our direction.

***

The next class was Health. Wouldn't you know it, now it was Rory and *Jeremiah* in the same class together. I wonder if another incident would happen.

The teacher was energetic. He went on a lecture about how we should appreciate our families. "I cannot stress this enough," he said with such emphasis in his voice, it almost sounded like he would cry. "You can't hate your family, without hating a part of yourself. No matter what they do to you..." Lies, lies, all lies. To hate someone who mistreated you meant to hate yourself? I begged to differ.

One girl got to get out of this class early. "Thank you," he said taking her pass. "And when you get home, make sure to tell your parents that you love them." The girl smiled and nodded on her way out the door.

I looked over toward Jeremiah and Sidney, who'd previously been in better moods before class started. Outside the classroom he'd hugged her from behind and startled her, and she'd erupted in a fit of giggles. But now both looked uncomfortable. They'd stopped passing notes and messing around under the table. Was it the subject matter that was making them uncomfortable? I'd thought they'd both had loving families. Well, I hadn't exactly met Jeremiah's family, but...

I noticed they'd stopped whispering conversations and glanced over to the far-left corner of the room—Rory. I became as curious as them when I looked at him as well. He had a mixed expression on his face. At first glance, you might think he was just a little moody. If you looked a little longer though, you'd see that he was severely upset. Trying to hide something with a tough face.

***

It was nice outside, even on an early December day. While it may have been snowing up in Maryland, it was normal room temperature down here. I sat beneath a tree, letting its leaves fall around me. I watched a group of kids walk by, some of which I had finally got to hear a real Texan accent from.

"I don't care that she gets to go to Rome and Germany over break," someone said. "It ain't Texas."

I would've sat under the bleachers to read the graffiti there, but there were other things going on there too. Unfortunately, Sidney, Jeremiah, and Sonny didn't have my lunch shift. It would've been nice to have *someone*. I supposed I could've gone up to one of the groups sitting down and asked to join, but I didn't really know anyone. High school students weren't all scary—but it was hard to tell which were.

Turned out it was good that Sonny, Sidney, and Jeremiah weren't here after all, when I saw Rory sitting not far from me with a few guys, laughing and looking normal. All the anger I'd seen earlier had vanished.

I passed them when I got up to throw my trash away. They were smoking, and without meaning to, I started coughing.

Rory started laughing, like it was the funniest thing he'd ever seen. "Aw, I'm sorry, are we hurting your fragile little lungs?" he snickered.

My back tensed and I almost turned around and shouted back. But instead I walked away, trying to act like I didn't hear a thing.

This morning I'd seen him come out of his house. I'd heard yelling in there and it'd looked like he got nearly thrown out of his front door. I'd felt sorry for him then. Now I was too angry to care.

Chapter 5: RORY- A Smile For Cover (Monday, December 16, 1996)

As soon as I left my house this morning, I went straight to *Sonny Morning* where Todd worked on Monday mornings. Only Monday mornings though. Every other day of the week he worked at *Todd's Music Store*, aka his very own guitar/piano/trumpet/every other instrument store.

Todd had been my brother's guitar teacher for a few years, when Jason was really young. He'd also given him a part-time job at his store, letting him help out with organizing merchandise and cleaning.

My brother Jason, who by now was twenty-two, had worked with Todd at the store much of the time. Sometimes I would get jealous of the time he spent there. I couldn't really blame him—Todd was much older, and had a better taste in music than most of the kids in our school or neighborhood. It was natural for someone to want to hang out with an older, cooler person—I wanted to spend time with Jason because he was popular, a part of the dominant crowd, and knew how to impress girls. But there was a little more to that in our case. As much as I had loved Jason, I had resented him for how he never helped me with certain things.

He GAVE me a lot. And I knew it was out of love. He hadn't even gotten to the end of high school yet, and already, he was outgoing and confident, always knowing the right words to say, the right facial expressions to make. Everyone looked up to him—I looked up to him and admired him. I wanted to BE like him. He was strong, talented, and intelligent. But even when he was invited to the biggest parties of the year, he sometimes turned those down just to take me for a night out to eat at my favorite restaurant, even though he sufficiently hated it. He taught me how to play the guitar. And occasionally, I still pulled it out to calm me, even when the memories behind it stung. He bought me all sorts of things I never asked for but he knew I liked. He would always give me cards on my birthday with his extraordinary drawings in them. Jason was an artist. He turned down the money people offered just to keep his own creations. Sometimes I sat there and watched him hard at work, observing his hand movements, him not even minding me looking over his shoulder. Yes, Jason gave me much of his time.

But all that he gave me still didn't add up to what he could've given me—how my old man threw swings and sent his foot flying down on my head, even when I was completely defenseless. He never did that to Jason. Jason was the golden boy, always got perfect grades, also did every single house task exactly correct. And he always kept his cool. He wasn't clumsy or emotional like my mom and I. No one was perfect, not even Jason, but somehow, he managed to never really piss my old man off. The worst he ever got out of him was an eye roll or a raised voice. Not a raised fist though. I knew Jason was afraid to watch as much as he was afraid to get involved, but I always looked to him for safety, and he just stood and watched, frozen, never even running to get mom. He didn't dare even speak. Maybe he'd thought he'd be next, which he was probably right about. He'd had a clean record with our dad, and probably wanted to keep it that way. The most infuriating part was that deep down, I knew I couldn't blame him for that.

Then, one day, everything changed. I was so fond of him, despite him not sticking up for me, that I would follow him places. And learn things. And discover what was going on and how he kept getting me numerous items, how he kept collecting large amounts of money when his little job at *Todd's Music Store* didn't pay him nearly that much.

I waited a couple more years. Until he was eighteen. Because a small but strong part of me wanted him to be at an age where he could handle himself when this happened.

I told on him.

I was so angry that he lied to me, and was fed up with having to be whipped in front of him, in front of anybody for that matter, and reported him—not to the police—I was never quite fond of them myself. But to mom and dad. I knew they wouldn't tell the police either.

The most my old man did to him was yell at Jason. So did I. I was so quick to scold Jason when he came up to my room I almost had him in tears. When I thought back about the words I said, they stung so deep. I swore, if I could take them back, I would.

One angry outburst from the one he loved the most seemed enough to send him running. Whenever I forced myself to think logically, I knew it was more—trying to escape Tre's gang, the trouble they had all caused, and start over a new life. Not to mention, if they went after him, from knowing that he was gone, they would probably not target anyone in his family. Perhaps Jason thought he was protecting us, protecting me. Jason packed his bags that night, left a note, and to this day has never returned or phoned. And I never received another card of any sort with his beautiful artwork gracing the paper.

I still had that note with me however. I always carried it in my pocket. I would never let it go. It was the only little piece of him I had left.

In the bright breakfast restaurant of *Sonny Morning*, despite there being only a few people sitting around and Todd in the back, I covered my marked neck and headed quickly toward the far left, where there was a restroom. I focused my neck in the mirror, took wet a towel, and slowly wiped away the little bit of cracked dry blood. It had started bleeding a little bit after my old man left a massive bruise there from punching me this morning. It was nasty but I was used to it. I covered it with a bandage and went to work on the big bruise on my knee. There was also a bruise on my arm from the night before. I covered it as much as I possibly could with the make-up, which didn't really match my pale skin-tone too well. It was too tan. I grimaced and put it away.

I came out and sat on the stool. Todd scowled at me as he was drying a plate and sauntered over. No, he wasn't scowling at me. He was scowling at something that was on me. *Oh fuck,* I thought.

"What is that?" he asked, motioning toward my wrist. Shit. I forgot to cover *that*, and left my wristbands at home.

"Oh..." I said very slowly. Then finally, "I just slid on a bunch of gravel, and—"

"Really?" Todd said promptly, and then it was just silent. "Did the gravel pebbles happen to be some kids at school, or in the park, that pissed you off? Did you get into another fight, Rory?" I didn't think he was fooled. Even though Todd and I didn't always see eye to eye, both of us were torn apart when Jason left, and we each took it different ways. Neither of us took it well. Todd was severely depressed, but he was strong. He knew how to get through it while keeping his life balanced. He always kept himself busy, not really allowing himself much free time anymore. I, on the other hand, just fell rock-bottom. That first night without Jason I cried for several hours in my bed. After that, never again. I started smoking, getting into fights, pissing off authority—I even got arrested once. I was surprised I hadn't gotten kicked out of school yet. I was surprised I wasn't dead yet. Todd got so scared whenever this happened, afraid that I would make it a routine and that's all my life would be wrapped around—anger, and recklessness. But anger had energy—it kept me going. I didn't have the strength to merely hide depression. It would've eaten me alive. Todd kept my anger in check. He sort of took me in under his aid, as an unofficial guardian. He must've figured my parents weren't doing such a hot job, that they were merely neglectful. If *only* that were it. He thought every bruise and scar and mark I had was from fighting. Since then, I'd been getting into less trouble and doing somewhat better, but there was still a lot of work to do. There were nights I'd wake up in his house, all bandaged up, having no memory of the night after I'd left my house, because I'd gotten into a fight with somebody. He'd call my parents and let them know I was alright. I was grateful, but careful not to let him too close to my family secrets.

I looked away from him, embarrassed. He never took his eyes off me.

Gabriella came walking over, curiosity in her eyes. Gabriella was Todd's girlfriend who lived with him. She had wavy blonde hair, a curvy body, a shy smile, and she was very calm and laid back, unlike him. Maybe opposites really did attract. It was hard to believe she could be with such a non-down-to-earth type of person. But it worked somehow. Todd never talked much. He usually just gave quick one-to-three word responses or grunts, and that was that. He was always completely consumed with something.

"It was just gravel," I said uneasily, not daring to look at either one of them. I couldn't completely lay all my trust with them even though they were pretty much the only friends I had.

Todd's jaw clenched. "Rory," he said in a stern voice, "if it's something else—if you got into another fight—"

"I didn't get into a fight!" I spat angrily.

The look in Todd's eye made me realize what a mistake it was to take that tone with him. "I'm not accusing you, Rory—I'm asking. And I'll keep asking. Perhaps if you weren't always getting into fights in the first place, I'd have no reason to ask at all. But I'm just looking out for you—so don't you dare speak to me that way."

Todd had a way of speaking in a low voice that somehow still felt as though you were getting shouted at, and he also had a way of keeping you looking at him, as though his face were a magnet you couldn't turn away from. His glaring gaze held my attention in place, until he finished.

I sighed and swung my bag over my shoulder and walked out the door, trying not to be irritated. I knew he was just trying to help, but I didn't want it. Not now, anyway.

"Calm down Todd," I heard Gabriella say soothingly. "He's a teenager. You know how they are. They have an ambitious mindset and think they're invincible."

Maybe some did, by I in *no* way thought I was invincible.

As I walked down the streets, some people glared at me. Some because a teen wearing mostly black screamed *Danger!* Some because they actually knew me, so that was reasonable. Like Mr. Schmidt, my former teacher. An old man who could never teach worth a damn. How he would dare to play counselor with me back in the days of grade school. Admittedly, I didn't appreciate teachers just stopping by my desk and looking over my shoulder, or for that matter, AT my shoulder. Just to stare at me instead of my work. They'd be baffled when I'd tell them that I accidentally spilled hot water on myself. They should've been. It was a silly explanation. But they believed me anyway. But Mr. Schmidt had always known I was a troubled kid, and there were other kids of trouble, like the ones currently wrecking his car. I didn't want to screw things up even more. My emotions always got the best of me. It seemed as though using a mask to cover it up from the rest of the world was the only way.

School was difficult in a sense that it was the one place I had to control myself best. If I got expelled, I was history. He would beat me black and blue, and more. But some people just made me so mad I wanted to make them choke on their own blood.

Even though this morning was quite chilly, the day proved to be warm. I wanted to take my jacket off so badly, and at one point, I did, but was so afraid someone would notice the scars under the badly done make-up. Who put make-up on their arms? People probably thought I was weird, but I didn't care. If I cared how others perceived me by now, I might as well had told myself goodbye a long time ago.

English would've been okay if Sonny had kept his catty mouth shut. We had begun *The Outsiders* today. I hated reading, but it was an alright book. Health was okay. It was good not to get dressed in the locker room. Some people would stare indiscreetly. One time I lost my temper and snarled at someone, "Are you checking me out?" He went red and made a constant effort not to look at me again.

The whole lecture about parents cut real deep. What did this so-called 'teacher' know about parents?

The people at lunch were the same as usual—they weren't really my friends. They were just kind of there. People to talk to. Acquaintances.

Before I had crossed paths with Sonny and Jeremiah in the hallway, Ms. Johnston, my English teacher, stopped me because apparently she was "concerned". First I tried to laugh it off, but then she got firm.

"Rory," she had said, "This is not funny. You're an A student, and this is about the third time you've arrived late to class. Is there anything I should know about?"

I knew she was just worried, and deep down, a part of me lit up. I just couldn't handle it. I didn't like appearing weak or vulnerable; I didn't like having to rely on someone else's comfort, no matter how tempting it was. Most of all, the more and more they did that, the more and more guilty I felt, and undeserving of anything good. Whenever I got close to someone, I hurt them in some way or another, and didn't realize the consequences until after they were gone. I wasn't planning on going through one more cycle of that, so I shut myself off.

"I'm fine," I snapped, and opened the door to leave, intentionally knocking a chair over in the process.

"You're extremely smart Rory," she continued, trying not to let it be obvious that she was now really upset, "and I just don't want to see you throw that away. If you ever need someone to talk to, I'm here."

If I had stood there any longer, looking into her blue eyes that reminded me of Jason's, I would've lost it. So I just gave a tight smile and nod, and entered the normal, unwelcoming hallways. I said that I almost got detention so I wouldn't have to admit what was really discussed. Sidney looked at me with the disgust she regularly looked at me with. The kind of disgust you looked at when gum was stuck on the bottom of your shoe. She didn't used to look at me that way.

It was a gradual loss over time, her getting less and less patient and sympathetic, and more and more irritated with my behavior towards others. She didn't know about the extent of what went on at my home, but I hadn't wanted to burden her with it. Besides, it wasn't an excuse anyway. I used to think it'd only matter how I treated her (and her family). But she'd hated it all the same if I was rude to a stranger. And the day I really lost her...the official breaking point, the last straw, was when she witnessed me committing arson to an empty nearby house. No one lived in it, but Sidney had scrambled to put the fire out anyway. That day, I was so destructive and the anger was so strong, that I all but put my hand on someone. The fire had only been the finale though. Before that, I broke all the windows with a hammer, spray painted the shed, kicked at the doors leaving scuff marks, and yelling about how shitty the world was.

When she finally showed up, using a fire extinguisher to put out the beginning flames, she stared at me with such disgust and resentment, I almost shuddered. I knew it must've been terrifying for her to witness this. I took a step toward her. She took a step back. Without her speaking any words, I knew that it was over.

After that, she must've told Sonny what happened. I was sure that she hadn't exaggerated or told half-truths. She didn't need to try to make it sound bad, because it *was* bad. He never really forgave me for wasting his sister's time, and potentially traumatizing her with my tantrum. She was too good for trash like me.

After I had left the confrontation, I overheard Sidney talking to that new girl at their lockers. She explained the beef between me and Jeremiah—something that even I knew wasn't Jeremiah's problem. It just seemed reality threw salt in my wounds given that he has the life I never had—or that Jason never had. He was going to be a talented and successful musician one day, with a fun group of friends, and nothing to frown over except homework. That sounded like heaven to me. It also didn't help that he was going out and going good with my ex, whom I still found myself daydreaming of at times.

The new girl—Renee—I didn't get what her deal was. I was very sour to her. Twice in one day. She did nothing to me to deserve that treatment. Make that three times. I also gave her a mean look when she accidentally bumped into me in the hallway. And yet each time, she just walked away or didn't respond. If it were me, I would've punched myself in the nose. I couldn't help it—something about her made me want to keep her away.

When I came home that day, my mom was just lying on the couch, out cold. Her face was very pale.

At first I thought she was just exhausted and sleepy, but then I realized it was something else.

I took her pulse at her wrist. Her heart was beating profusely and I didn't have to guess what the hell had happened while I was at school when the smell arose to my nostrils.

My own heart froze for a second right before her eyes opened and she began to yawn, like it was just a normal awakening. I was so angry, I almost kicked her, but suffocated the urge. "Mom, why, WHY are you always shoving the alcohol?" I screamed, and stomped out of the house, slamming the door. I would not deal with this. Not today. I had thought she gave up drinking long ago. I had thought *I* had suppressed urges a long time ago to kick people, especially my own mother. I was angrier at myself. Was I becoming like him?

I went out to the tree me and Jason used to go to. It was deep within the woods that lay beyond my house, the same place my old man would drag me out, at any time day or night, to whip me unmercifully and leave me lying for the rain to spill on.

The tree was near a lake. I sat by a group of rocks, leaning my head against the biggest one, me and Jason's carved initials face to face. I remembered this was the exact area he and I would play at and roll around in when we were kids and stupid but fun-loving. He would throw rocks at older kids who teased me because I was an alleged "tree-hugger". This place used to be loud, alive, and full of activity. Now it was eerie silence.

I liked being alone. I liked the outdoors. I didn't like dirt or being around bugs, but I guess I was just used to it from sleeping out here so many times. The trees were pretty. The air smelled nice. The sun shone down and made me feel warm. I saw what looked to be a family of squirrels nearby, fighting over an acorn. A rabbit was hopping along, stopped to stare wearily at me for a second, and continued hopping when it realized I wasn't a threat. It was rare that someone like me would say something was 'adorable'. I hated that word so much. But it was.

For me, being alone was a good thing. It was peaceful. Sometimes animals were nicer than people. There was no one to hurt me, but even more important, no one for me to hurt. I wasn't proud of hurting anybody. Sometimes it just happened like a cursed force that spread through my body and took control.

Some may argue that being alone was frightening or sad. No one to talk to. No familiar comfort of breathing next to you. If a big forest fire broke down all the trees that currently surrounded me and made them block my way, I'd be stuck, and there'd be no one to save me or to shield me from the flames.

I used to think this way too, but no use in making things more depressing than they already were. So I just shoved these thoughts out of my head and to the side for later consideration, because there's nothing I could do now. Although I never got to them no matter how much later it was. For me, it was just a matter of: Did I want to risk doing something regrettable? Or did I want to play it safe, with just a little boredom in the mix?

I had fallen asleep right where I was, sitting up against the tree, dreaming. Dreaming of Jason. How I didn't used to need an alarm clock to get up in the morning—I had him, a less difficult method of waking up. I would feel my bed vibrating, and open my eyes and there he was, jumping up and down, saying, "Get up Rory. It's Friday. Just one more day, and you can sleep in all you want." And even weekends when I could sleep in, the sunlight would pour through my window, birds would be right outside chirping, and he would come in anyway, begging me to come outside and play ball with him or help wash the car, where again, we cared about nothing but fun at the time, and would get each other soaked.

I woke up, my body aching, my sides jolting as I jumped from a painful spasm. My mind wasn't thinking clearly. *No, Jason, don't go, stay*, was all I could make out in my thoughts.

I got up slowly, stretched, brushed myself off, and turned toward that tree. I reached out and touched its rough bark. I forced a weak smile.

The statement *"It takes more muscles to frown than to smile"* was a flat-out lie.

6

Chapter 6: RENEE- Revelation
(Monday, December 16, 1996)

After lunch during Study period, a red-headed girl came up to me and said, "Hi! I'm April. I sit beside you in English class."

I nodded.

"Renee, right?"

I nodded.

"Well, I'm inviting the whole school to my party tonight. Would you like to come?" She must've seen how weary I looked because she laughed and added, "It's just a party, Renee."

I shrugged. "Okay."

"Cool! Here's my address." She scribbled it down on a napkin and waved goodbye.

Little did I know this party would end up being a disaster.

***

Why was he so mean to me? I thought on my way home. I always knew there were the usual bullies in school, but this seemed different. And it wasn't just me. He just seemed like he was angry at *everything*. Like absolutely everything set him off. It didn't seem like it was me specifically that bothered him—any bully I'd ever encountered targeted me for a reason, albeit usually a stupid one of course, like my braces or glasses, being a good student, how quiet I was. Sidney told me earlier today before lunch that he had a hard temper and that he'd do anything it took to keep people who were nice away from him. That was a pretty strategic method to go about doing that, I guess. *"He uses intimidation to look tough,"* Sidney explained. *"He refuses to admit that he has a problem; that's why I broke up with him. He's going to go too far one day. He lets his anger consume him."* All throughout the day, Jeremiah and Sonny kept giving me little warnings on how careful I should be whenever Rory was around me. *"He has a temper,"* they all said.

When I got home, I was relieved that Sheila and Jenny had gone out for the night, and wouldn't be back until late. Dad was working late too. I guessed I wouldn't need to tell anyone about the party I'd be going to. But I was enraged by the note left behind, scribbled in a sloppy attempt at cursive: *"Renee, we've gone out 4 dinner, and then 2 go shopping. Jenny and I need to get last-minute books 4 her classes at her school, so that will account 4 at least an hour. Your father will be home at around 10."*

My hands shook as I set the piece of paper down. It wasn't that she wrote like she was in junior high, but that she signed it *"Nicole"*. That was mom's name, and she always did it in a pretty and unique way, unlike Sheila's dirty attempt.

I became angry and also panicky. I had visions and memories of my mother flit across my mind, and the deep realization that I was never going to see her again. My skin began to crawl. I leaned back and tried to breath, but I just couldn't help but to jump up. I looked around my new room—it was decent, not the one I dreamed of, not a palace like Sidney's, but it was okay. I paced around and tried to calm myself. Still no help.

I phoned Jasmine. No answer. I phone Sidney. Then Jeremiah. No answer from them either.

But I couldn't be alone. The house was too dark and quiet. I hated it. I hated loneliness. It was almost like I was suffocating.

No, I *was* suffocating.

I sat on my bed. Tried to steady my breath. *What is WRONG with me?!* But I knew exactly what it was.

I grasped the sheets tightly, with both hands, sweating. These attacks came often. My chest was moving up and down really fast, my breathing too wild and uneven. Hyperventilating. My throat throbbed painfully from holding back tears, and that drove my body entirely. I got up and walked over to my desk, like a zombie. I was alone in the house. Now was a good, safe time when I would not get caught.

This was something that happened all too often. I'd been tempted to do it for a year, so I got something for it, just in case. I didn't know if it would work or not, I always chickened out at the last minute. I pulled open the drawer and pulled out the shaving blade, small but sharp, so shiny my reflection was as visible as if it were a mirror. Only I wasn't going to use it for shaving. Gently, I placed it against my arm and it rested there. Would it feel good? Would it feel painful? Would it feel neither, and just be numb and meaningless?

I stood for a whole minute, a whole sixty-something seconds, biting my lip, trying to work up the nerve. It was so sharp though, and I was so small and bony.

I dropped it back in the drawer and slammed it shut.

I couldn't do it.

***

I snuck out later while my dad was in the shower and Sheila was in the kitchen. It was easy to tip toe down the stairs and straight out the door when the kitchen was all the way in the back (and the television was on). Jenny was in her own room. They all thought I was asleep.

The party was right around the block from where I lived. I made sure to double, triple, quadruple- check the address. As soon as I took my first step in, the energy and atmosphere almost knocked me over. I wasn't used to parties. In the living room there was a bunch of people lying around smoking or drinking, with loud music. Toward the entrance, there were only two people, sitting on a single chair together, the girl on his lap, lacing her fingers through his hair. They hardly noticed me. I slowly walked past them, into the next room. I had walked straight into the house itself, since the door had been wide open, but was wondering why no one was standing there with a list checking people off as they came. Anybody could've just walked in. I was sure the place attracted many as well, considering the music could be heard down the block. Another reason it was so easy to find. I could've done it without the address.

Though I still had my doubts, and I was beginning to wonder if I had reached the correct house when I heard a familiar voice and saw that bush of orange hair come and greet me. It was a mess now.

"Nice to see you." April's words were a little slurred. She had a guy trying to pull her away, not noticing me. April was not the April I met earlier, a ditzy flirty girl with neat hair and a perky personality. The half-full glass she was holding sloshed around precariously.

There was the thick aroma of alcohol and quiet eerie music playing. Not exactly party music. I had expected some loud upbeat music, and something to drink other than beer or champagne, but at least there were people. People all scattered about, on couches, on the floor, outside, even though it was cold. Some were talking, but most were making out. The music and the darkness made me think of a graveyard.

I turned to leave. A hand fell on my shoulder. I jumped and turned.

"Won't you stay?" It was another girl. "You don't have to drink the beer. You don't even have to touch anyone. Just stay?"

It was clear she was reaching her point. She was a little less intoxicated than others, enough to fool you if she remained quiet and just stood or sat still, but I was a little afraid that some of the others might throw up. A few had red sunken eyes or lips.

I headed to the kitchen. There were little paper cups filled with beverages sitting on the counter. I stopped at something that caught my eye—a photo, sitting right on a collage of many, titled "Freshman Class". A couple years ago, things must've been different. *Very* different. For the two people sitting together in the photo were Sidney...and Rory. Where was Jeremiah? Both Sidney and Rory were smiling and it seemed a sincere smile, not the fake kind you used just to pose for a camera. Rory had his arm around Sidney. Rory looked so different. His face, revealing eyes that were warm and inviting, looked happy.

Speaking of Sidney and Jeremiah—and Sonny, for that matter—were they here?

I felt a tap on my shoulder. "Why don't you go sit down while I bring you something to drink? Soda perhaps?" I reluctantly went to the living room and sat down, trying not to breathe in the access smoke. I wasn't going to accept any soda from anyone. I didn't know anyone. Everyone seemed nice, but you never knew.

I felt the couch sink for a second as someone else sat beside me. It was a small couch, so their side touched mine. I looked over and saw that it was Rory. He appeared to be the only other person here besides me who wasn't dripping with alcohol. He rested his head on his hand, leaning on the arm of the couch.

Two girls stumbled by, giggling. I don't think they stumbled from being drunk though, just messing around. They were two of only a few here who didn't appear to be drinking. One of them let out a low wolf whistle, nodding in Rory's direction. He just continued to stare off into space, ignoring them.

There was some powdery stuff lying on a nearby table that I didn't recognize. Some people were getting up, taking some, and bringing it back to their friends. Someone else offered me a drink. I started to refuse, but she interrupted me. "NO, I insist," she said, shoving the cup into my hand. I took it with a smile just to get her to go away. I had never tried alcohol before, so out of curiosity I sipped some. And spit it out immediately.

"You don't have to drink it if you don't want to, you know," came an irritable voice.

I looked over at Rory. "Well, I thought I'd at least try it."

"Well did you like it?"

"No." I set the drink down gently.

"Me neither."

"You don't like alcohol?"

"No, I hate it. It's disgusting," he said sharply, glancing at the couple in front of us.

There was more silence. I glanced at Rory's arm as he took his jacket off. He was wearing short sleeves and I could see on his upper arm disappearing up behind the sleeve on his shoulder was a tattoo. There looked to be a foreign language written out on it, maybe Japanese. I guessed it was kanji. "I like your tattoo."

This was the first time he looked at me. He seemed to have been caught by surprise. His face looked younger now and he shifted his position. He looked uncomfortable. He joined his hands together, and started messing around with them, like a nervous habit. "Umm...thanks. It says, '*When you love someone, it's worth all the pain'.*" He paused. "M-my brother used to say that all the time." He swallowed.

Used to. "You okay?" I whispered.

"Yeah."

Radiohead was playing from the stereo, a dark song to match the quiet vibe going on in here. Or maybe I was just projecting my own quiet sad thoughts onto it. The couch shifted again and I looked up to see Rory leaving. Before I could say anything, he turned back. "I'm going outside to the backyard. Did you want to come?"

I nodded. Anything for fresh air and to be away from here.

The music could still be heard blaring from the house, even outside. Only at a more reasonable volume now. The song changed to a slow rap song that came out last year. At least they seemed to have a variety of music. There were a few kids sitting around chatting and drinking, and their overalls reminded me of what I wore when I was a kid, but not their language. It was a funny combination.

Rory paid them no mind and sat on the ground beside the bordering hedges of the yard that served the place of a fence. Maybe not as secure, but nicer-looking. I awkwardly sat next to him, still not sure if he wanted me there. But he paid me no mind too as he gazed up at the moon. I was beginning to think his mind was always somewhere else.

"Where are you from? I can't remember if you told me or not."

"Maryland," I said.

"Oh." He nodded. "I've only ever been to Florida, when I was little. That's the only place outside of here I've been to. It's really hot. How's Maryland?"

"Cooler, I guess. Though it still gets hot during summer. It's probably pretty cold there right now though." It was not something I missed. The warmer temperature here felt relieving. We didn't have to all stay holed up in the house.

Rory nodded again. He went on sitting there after that, not looking at me, for about five minutes. Then a song came on, slow at first with a deep bass, eventually speeding up in tempo and volume. Rory started bobbing his head up and down to the beat. "Good to know they have some of that here," he said. It sounded like a seventies rock song, but I couldn't be sure. "I used to listen to this song with my brother all the time when I was younger," Rory said. "First rock song I ever heard. I even have 'one guitar', just like the song goes."

I smiled. "Is it from the seventies?"

"Early eighties. Did you know that it was inspired by a real fan who stood outside an arena for five hours?"

"Jeez," I said.

I didn't know for sure, but I thought I heard him chuckle.

Due to my inability to start conversations, we sat in silence again for a couple minutes. Suddenly I asked a really stupid question. "You ever get any blizzards around here?"

He turned and looked at me like I'd asked a really stupid question. "No," he said. "Certainly not like the one you guys got last winter."

"Oh yeah," I said, remembering a nor'easter storm in early January. And before I knew it, I was talking to him as if I'd known him for more than a few minutes, as if he were a neighbor from next door who'd experienced the blizzard with me. I described it to him, how much of the east coast had gotten hit pretty hard by the blizzard, including my area. We'd gotten about two feet of windblown snow. There were whiteout conditions and power outages. We were scheduled to go back to school on Monday the eighth, but it had obviously been canceled. While it was no fun not having power, it was still nice having a legit snow day and not having to go back right away after Winter Break. I remember the kids in my classes talking excitedly about it when we finally did go back. Or when the phones were working again. Jasmine and I had been so excited by it, talking for ages. We didn't remember the last time we'd experienced snow like that.

"Wow," Rory said, nodding. His face was expressionless, but I could sense that he was genuinely listening. "How many feet did you say again?"

"Two feet. Some areas got four feet."

He raised his eyebrows.

"It was windblown snow. So it wasn't all necessarily even snow that fell."

"That sure is something." He fell silent again.

After about a minute, without really moving at all, Rory's entire demeanor changed. Very slightly, he hitched his chin up and was staring across the yard toward the thick abundant bushes on the far side of the house that overflowed into the next yard over, like a cat spotting prey. Seeing him do that was like having a string attached to my neck and making me turn too.

I didn't see anything though.

Regardless, he got up quickly and walked away, through the kitchen door. I followed him from there through the living room, toward the entrance. As he did, my eyes zoomed toward his back pocket, where he was hastily shoving something in. Whatever was on that paper, it was very important.

I glanced down, and noticed that something else fell out of his pocket. It was neatly folded. "Rory!" I called, but he was already out of sight. Automatically, my body jumped up and seized it before anyone else could. I promised myself I would not even open it. I would return it to him when I had a chance.

His personality was different tonight. It was like he was a chameleon. Was he always like that? Did he have mood swings? Or was he just lost? Because those frightened eyes, that shy and quiet tone, and that awkward position was nothing like what I had seen or how he acted today at school.

I stepped into the night of cool and crisp air and made my way around the corner and down the sidewalk. I could see my breath as I breathed out. It was dark out, with a few streetlights to lead the way. Thick black bushes lined both sidewalks on either side of the empty road. I jammed my hands in my pockets and started walking a little faster, not sure why I was starting to feel so afraid. Suddenly, I felt a hand clasp over my mouth, and thick breath in my ear. I could hardly breathe, and my body went into panic mode. "Hello, how are you tonight, darling?" There were a couple of snickers. There must've been more than one person. I could see a few strands of blonde hair. "Boy, I bet under those glasses you look real pretty. You've got hair for days...are you a long-lost princess?" More snickers.

Out of the corner of my eye, I saw Rory walking towards us, whoever had a hold of me.

"Rory!" the voice exclaimed, sounding honored. "Rory, my man, long time no see."

"Tre," Rory responded. His voice was unreadable. Toneless.

"Know what?"

"What?" he answered. Still unreadable.

Yell for someone. Get the police, dammit!

My head was shoved up against Tre's chest. He shoved me in Rory's direction. Rory caught me as I stumbled, and then took his other hand to clasp over my mouth so I couldn't scream.

I got a clear view of Tre. His was a little less muscular than I expected, but it was hard to tell under the jacket. He had greyish eyes and looked older than a teen. He seemed to have a permanent scowl, even when smiling. Like he always had bad intentions.

"Rory, I caught you a present. The one you were talking to earlier." Tre glanced at me with a Cheshire grin. "Why don't you be a gentleman and give the lady an adventure?"

Rory cocked his head to one side. "What?"

"You know." Tre raised his eyebrows. "Give her an experience she'll never forget."

My heart pounded a thousand times faster. I had a feeling I knew what he meant by 'experience' or 'adventure'.

"If you do, the deal tomorrow is off."

I looked up at Rory. His face had softened a little.

Tre took a few steps forward, so that now, he and Rory were eye to eye. I was stuck in between them, like I wasn't even there, like a little twig. Tre whispered, "And we both know you can't provide what is necessary for this deal, Rory."

My entire body was an earthquake. Not because it was thirty-eight degrees.

"And what if I choose to do neither?"

"Well then, you know what happens." Tre smiled. I couldn't help but to guess there was something sadistic on his mind, whatever this 'deal' was that Rory didn't want to participate in.

Rory looked at him long and hard. "I'm not doing it in front of you."

Oh no, I thought. *He's not really bad enough to do this, is he?*

"There's a corner," Tre said, pointing. "You can do it around there."

Rory immediately started pulling me, my feet dragging on the sandy gravel. It was so fast, everything was a blur. I couldn't breathe *at all.* All I felt was my head firmly against his chest and the ground beneath, as if my body were two separate parts. The worst part was I couldn't make a sound. *NO!* I started flailing my arms to fight back, but he just released my shoulder and locked both of my wrists behind me in one strong grip. It could've been a pair of handcuffs for all I knew.

Things slowed down and the surroundings looked different. The next thing I knew, my back was up against a brick wall, his hand still on my mouth, and his other still had both of mine pinned against my back. Rory was an inch away, panting, staring right at me.

By then, my whole thinking process had gone numb. Though I still prayed there was someone nearby to stop this, I stopped panicking, and stopped even forming coherent sentences inside. *He'll kill you...me...need help...* I couldn't hear my heart anymore, nor could I breathe against his palm. I closed my eyes. *Mommy...*

"Don't scream. I'm not going to hurt you." It was familiar and low, whispering in my ear. I opened my eyes, and very, *very* slowly, he released his hand from my mouth, removing his fingers first, and then his palm, as if ready to cover me back up again in case I did decide to scream. Once he saw that I wouldn't, he let go of my hands too. All sorts of oxygen hugged and greeted me. "You need to get out of here—"

"HEY RORY! WHAT'S TAKING SO LONG? PLANNING ON DOING AN ENCORE?" There were howls of hideous laughter in the distance, and I knew we couldn't be far.

Rory made a disgusted look and turned back to me. "Go," he hissed. "And not back to the party." He stepped away from me.

I stared at him for a moment, confused. There were all sorts of questions I wanted to ask him. But he was saving me and I wasn't going to make that any more difficult. I started running in the opposite direction, still looking back at him, until he became nothing but a spec. By then my sides ached with pain. When I got to my street, I couldn't run up to my front door soon enough. I went inside my house, where my father was cleaning up in the kitchen. He glanced up, stunned to see me coming through the front door. "Renee, what—" I raced up the stairs, to my dark room, sat on my bed, pulled my knees up to my chin, and wrapped my arms around them. And thought about how *stupid* I was to go to that damn party. I would hear about it tomorrow from my dad, but for now all was quiet, and the moonlight shone down through my window. I could vaguely make out fading lights and hear the distant sirens of a police car somewhere far away.

Chapter 7: RORY-The Silence is Too Loud (Monday evening, December 16, 1996)

She was finally out of there.

I walked back around the corner. "How'd it go?" Tre asked casually.

"Good," I replied quietly, trying to sound apathetic.

"You didn't do a thing, did you."

I wasn't surprised. Tre was too good to fall for this. "Of course not."

"I wanted to bring back the Rory that left us...whatever happened to him?"

"I *never* raped anyone," I snapped. "Would never even think of something like that." I'd hit people before. I'd broken into stores. I'd stolen before. But I never did the unthinkable.

"Good thing we got me now to lead us now," Tre continued. "Man, I always thought that Jason was the biggest disappointment to us, but you..."

I lunged at him.

But he grabbed a handful of my shirt and in a second, my back and head were on the ground, and I couldn't get up. His big foot was pressed down on my chest. He chuckled for a second, then his face immediately flashed to anger. I gasped for air. Tre was so much bigger and stronger than I was. His golden strands of hair tried to scratch at my eyes like cat's claws as he bent down. He was about to say something when one of the others said, "Dude, c'mon, they're coming!"

A whole bunch of commotion started happening. Feet ran around everywhere, and I was finally able to inhale again. I sat up coughing, my head spinning. When my vision was decent, all I could make out were the silhouettes of Tre and the others, like rabid wolves, thrusting over the caged fence and into the misty fog of the night. A car zoomed louder and louder, until it was so close to me, I thought I would get hit. Instead it sprayed dust everywhere, fogging up my sight. There were bright flashing red and blue lights that were so blinding, they reached through the dust anyway.

I heard a door slam, and the next thing I knew, a police officer was standing above me looking down with a flashlight. Someone must've heard what was going on with Tre right outside their window.

"Rory Silverman," the policeman said, gently pulling me up. "When will you learn to stay out of trouble, eh?"

He shoved me up against the car, and tightened his grip around my wrists behind my back. I could feel metal brush them. "Ouch," I growled.

"I'll take him officer," a familiar and quiet voice said. Todd.

"Obviously, you can't—"

"I know how to handle this kid." Silence. The words could've broken through a brick building. The monotonous manner of his voice didn't matter.

The officer sighed, letting go of me. He took a few steps over to Todd, and said through gritted teeth, "You keep this kid in check, or else he'll be in prison before he turns eighteen." Todd gave a curt nod.

When the officer drove off, Todd walked over to me. I knew I'd have just as hard a time—harder, actually—than I'd had with the police officer just now.

"Todd—"

"Don't look up at me with those puppy eyes," he said in a harsh voice. "What did you do this time?"

"I...."

He stared at me a bit longer, trying to figure me out, raising his eyes as if to say, *Well...what?* I bit the inside of my lips and cheeks, tasting blood. I didn't want to speak or have my face betray my fear. I didn't want him to think I was pathetic. Todd rarely had sympathy or solace for anyone. He had been through some of the most brutal things. He'd been through some vicious assaults too, and was in a gang himself when he'd been a teen. Todd pitied nobody.

I thought we would stand there all night until Todd finally said, "Did you *do* anything, or was it all Tre?"

I just shook my head, confused. "Uh, Tre," I finally said as firmly as I could. "There was a girl...but she's okay...I think."

"Why didn't you say you didn't do it then?"

"I just..." I shrugged. I'd forgotten how to speak English.

"Look, let me give you a ride home."

"Okay. Thanks."

"Get in the car."

Todd wasn't always that cold and blunt. He used to be talkative and open, just like Jason. What the effects of someone leaving your life could do, nothing could describe it as well as Todd's drastic and scary change in a person. Years ago, people could go up to him and spark a fun and happy conversation. This was the last thing that was possible nowadays.

***

This was not the typical day of a five-year old.

I heard the door slam. He was home. I hid under my bed, trying not to make a sound. Then I heard the steps start. It was coming and I knew the drill. They got louder and closer, until finally they were standing right outside my door.

The doorknob turned, opened, and there he was in my room. I didn't need to peek to know what his face looked like. I didn't care that it was incredibly dusty where I lay—I only attempted, once again, to save my own self, even though it never worked before. My teachers said I was always striving. Yes, I always was, but for more than grades.

This time was like every other. Dust got in my nostrils and a sneeze flew out involuntarily. The next thing I knew was a big, large hand coming to get me, and yanking my entire body out from under the bed. My skin scraped against the chipped wood. Now I was outside of my room, and thrown up against the wall, hanging onto the stair railing, trying not to fall. The hardness of it was so abrupt, I thought the ceiling would collapse and cave in...I thought my heart would too.

BANG! BANG! BANG! Each slam against the wall sounded like a gunshot. My back was rattling and aching as I struggled to exhale the air from within. I started apologizing, for what? I still didn't know.

All that time, I felt another presence beside me. It was a nice and pleasant one that made things a little better. Jason...make him stop, make him STOP. But he didn't. He just stared throughout the whole thing, and held my hand afterwards. As if that useless gesture did ANY good. I tried to keep him in my line of sight, just look at him, during. Sometimes the sight of him would slip away from all the impact, but at least I tried, and at least he was there. And useless as he was afterwards, I was glad he did at least that. And my dad didn't even acknowledge his existence.

Then the phone rang. The slamming ceased. The yells, the punches...the beating had stopped. My dad stood there for a second, then left.

I felt so dirty, from both the dust and the blood. I turned slowly, so as not to agitate my bruised back. There was a small circle of red on the wall where my head had been.

Jason walked over and softly caressed my hair. He didn't try to pull his fingers through when the drying fluid stopped them.

"I'm done now. And I didn't use any hot water," he whispered into my ear.

"Thank you," I replied. This would be my third bath today.

I climbed into my window at about three a.m., closing the curtains behind me. Immediately, sleep fell upon me and I didn't wake up again until six. It was still dark. I sat staring up at the moon for a while. I wondered if Jason was up looking at the exact same sight I was right now.

My room was the one thing that's been constant in my life. All my room consisted of was my bed, my desk, some CDs, and a closet full of clothes. There were a few posters too. Marilyn Manson, Mötley Crüe, and Def Leppard to name a few, graced my walls. Other than that, not much else. Except that my window was always shut now instead of open. I couldn't bear the sound of laughter out there anymore, the sound of happiness—to see kids playing around or walking their dogs.

And my guitar, though it had always stood proudly against the wall for display, now sat up on the dusty shelf in the closet, alone and forgotten, with numerous guitar books, not having been opened in ages.

I got up and walked over to the notebook sitting on top of the computer. At first it had just been a regular, boring composition book—then I glued me and Jason's painting on it. Both of us had been suckers for messy finger painting, even when we grew older. But he was always better than me. The picture on the cover consisted of both Jason, who was holding a guitar, and me. Besides an artist, Jason had also always wanted to be a musician. I knew he could do it. As young as he was, he was always out playing late at local shows, and everyone wanted to see him perform. He made me want to become one too, but I was always a person of stage fright. My awkwardness would surely gain me more laughs and taunts then it did when presenting a project to class. My physique was so weak, I could barely hold a guitar without becoming sore in just a few minutes. So I just stuck to classes and lessons—but now I wasn't stuck to anything at all. It just wasn't worth it anymore.

I opened it to a crooked and sloppy page. To me, writing was easy. Everyone always complained about it. But it was easy and vital for me to just put words down together on paper, and try it different ways too, to see which came out the best. I wasn't looking to become some author or anything—they were for *me*, and me only. Plus, it was so much more fun than reading. Even if my poetry was crap.

Second after second, I watch him die
Nothing I can do but see it and cry
He demands for something greater than life
Greater than his own salvation.
Redemption is impossible now
I can't change the past
People say it'll be okay
But this pain will always last
Where's an angel when I need it?
Just trapped inside, crying, bleeding.
He took something that was dear to me.
No matter how much I pray, beg, and plead

Something warm erupted in my eyes, so I quickly put it down. It was the first one I had written since the night Jason left. But it surprised me how comforting it was at the same time to read it too. Knowing I could express the truth to myself privately. I denied it to everyone else—why deny it to myself? I could look at my life, and know that I wasn't lying. It was relieving, because now I knew I wouldn't go—*completely*—insane.

I traced back to another page. It was blank. No, the page before it was blank. The page I had turned to was ripped out. I felt both my pockets. One had the note Jason wrote. The other was empty.

Oh well, was all I thought. *Nobody knows I wrote it.*

I glanced at my clock. 6:15. *Better get moving.*

"Rory," my mom said sternly as I came downstairs, "where were you last night?"

"Surprised you noticed," I responded bitterly, walking right past her without giving so much as a glance.

"YOU HAD ME WORRIED SICK! And you upset your father." This time I turned and stared at her. She took a few breaths, and then in a more steady voice, she said, "Rory. You're not skipping classes are you?"

"No...what does that matter?"

"Because it's your only chance out of here. Education is a dream for some people and an escape for others."

I stood there, stunned. Before I could say anything, the door to the kitchen slammed, making us both jump.

"Who...threw it...away?" he asked.

I had. Yes, last night before leaving the house, I roamed through that fridge, and wiped out every last bottle. Sent them flying in the dumpster at the end of the street, which was where I probably would end up next. I couldn't see my mom like that again.

Mom turned to me, eyes wide.

"You son of a bitch," he growled. There was a loud crash as my head exploded and my back hit the wooden floor immediately. He must've gotten another pack the other night and hit me with the one he was drinking just now. Glass shattered everywhere. My mom screamed. I tasted blood in my mouth. I didn't cry, but I moaned a little, taking a piece of glass out of my skin. He walked away.

My mom sat over me, wrapping her hands gently around my face, patting it with a damp cloth, still sniffling. "I *drank* his beer..."

No. I hadn't thrown his beer out. That was a lie. But I had to have him think it so she wouldn't get hurt.

"I'll take them for you," I replied weakly, forcing myself up. "Th-the...beatings." My voice came out in a whisper, I was so tired.

"NO!" And she went from looking down at me to looking up at me as I got up. "But...if anyone asks...just...tell them you slipped on a piece of glass."

I nodded, knowing I had to follow the drill. Even if I had to go around all day awkwardly trying to hide the remnants of what was left behind from it, it was worth it so that no one would find out. If they did, I'd get sent to a foster home, and never see my mother again. It was only a few more years until I was eighteen and in college hopefully. I could try to raise enough money to get me *and* my mom out of here. I wanted to live with Todd, but he wouldn't allow that unless I promised to stay in school. And right now, I didn't want to leave my mother. I *hated* school with a passion, but my options were limited.

***

A strange thing happened this morning. Instead of the usual routine of going to first period, everybody was sent to the auditorium. It was pretty hectic in the hallways. Tre was pissed. He spends every one of his mornings just leaning against the wall, having his pick of the girl for the day. They all swarmed around him like a bunch of bees. He was usually calm and collected, but today, like everyone else, he was in a mad rush toward the auditorium to get the best seats, which were in the back.

"Out of my way you little freak," he growled, pushing me so hard, I almost fell back against a locker. Then Mr. O'Hara, the Physics teacher, scolded me for the chains on my pants. I started to take them off, and when he disappeared in the crowd, I left them alone.

Several administrators were standing on the stage, whispering frantically, until finally Principal Page came to the podium.

"Ladies and gentlemen, may I have your attention please...ladies, gentlemen...please..."

"SHUT UP!" one of the assistant principals roared when he leaned into the mic. Everyone did.

Ms. Page sighed. "Thank you. First and foremost," she said in a raggedy, pissed off tone, "I want to say that last night's behavior was absolutely unacceptable. According to the police, they've concluded that about fifty-four of the teens at that party came from *this* school."

That party had been on the news the previous night. I had heard it playing on a TV through a music store when I was heading back late, well after two a.m.

"Drinking alcohol and smoking weed or pot will not help you to graduate with a clean record." And the lecture lasted about ten more minutes. They even considered canceling the pep rally that was scheduled for today, not too long from now. But once the auditorium erupted in protests, coming from both students *and* teachers alike, the administration decided it would be unfair to the innocent.

At least I got to miss some of Chemistry. Now it was twenty minutes shorter.

Sonny and Jeremiah sat there and idolized their science fair project. What was weird was that they cared about school, and I didn't, but I got higher grades anyway, just because I *needed* to. Usually I needed something to distract me at home, AND I always had a fear that I wouldn't have a good enough GPA to go somewhere far away, out of state, out of sight and out of mind, so I could dorm and for once, have a restful night instead of a sleepless one. But...something always pulled me away from that fantasy. My mother.

"Can anyone explain to me the difference between an ionic bond and a covalent bond?" Ms. Hope asked the class. Naturally, we acted as though we didn't hear her. She picked up the seating chart with the roster and said, "Rory."

"The covalent bonds share electrons." My voice shook. I hated being called on.

"Speak up," she hissed.

I sucked my teeth and then repeated, in an annoyed tone.

"Don't you take that tone with me," she snapped. She went on with the lecture, while I heard Sonny giggling in the back. I turned around sharply. He turned his head innocently towards the window, like he was busy in thought, with his finger on his chin. Then he smiled and waved at someone outside. I slowly turned back around.

"Sonny...*Sonny*?"

Sonny's head snapped back to the front and recovered with a grin. "Yes Ms. Hope?"

"Who are you talking to?" She walked over to the window.

"Oh...I guess I was just seeing things," he responded calmly.

She turned to face him. He looked up at her, displaying the goofiest smile I had ever seen in my entire life.

She glared. "And I thought *I* had horrible vision." She went over and sat at her desk, done with the lecture, intent on grading papers. "Now there is only five minutes left of class until you kids get to go out and have your little fun," she said, as if we didn't deserve a life. "In the meantime, I'm grading your term papers, and they had better be good. So far, I'm not liking what I've seen. This is *not* a hard class, ladies and gentlemen."

"Somebody's on PMS," Sonny whispered in Jeremiah's ear.

"*What?*"

"I said...that's a really nice DESK," Sonny said, nodding his head.

The bell rang. Everyone walked out, Sonny casually shoving me on the way, not a very heavy shove...but nonetheless, I shoved him back.

He put a hand up to stop me. "Rory, hey listen," he said, "you need yoga in your life or something. You've got too much pent-up stress." He walked out before I could make a smart comment back. I realized I was the last one in the room, alone. Until I turned and saw the new girl, Renee, gathering up her books and heading out.

She accidentally bumped into the statue that stood on the side of Ms. Hope's desk, who had long gone to the teacher's lounge to complain. It was an enormous statue of one of the famous scientists she always talked about. It tipped over and since it was heavy, Renee was having a hard time balancing it back in place.

I came over and lifted it from her hands, struggling a little myself, but gently putting it back.

"Thank you," she said, glancing at me before bending down to pick her things up off the ground. She had long, wavy, dark brown hair, light brown eyes, and she looked a lot younger than a junior in high school.

I turned my head quickly, playing like I was busy with something else and not noticing the small razorblade falling out of her pocket. I heard her draw in her breath and pull it out of sight as quickly as possible. There was also another one lying on the ground that she didn't see. A small shard of glass. The razorblade (although a male one,

I realized) was a perfectly reasonable thing to have, though probably would result in expulsion if caught on school grounds. At least, that's what happened to a girl last year who got caught with it in the locker rooms. Yes, it was true—students got in trouble for the stupidest things as it was. You didn't *need* to be a bad kid in order to get in trouble.

But the shard of glass though, I wasn't sure what could possibly be the purpose of that.

When she was finished I looked down at her and put on a cold face. "Whatever. This is the last time I will lift some weight for you."

I stopped by the bathroom on my way out to the pep rally. As I passed the mirror, I couldn't help but notice how my eyes were a little glazed. I went up to it and examined them.

The mirror had my mind going back to Chemistry. And what fell out of Renee's bag.

I *needed* that glass shard.

I glanced down at both of my pockets, to make sure both things were safely secure in each one. There was the note Jason wrote me ages back. That thing itself was starting to age too. When I first received it, it was pure white, and every letter was neatly in place. Now it was on the yellowing end, wrinkled, and some of the ink was blurred. Tears from that very first night had the first effects on it.

Then, in the other pocket, was the shard. I had to steal it from her. It wasn't for me. Well, I guess it kind of was. It was for my mom too. To protect both my mom and I. I didn't want to use it as a weapon, and I avoided the thought completely that that might ever become necessary. All I wanted to do was hold it out in front of me, whenever he threatened to do something. Sort of like a threat in return. Maybe it would let him know I meant business and was through with his crap. Ward him off with it, the way garlic or crosses ward off vampires. It wasn't the best item, but it would have to do. *Please do,* I thought, staring down at the tiny but sharp shard.

My thoughts shifted to Tre, who I'd have to meet in a little while. The guilt of what I had that I was supposed to give him today weighed down on me, weighed down in my backpack even though it was a simple, light little item: The keys to Todd's music store. Tre never liked Todd; but now he resented him more than ever, since he'd gotten himself banished from the store permanently for being caught shoplifting. Now he wanted to sneak back in and vandalize the place, from the inside. The outside was too amateur for him—*anyone* could do that.

So I'd stolen the keys from the front checkout counter when Todd wasn't looking. Tre wanted to take merchandise and resell them for money. I kept trying to justify it to myself by thinking, *He shouldn't have been irresponsible enough to just leave them there like that.* It didn't work though, because I knew I shouldn't have taken them and he'd probably trusted me enough to not go sneaking around. The deep pit of lousiness grew deeper and deeper trying to consume me, so I moved away from that fact and moved on to why I was even willing to do this for Tre in the first place.

He'd said he would harm Sidney if I didn't comply.

I didn't know what he meant specifically. I didn't know if he meant assault her or try to run her over, or do something more subtle and that he would be less likely to get caught for, like throw stones at her house to scare her, or slip something into her locker.

Either way, I would *not* let that happen. Sidney's wellbeing was more important than a store getting vandalized. Hell, *anyone's* wellbeing was more important than a store. So I kept that on my mind as much as possible. If I was forced to explain myself later to Todd, that would have to be a good enough explanation. Surely he'd see the logic in it.

And if Todd wanted to call the police on Tre, he could be my guest. I wasn't going to be the one to rat that guy out though.

Tre was nineteen yet still in high school. I suppose anyone would be bitter if they were in that situation, but it didn't give him the right to be so needlessly cruel towards people. There was seriously something wrong with the guy's wiring. I didn't think he was just a troubled kid, I thought he was genuinely sadistic. He was only a freshman when Jason went to high school, but he'd already willingly joined in with Jason and the rest of the big cats in all their sprees. Whereas while Jason only felt a lack of guilt in things like vandalism, loitering, shoplifting, or smoking in nonsmoking areas, Tre liked to hurt people. He *liked* it. I shuddered at the thought of what he was going to do to Renee last night—might've done if I hadn't showed up. Tre got a strange kick out of hurting people, and it didn't matter who—men, women, children. The asshole probably kicked cats too.

He didn't even really know Sidney. But anyone that knew me well (and shamefully, he did) knew I would do anything—ANY-THING—to protect Sidney.

That's fine. She wouldn't give a damn. In fact she might even be disgusted by it. After all, she's got her buff brother and tall, handsome, funny boyfriend to flatter her now. The kind who knows how to be enticing and says all the right things. Makes all the right moves.

The worst thing of all was that what Tre was doing was the exact same thing Jason did—that I got him in trouble for. Except Jason never directly hurt anyone for it. He would steal and shoplift for Tre sometimes, which wasn't good. But he was above mugging people and assaulting them, which was more than one could say for Tre. Money. And adventure. It was all about the money and adventure. And revenge. Revenge from a society they deemed unfair to our generation, our class, etc. And fear from people. And getting things without having to really put in the work for them.

I tried to think all of these thoughts without having the dizziness rush through my system.

***

The field outside had been completely transformed. Now it was filled with banners, loud cheering, and four bright colors each representing a different class. Skilled dance moves were being displayed as music flowed throughout the place. But my head was somewhere else. I knew sooner or later, Renee would discover her blade missing. I also snuck the keys into Tre's bag. It was in his bag as of that moment—I had snuck it in when he got up to use the bathroom before the pep rally began. And I didn't want Renee to worry. I wanted her to know that I wouldn't rat her out or anything...I didn't know what she had the blade for, if there was any malicious intent or not. But if there was anything I wanted someone to acknowledge me for, it was that I kept my mouth shut. So I had left a note in her locker. Hopefully she would read it and meet down where I was, under the bleachers.

My thoughts were broken as Jeremiah and Sonny's band came on stage. I got a sick feeling in my stomach. Jason had been a musician. Not a famous one, but one nonetheless. I knew if he hadn't run off, he would've been successful in a matter of time. He worked the guitar like it had a life of its own, and his voice was superb. Sometimes he would even let me write some of his lyrics. I was always so excited when he let me do that, so honored—he didn't have to let me do that. How many people would? I knew if I was a musician, I'd want to write my *own* lyrics. And I couldn't imagine how terrible the lyrics I gave him really were.

I felt like running a chainsaw through my thighs. *Why'd you have to throw that away, you self-centered son-of-a-bitch? All over jealousy too...* His lyrics, his tunes, his voice and soul, his OVERALL PER-

FORMANCE was a better world to me than this one. Anytime I looked at a guitar, all I could think of was him.

I spit at the ground, beginning to get grumpy despite the massive event. Jeremiah couldn't sing...he didn't know the first thing about it. Same went for Sonny and the drums. Neither of them could measure up.

Maybe if I kept focusing on the negatives, it would distract me from realizing how good they really were, and how much alike Jeremiah's vocals sounded to Jason's.

I glanced down at my watch. Ten o'clock. Where was she? *Here I am, actually trying to do something nice,* I thought furiously. *I mean, I try sometimes to be a decent guy, and no one wants to cooperate.* I gritted my teeth, forcing long, deep breaths to cool down.

I heard someone stepping in the grass. I turned around, hopeful—and it was Sidney. "Hey, Sid," I said casually, stopping the impulse of reaching out and touching her arm just in time. I should know better. "What are you doing here?"

She turned. "Huh?"

"What are you doing here?"

"I was just going in to refill my water bottle."

True. The water fountain out here was not very good.

"Where's your little friend—"

"Uh...you mean Renee?"

"Yeah, her."

"Why do you need to know that?"

"Why not?"

She shrugs. "I don't know. I'm very protective of my friends, so..."

My heart started to pound harder. "Have I ever put my hands on a female before?" I asked as slowly as possible, burning up. I regretted the words as soon as I saw Sidney's mouth hang open.

"Did I say a damn thing about you 'putting your hands on some-one'? NO!"

I sighed, wishing I wasn't such an idiot. It was true, she didn't. I had overreacted. "Why are you so difficult? Just tell me where she is."

Sidney sighed. "She's in the clinic."

"What?" I asked, trying not to sound too concerned.

"She's not feeling well. It all started when she was on her way to her locker. She looked real pale, and she started saying things like, 'I need my mother...'" Sidney shook her head, and continued. "So I brought her to the clinic—Sonny and Jeremiah were already at the show—she's resting there for a little while, but they said she should be okay." She looked up at me and glared. "Happy?" She strolled away, empty water bottle swinging by her side.

"Fuck you," I said under my breath. I had just wanted to know where someone was.

I stayed there, however, in case Renee ever did show up. Sidney had mentioned that Renee was on her way to her locker, but...never made it. She would go again—and get the note.

My prediction turned out to be true. Renee showed up about ten minutes later, wandering around, not knowing exactly where to go.

"Pssss," I whispered sharply.

She turned, startled. "You wanted to meet with me?" she mouthed.

"Yes..." I paused, trying to think of the right words. "Um, why don't you come over here?" I asked, beckoning her.

She just stood, rooted to the ground.

"Stop it," I said irritably, "I'm not going to hurt you. Don't you remember last night?"

She still just stood there. This had gone on long enough.

I did something very risky and stupid just then. I pulled out the switchblade I had tucked away in my jacket, the same one I'd stolen from Tre years back. I held it out, making her lose her breath for a moment, before she realized that I had voluntarily dropped it in the dirt in front of her. Then I backed away about five more feet, so that she could easily bend down and reach it, in time to defend herself if I came running towards her immediately. It was simple common sense—you wouldn't go and attack someone if they had a knife on them. I didn't know why people were afraid of me before I even did anything. I probably gave off a bad vibe.

"There," I said. "Now, you can come and protect yourself if you need to."

She looked ashamed. Good, she should've. She should've felt *awful.* She stepped forward, without the knife.

"Hey, pick it up and give it back if you're not going to use it!" I hissed, my eyes darting around cautiously. There was hardly anyone about. We were under a far bleacher that was distant from the specks of people rallying and from the muffled sounds of a marching band and cheerleaders. Still, I didn't feel like getting expelled. Or for that matter, arrested.

Renee handed my knife back and blurted, "Why do you have this?"

I opened my mouth to respond, but shut it. The truth was, I felt safer with it when I was around my old man. And Tre. It was exceedingly stupid to bring it to school and I would decide to not do it anymore. Instead of saying all this, I just snapped, "That's not what we're talking about right now, and *you* are one to talk." I paused. "I have—well, had—your shard," I said.

"What?" she asked astonished.

"I can give it back if you want. But..."

"But why?" She wasn't angry, just perplexed.

"I feel safer with it." I sighed. "You remember how last night he was ranting on about some 'deal'?" She nodded. "Tre wants me to give him the keys to a music store that he wants to break into. Only it wouldn't technically be 'breaking' if he had keys, but he's obviously not supposed to have them. He was banned from the store a long time ago. I have the keys with me right now. I hang out there a lot and I stole them." *Because I'm an idiot who wants to get banned by Todd too.* And he would. He'd do it to his own child (if he had one). "And he said if I don't give them to him, he'd hurt Sidney. So I need to hand these right to him, I can't just slip them into his locker or bag, and risk having someone see or steal them—"

"Wha—" She couldn't find the words. Her eyes narrowed, dismayed, and she held her hands out like *what the hell is going on?*

"He's doing it, to screw with ME. He doesn't have anything against her, he doesn't even KNOW her."

"Excuse me!"

We both jumped and turned, startled, to see an administrator walking toward us. Renee dropped the bottle. I tore my gaze away, bent down quickly, and retrieved it. I went to place it firmly in my pocket, but the administrator was here now and yanked it out of my hand. Just as well, really. Otherwise he would search me and all my belongings, and find the knife.

He had a walkie-talkie and hissed something into it, too fast and low to catch. Then he turned back, glared at us, and motioned for us to follow him.

***

We sat in the big, quiet, gray room, just the two of us, waiting. All I could hear was a phone ring in a nearby office. The silence was way too loud, and awkward.

I had to think of a way to break it. I had to think of something normal and comfortable to talk about. I relaxed my shoulders and took a deep breath. "So...where did you say you were from again?" I asked.

"Uh, Maryland. You?"

"Florida. I moved here when I was three and a half."

Her voice was quiet and shaky. "What did you need it for?

I turned toward her. She was still staring straight ahead. "Huh?" I asked stupidly.

"The shard of glass you took. It's not hard to come by, but...what do you need one for?"

"Oh...well..." For Tre. And didn't feel like breaking anymore mirrors, especially school property.

There was some more awkward silence. I didn't want to provoke more talking, but it was uncomfortable being surrounded by quietness, at least this type. It wasn't the same type of quietness you find in the woods, or on a mountain, or in an open meadow.

"What do you think our punishment will be?"

"For simply straying from the event and hanging out under the bleachers, like a lot of kids have done? Nothing," I said defiantly.

"Suspension," said a kid sitting in a seat across the small room from us.

"What?" I almost yelled.

"This school has really cracked down on stuff like that. My buddy got suspended for three days last year for doing the same thing."

"You're lying," I said, glaring at him.

"I'm not." He seemed so nonchalant about it. What was he in here for? Reading too much during class?

"That's the stupidest thing I've ever heard." I sat back with my arms folded.

"Never said it wasn't stupid. Only that it's what happens."

"Well, fuck."

My head snapped over at Renee. I was surprised to hear her swear. She seemed like the type of girl who never did anything even remotely against the rules. A good girl, that wore flowers in her hair and sang about world peace. I'd thought she would've been a hippie if this was the seventies. But now I was thinking she might've been more of a rebel.

"I shit you not," the guy said. I turned to Renee and quickly changed the subject before he could continue on this infuriating discussion. "How'd you convince your parents to go out last night?"

"I didn't. I snuck out."

It was so blunt. "Oh."

"I didn't bother asking him, since I knew he would say no."

Then came the question that had been burning a hole in me. "Renee?"

"Yeah?"

"What happened to your mother?" I blurted.

She turned toward me and stared.

"I'm sorry," I said immediately. "I mean—I just—"

"No, no it's alright," she replied.

"It was just straight curiosity, but you don't have to tell me if—"

"She was in an accident five years ago and died."

"Oh," I said quietly.

"Um, do you have a brother?" Now it was her turn to blush a little. "Oh! I'm sorry, I—"

"S'okay," I responded. "Yeah. One older brother. His name's Jason. You?"

"No siblings. Just one older cousin who lives with me named Jenny."

"Do you like her?"

"No."

"Well, keep her close. You might be glad you did one day—"

"Rory? Your mother's here," an administrator said, the door flying open.

I sighed. I glanced at Renee one last time, and then turned and walked out.

Chapter 8: RENEE-When Rain Falls, the Storm Calls (Early morning, Wednesday, December 18th, 1996)

I stared out my window that night, watching the rain fall.

The car ride back yesterday was silent, and I knew I was in for it. Until we arrived home and all my dad did was shake his head and point toward the stairs. It meant, *Go to your room*. Really? That was it? No. That was just until he could figure out exactly what things to say to me. Until he calmed down and cooled off instead of throwing a raging fit. But...I sort of wanted that. I sort of *deserved* that. No, scratch that—I *did* deserve that. I guess it just really bothered me because he used to be a lot tougher, and now, ever since mom died, he wasn't. He had little moments when he'd burst out, like the first night we were here. But that was it. What happened to my father?

I looked over at my still-packed belongings. On them lay the small and crinkled piece of paper Rory had left behind at the party.

A couple hours earlier, my secret had been unleashed. And it was all Jenny's fault.

"Turn down your music, Jenny!" Sheila yelled from downstairs.

"*Hey, don't go in there!*" *Jenny shouted at me, thinking I was about to go through the biggest bag she owned. It was the same one I had to carry in two nights ago. Why or how it was in my room, I had no idea.*

But it wasn't until Sheila screamed that Jenny turned her music off completely. The entire house went dead quiet.

"*What's wrong?*" *dad asked, striding out of his room. He looked tired and weary. A little older than thirty-eight.*

"*What are these? Who's are these?*" *Sheila came stomping into my room through the bathroom, two broken pieces of glass sitting delicately in her hand, her fist shaking violently. Sweat was accumulating on the back of my neck, which I massaged with my hand, trying to look casual. My heart started beating and had sunken to the bottom of my stomach.* "*You!*" *Sheila pointed her finger at me.* "*Come in here with the rest of us!*"

My legs felt like jelly as I followed Sheila into Jenny's room, where Jenny and my dad were currently standing, all accusing eyes on me. Damn it, I thought. I should've stuck to razors for shaving. That would be more normal.

I'd forgotten to take them out of my jeans pocket, the ones I put in the dirty laundry when I'd changed. Nothing strange about a broken piece of glass in your pocket that you could've picked up anywhere. Nothing at all.

"*What is this?*" *Sheila shook her hand, the pieces fluttering a little.* "*I found it in* your *pants!*"

"*How disgusting,*" *Jenny remarked quietly.* "*You know Ren, you should really make sure things are at the bottom of the trash can if you want to get rid of them from everyone.*" *She paused.* "*But I guess you didn't want to get rid of them.*"

Though horror had stricken me in the gut, it didn't show. I looked up at her, combing her wildly messy hair from the shower, and glared.

"How do you know they're mine?" I asked in a not-so-convincing tone. My mouth almost went numb.

"I see you with stuff like that sometimes."

I grimaced. "And?" I said through clenched teeth.

"Renee!" Sheila shrieked. It was the first time I saw pure terror on her face. Not smugness. Not arrogance. Just straight terror. And, it was the first time she called me by my real name. In my life.

My dad came over and clamped a big hand around my arm. I tried to pull out of his grip but there was no way to budge. I looked up at him, and I knew I shouldn't have—he had a cold, angry look in his eyes. The phone rang. "I'll get it," he said through gritted teeth. He slammed the door on the way out. All three of us flinched. I was grateful for whoever called—I didn't want to know what he was about to say or do.

Sheila just threw the two pieces in the garbage before bagging it up, even though it wasn't full enough to bag up yet, and walked off quickly, mumbling inaudible words. She didn't have her usual conceited strut. She was walking as if it was her first time learning.

And then there was Jenny. Looking at me with narrowed eyes, like she was the one who'd been wronged.

"How dare you..." I began, not knowing exactly where to go from there.

"Sneaking those little monsters around," she said. "You're so sick. Who's to say you weren't planning on stabbing somebody else?"

I exited the bedroom, went down the stairs, and walked outside into the rain, pouring and cleansing my face. Jenny followed and continued her tirade.

"You see, your dad and my mom may not have suspected, but I knew it all along. One child was bound to inherit her mother's idiocy—"

"You bitch." I turned and faced her, stopping her dead in her tracks. We were now behind the shed, where nobody could see, and there was no protection. Her face was an inch away from mine, a couple inches higher.

"Of course, there are always those rare occasions when you think you can go the day without them, too. But very rarely."

BANG!

Jenny lay there in the mud, blood spilling from her nose.

I drew designs on the freezing, wet glass. My heart was now steady as the rain outside, and I was currently the only resident up at this hour, as far as I knew. The wind blew the leaves and swayed the trees. There were distant sirens in one direction, some pulsing music in another. The typical neighborhood sound like the one I had tossed and turned to all night long when I had escaped the party.

No. Not the party. Tre and his clan.

I had been worried about Rory and I was relieved when I saw him in school the next day. I found myself still hoping that he was okay at this very moment. I even hoped I would meet him sometime again soon. He seemed like a very troubled person, which might've been rich coming from me, but he seemed even more severely troubled than me. And I could admit that that was saying a lot.

Down below, I heard the giggles and chuckles of delinquents and preteens fooling around, spray-painting walls with curse words and obscenities. Then, a woman (must've been somebody's mom), came and grabbed one of the little boys by the hair. He screamed and started trying to fight back, but all that did was make the already-angry woman shove him against the wall. There was a brawl of cursing, then silence and God knew what happened next. I had started tuning out by then. The sun began to rise. I had to escape for a little while. I wasn't ready to face my family again just yet.

I was not sorry for what I did. Jenny was in her room, probably pressing an ice pack to her face right now. I wondered if dad or Sheila knew about it yet. But I would never forgive my cousin for what she said.

Yes, mom had an addiction once. A cutting addiction. But she dealt with it. And she was okay afterwards. At least she and I could admit our problems, unlike some people.

I picked up my purse from my desk. It didn't have much, but I felt naked without it. I left a note for dad on my bed. It said, *"Went out for a little while. Be back in a few hours. I won't be too far."*

Before I left, and before I could think, I took one little peek in Jenny's bag that she carelessly left beside my bed. It was filled with several packets of condoms, and a stack of polaroids of her and a guy I'd never met (and Sheila probably hadn't either). They were making out. I never understood why people took pictures of themselves kissing. What were you going to do with them, hang them on your wall?

"Idiot," I said quietly to myself, trying to deny my surprise, and the fact that it didn't really make her an idiot at all. She was being responsible. Then I turned and left, quietly slipping out the front door.

***

I sat on a bench in a park where there were plenty of people around. An old couple smiled at me politely as they walked by. I smiled back. I sketched pictures of random people around me, only in different clothes. In life, if there was something in me I learned to depend on the most for strength, it was a pencil, a pad, and my hands. But it wasn't long before I fell asleep right there on the bench.

I awoke about an hour later with a searing hunger in my stomach. It was still the same day, Wednesday. And eight in the morning, according to my watch. *I must've left earlier than I thought.* It felt like I had slept forever.

I wanted to call Sidney. She knew Rory and I wanted to tell her what happened to us. She was probably in class at the moment, and by now, she would learn about what happened. Her, Sonny, and Jeremiah all hated Rory. What if they judged me for even having met up with him in the first place? Was I overreacting? The nerves in my stomach made it too stressful to try talking to anyone right now.

Just when I'd made friends. *I knew it was too good and too easy to be true.* Tears sprung to my eyes, so I quickly got up and started walking somewhere else.

The day was nice. Warm sunlight poured on me. I got a heavenly-tasting breakfast bar out of my purse and soothed my stomach. It started to get a little nauseous again as I saw a woman walk by, holding her little daughter's hand while in the other, the girl carried a stuffed teddy bear. She also had a *Disney* backpack on. It didn't seem so long ago now that my mom had bought me a stuffed animal. She'd take me on vacations too during summer, usually to Walt Disney World in Florida. I used to be such a good little girl. I wondered how her reaction would be if she knew what I'd become.

Unfortunately, the breakfast didn't sit for long. It wasn't because I grew hungry again. Hungry for food at least. I knew what the real problem was and stopped denying it. It was so bad I wanted to scratch the skin off my arms.

I stopped by a small bench on a deserted street corner. The wind started picking up and dark clouds were slowly making their way in. I was surprised by how quickly the weather had changed from that morning in a matter of minutes. I zipped up my thick black jacket and snuggled around in it.

A little kid, maybe seven or eight, had been sitting behind the bench and blowing some bubbles. Then he started crying.

I got up and walked around the bench. I approached him slowly and gently. "Hey kid," I said softly, "Are you lost?"

He sniffled. "Y-y-yes. We-well...n-not really." He pointed toward his pocket. "B-b-but...I need to catch the bus home, BUT I LOST MY MONEY!" he wailed, so loudly it echoed throughout the empty and deserted street.

I felt in my pocket. It turned out I had more than enough money left for the bus for both of us, and the bus wasn't going to come for at least another ten minutes.

I bent down toward the kid. "I can give you some money."

The boy stopped crying, looked at me for a second, and nodded.

I had really wanted to go into the small drugstore on our right to get some Aleve. I was now getting a killer headache and I hoped desperately that it wouldn't become a migraine. A migraine was the last thing I needed right now, and if it happened, then being out would be the last thing needed right now. I would need to be at home, but people like Jenny and Sheila—and even my dad, to an extent—were also the last things I needed right now. *Everything* was the last thing I needed right now and it drove me crazy. But I couldn't just leave the kid stranded here.

He got off the bus to what looked like his neighborhood. I prayed it was, and that I wouldn't hear a story later about a kid of his description having gone missing. I walked into a little coffee place further down the street, despite already having breakfast. I was tired and cold. A little coffee helped sometimes.

There was an Asian girl who looked to be about eighteen or nineteen, with a streak of bright blue in her otherwise dark hair, along with black lipstick, sitting near the counter talking to what I thought was her boyfriend at first, but soon I figured to be her brother. I envied her looks and confidence. She had the little TV in the top ceiling corner on, the kind that never had the volume up enough, and it was on the weather channel. "There is currently a Severe Thunderstorm Warning for the following counties..." He named several places within the vicinity, including ours, and then added, "Likely to be severe wind gusts and possibly hail."

As I made my way to a table, I accidentally bumped into someone. "Sorry," I mumbled without looking up at the person and went to a table to sit down.

Then, I felt that presence again, right beside me. And somehow, I knew.

"Rory," I said without looking.

"Yep. It's me."

"What are you doing here?"

"What are *you* doing here?"

"I...I ran away from home for a little while." It sounded so childish.

"Did you now." He sounded more like he was talking to himself than another person. "Do they beat you?" he said starting in his regular voice, and ending in such a low whisper that I could hardly catch the last bit, the 'beat you' part.

Startled, I responded, "No. I screwed up on my own."

There was silence. So I finally decided to ask the one question that was burning a hole in me.

"Why does Tre want to screw with you?" I asked.

"He's always wanted to. It's because I called it quits with him a while back."

"Called it quits?"

"I was in a gang with him and my brother. Back when Tre and I were just freshmen and my brother was a junior."

"How did you...become a part of it?"

"Jason used to be a part of it." He sighed and took a deep breath. "My bro. Before he left. He left when I was only twelve years old. So then they looked to me."

"At you? You were twelve!"

"You'd be surprised how young some people are when they join a gang," he said somberly.

"So...how come he left?" I was still trying to wrap my head around all of this.

"He felt guilty. Jason was—is—actually a very innocent guy. He doesn't like doing wrong. He only did it to make money. So eventually, he wanted to leave the gang." He paused. "I think he was doing it to try to protect me. In all honesty, I was never *really* a part of the gang. I was just his kid brother, and they don't see me as a threat. Even Tre, who was pretty young at the time, was older than me. Because he got held back. He's nineteen, you know." Somehow this didn't surprise me. I'd thought that guy looked a little old to be in high school. "He should be out of school by now, at least high school. I can't really see him going to college." Rory grimaced. "Idiot doesn't think hard work is something his entitled hands should have to do for anything. But they really looked up to him, especially Tre. Everyone was enraged when he left."

I knew what that meant. I didn't know much about gangs, but I knew a lot of them weren't okay with someone just leaving.

"But I did worse things," Rory continued. "The most he had on his conscience was stealing things." And to think, I used to feel like a felon for shoplifting bubblegum from the store when I was eight. "He didn't hurt anybody—he didn't even threaten anybody. All the money he made went to good use too."

I waited for him.

"Neither parent had a job back then." They had to fend for themselves. *And what did you do...that was worse?*

"I beat people sometimes," he said, as if reading my mind. "Sometimes beat them bloody, if they were a threat to us." I winced. "I also stole so much money—all to keep my alcohol-loving father satisfied."

"But that part isn't your fault."

"Yeah, but..." he shrugged. "You know, I really did mean it when I said how that wasn't the type of person I was. You know, about revealing your glass and everything?"

I flinched. "I know," I said.

"That *is* what it was, right? You weren't planning on cutting somebody else?"

"No," I responded promptly. Though I did fantasize about it sometimes.

"I'm far from it. Nothing could ever make me go that way. It's not my place to tell anyone how to live their life." He paused. "Just...don't do it to any major arteries or veins."

"Uh, of course not." I didn't bother telling him that I hadn't tried it at all yet, even after a year of contemplating it. And that now I probably never would, even if I wanted to. Mom had always used to say, *"People who get no love at home, have difficulty giving it to others."* But he was giving me some. Or at least, a warning not to fatally stab myself. It must've counted for something.

Good thing I had you, mom.

I looked out the window. Raindrops started to fall lightly, and then got harder and harder, smearing and streaking the glass. The clouds outside were becoming almost black now. Wind was blowing around so hard, some of the tables shook inside. Somebody's glass dropped and shattered to the floor, water spilling out of it. There was dead silence everywhere.

I looked out the window again. Things were flying around, rather big things too, such as potted plants and statues people decorated their front porches with. The air seemed to be...rotating.

A big red message appeared on the TV, with that horrifically loud distorted alarm sound, signaling a Tornado Warning. Words ran across the bottom of the screen listing counties, and one of them was ours.

Something loud hit the window and made me jump. People starting panicking in a rush. Some ran out to their cars, some went towards the back room, others huddled together in the corners.

Rory grabbed my arm and pulled me under a table. "Those people," he hissed in my ear, "what are they doing going out to their *cars?* Don't they know you should stay put?" Though it was hard to hear because the wind outside was very loud now, almost deafening, and the floor—no, the walls—no, the entire *building* started to shake.

I didn't know how long it was between that and when it actually happened. Time seemed to have come to a standstill, so it could've been seconds to hours for all I knew. Realistically it was probably about a minute or two. The noise in my head seemed to have been louder than the noise outside, though that was certainly coming around to drowning any and all thoughts out. My mind was blank while desperately trying to remember what I was supposed to be thinking about. Mom...Jenny, Sheila...dad...this boy sitting next to me, practically shouting something frantically into my ear...Rory? Yes, Rory, from school. School. I wasn't in school anymore for now. I was inside a place, one that smelled like coffee, and I was under a table, and there was loud noise outside, and—

The next thing I knew, a window shattered, and a big pair of hands gripped my shoulders. The lights flickered and then everything went dark. Any and all light was devoured by the coming disaster. I closed my eyes and my body felt as though it was being separated in different directions. My mind was shaking in my skull, I could not think straight. Couldn't form any coherent thoughts. Everything was just pure chaos. I didn't know where I was, and it sounded like a train so loud, my ears popped, and then went numb. I tried opening my eyes, but everything was black.

***

I remembered breathing heavily before I even opened my eyes. There were raging noises all around—fire engines, screaming, sobbing. I heard a quiet whimper right in my ear. There was an arm behind my back. It cradled my head in its shoulder. I could smell his shirt. I slowly opened my eyes. There was nothing but debris, wood, trees, plaster, and broken pieces glass lying around. Fresh water was being poured into my mouth and I felt something warm in my hand. But it was not another hand. It was something soft and furry.

I tilted my head back while another pair of hands cradled it gently. The last thing I heard was a deep whisper into my ear. "It's gonna be okay."

Chapter 9: RORY—It Happened One Night (Wednesday, December 18, 1996)

Earlier that day

I sat up against the trees and leaned back, watching the leaves fall lightly. I wondered what it would be like to live in isolation, away from the rest of mankind. It might've been hard, but in a way, a lot easier too. Sometimes being alone was safer and more pleasant.

I stared across the grass to a lake that was isolated itself, a cool mist sprinkled around it, making everything icy in its path. This lake was not something I paid much mind to until the incident four years ago—rumors were still wrong about the whole thing. I remembered the day clearly—I had not known what I was in for.

"You! You're the one who drove Jason away!" My dad shoved me so hard, I tripped over a rock and fell into the deep, cold water. He splashed in after me, not to save me, but to hit me some more. "But now I know, he was an IDIOT just like you!" He gripped my hair and shoved my face downwards. The water was so cold it didn't even feel like liquid, but solid ice. It scratched at my face and smothered me unmercifully. I was drowning.

I awoke in wet, muddy, grassy clothes on the ground beside the lake. I was coughing and gasping for breath. I heard footsteps walking away. I slowly lifted my shirt up, seeing a huge bruise on my ribs. It ached like hell so it hurt to sit up. Sunlight was shining down on me, drying me up, slowly but surely. Hours must have passed by, but I'd never know how I got out of there alive.

Talk of this started to spread around town afterwards. Neighbors claiming they heard me trying to commit suicide. It figured. I was practically the kid from hell to them. Others said they just heard screaming. Well, why didn't they try to call the police then? Not that it would've done any good, but doesn't the action count for something?

I heard stomps and was about ready to get up and leave—THUD! I couldn't tell whether it was his knee or his foot that whacked me in the side of my face. My eyes couldn't see straight for a second.

His face was in mine. "Get up boy!"

I closed my eyes, and instantly opened them back up. *Don't be a coward.* I drew myself upward, slowly walking past him, keeping an eye on him as he eyed me back.

"Get inside. You're just like your brother."

"Good. And I hope he's still like me more than you."

I tensed, bracing for the blow. But my dad gave a hoarse laugh and walked inside.

We parted ways in the hallway. I peeked into the living room to make sure my mother was okay. She was still breathing evenly. I turned a corner and found the closet door open. It was near the front entrance of the house where we kept our coats and shoes. It was no surprise that someone left it open. It matched all the unwashed dishes and clothes in the house.

Just as I was about to shut it, I noticed a box had fallen to the ground, spilling its contents. Most of it was just old bills, notices, and cigarettes. One thing stood out—it was a photograph. My family didn't exactly keep that many.

I heard the back door slam shut and looked down the hall. I could see him through the screen, sitting on the porch, his back to me.

I turned back to the closet and bent down, picking the photo up delicately. There were two people on it—a boy and a girl, probably not much older than I was. The boy was tall, wearing a black leather jacket, with his hair slicked back with gel, and his arm draped around the short girl. In his other hand, he was holding a red rose. The girl was almost a foot shorter than him, with a red, polka-dot dress on. She had bright red lipstick and was smiling, showing a mouth full of white teeth. The guy was smiling with his lips closed. He looked a little shy. But they both looked genuinely happy.

I turned it over. On the back, there was tiny writing that said:

I have more than any man could ever ask for. I have a beautiful girl who loves me and a working job to help support anything we need. One day, we'll have a nice big house with a vast backyard and a swing set for the kids. She and I are going to have at least two, maybe more. We will love them and care for them, and give them anything they need to make sure they grow up in a nice, loving environment.

-Darryl Silverman, 1974

It was probably the longest time I'd ever gone without blinking. *I'll be damned*. It was my parents. He looked...different. When I examined it closer, however, it *did* kind of look like him. Younger, thinner, happier...just take away all the bad, and put in some good, and there he was.

I quickly put the photo in my bag. I was probably risking another beating, but I didn't care. Somehow, I just had to have this photo. They probably forgot about it anyway.

I walked back down the hall, toward the back of the house. The wooden floor creaked ominously beneath me. I came to the screened door, and cracked it open, inching my way out.

He had a lighted cigarette, but he wasn't smoking it...he was touching it to some pictures. I couldn't tell what they were, because they were already burning.

Cautiously, I sat down on the porch next to him. I could tell he was distracted. This was one of the few times it would probably be safe.

"What happened to your life?" I blurted out without thinking.

I braced myself to jump up and run back in the house, but surprisingly, he answered, "My father happened. That's what happened. He was *always* happening."

I took a closer look at the photos and realized now that *that's* who was on them—my grandfather, whom I never knew. I had occasionally heard my old man talk about him when I was little. He'd get really angry whenever he did. But other than that, I knew nothing about the man.

"I never knew him," I said.

"And you never will. I'll NEVER let him near this house. You think I'm bad? He'd try to kill you if he were your dad. Tried to kill me once. Nearly burned me alive once. Another time he locked me inside the car for almost an hour in the heat."

Involuntarily, I glanced down at his waist. Since he was sitting, his shirt was raised up a little bit, revealing some flesh. Some reddish-brown flesh, not recent, scarred and twisted from something very long ago. When the rest of him was fair, like me. And I'd always assumed that the reason for his constant limping was that he was drunk a lot, but now I was starting to have second thoughts.

"You tried to kill me once," I reminded him quietly.

"No. *I* saved you. I pulled you out and then gave you CPR. I think I may have broken a few of your ribs in the process, because you're just so damn tiny, but I saved you."

My mouth hung open. So *that's* why I had a bruise on my ribs.

"Thanks," I mumbled. He didn't say anything. "Would you ever let grandpa—"

"*Not* your 'grandpa'," my dad corrected.

"Fair enough. Would you ever let him near Jason?"

"Rory, I'd burn my scalp off before allowing that to happen."

It was the first time he'd said my name. In a while, at least. "How do you know he won't? Jason, we don't know where he is."

"I know where *he* is. In hell," my dad said, pointing downward. He shrugged. "Hell. Maybe you'll even find Jason one day. Maybe."

I will. I would see Jason again before one of us died. I would find him, somehow, and try to patch things up. One day.

***

I got on the bus, heading nowhere in particular, and stared out the window. Trees, houses, and kids playing in playgrounds all passed by. So did Wilcox High. But there were no cars or buses in the parking lot. No lights were on inside either. An old, worn out, metal post held a sign beside the entrance that said, *Closed. Power Outage not expected to be fixed by afternoon.*

I took out a cigarette, and was getting ready to start smoking when something caught the corner of my eye—a dark-skinned girl, sitting a couple seats up in the opposite isle of me. Glasses, braces, small hands...she was shivering and wrapping her coat tightly around her. "Renee?" I asked myself quietly. I leaned forward for a closer look. Yes, it was Renee. She glanced behind her but didn't see me.

I looked back at my unused cigarette. I quickly put it back in my bag.

She got off the bus before me. I almost called out her name, but she was gone.

***

I got off at a stop between the movie theatre and surrounding neighborhoods. I put on my headphones and started walking in no particular direction. I stopped abruptly, fear stabbing my stomach when I realized I was right near Sidney's front yard. Her, Sonny, their little sister, and Jeremiah were all sitting around. None of them saw me. I tip-toed a few steps back, behind some trees.

Sidney and Jeremiah were sitting on the bench beside the front door. It was one of those entrances with a roof still over your head even when you stepped outside, before you approached the steps. Then there was a little path with patches of flowers on either side, though they were dying slowly as the cold season drew nearer. Sonny was trying to get some ice off of his windshield and a little girl with long black braids and neatly-arranged beads in her hair was running around with a golden retriever.

"Awww, Brooke, I think he likes you," Sidney cooed.

Then Jeremiah leaned down and whispered something in her ear. She immediately burst out laughing. I found myself laughing along with her, even though I didn't know what the joke was. That's how contagious Sidney's laughing was. Then I felt a pang in my stomach. Jeremiah was awfully lucky to have her. I was lucky at one point too, but I blew it.

"Hey guys, I'm going in to make some s'mores," Sonny announced. "Who wants to come with me?"

"Oooh, I do!" Jeremiah said excitedly. So excitedly that he slipped on some ice and startled the dog.

Jeremiah busted out laughing, and so did everyone else. Including me. He really was an okay guy. There was no reason for me to hate him. There was no reason for me to hate any of them. I just naturally made an enemy of everybody.

I sighed. I felt so sick, standing there in the trees like a damn stalker.

I continued backing my way out of the trees, until I was near the street again, turning my route around. I regretted ever looking in the first place, and now I would be much more careful about where I walked.

***

It turned out that Sidney's neighborhood had a nicer pack of woods than mine did. I leaned back, smelling the crisp air. I breathed, stretched, and yawned, wondering if I would fall asleep for a nap. A very stupid and dangerous thing to do, but I had done so before and I really didn't care.

Suddenly I heard leaves crunching. I stilled myself and jerked my hair away from my ears to listen some more. Around the corner of a nearby tree, a little dog, a pug, came walking over to me. I stared at it, confused, and started to get up. It let out a soft yelp and started to back away. "N-no," I said, losing my balance, "I won't hurt you."

The little puppy stopped in its tracks when I said that, as if it could understand. Then it slowly turned and looked in my direction, hesitating. I held out my hand in greeting. Reluctantly, it came walking back in my direction. It started sniffing my hand and licked it. I pet it on the head, and it jumped into my lap. I giggled like a little kid, putting my arm around it, and rubbed its soft little back. Now it was panting up at me, its tail wagging.

I checked its neck, but there was no collar. I carried it to the local animal shelter to see if anyone had lost a puppy, but there were no reports of a missing pug. It belonged to no one. I named it Patches. Him. I named *him* Patches. The people there told me he was a boy and that he was about seven. They also gave me some food to feed him, and assured me he was healthy, after giving him a free checkup. I wish everything was that free in life.

Patches continuously jumped into my backpack, as if it were the most comfy place ever, nibbling away on his little snacks. I guess it *would* be more comfortable then sleeping outside. Worked for me—animals weren't allowed in certain places, and I wasn't going to stay in the woods all day and night.

I entered a coffee shop. Shawna was there. She was twenty-one, only a year younger than Jason. She used to date him. Before that though, she used to date Tre. She was very pretty, with her blue-streaked hair and black lips.

She turned and looked up at me with surprise. "Rory."

"Yes." I sat down on a stool.

She sat across from me, her eyes lined with years' worth of depression. "Wow...you were shorter than me the last I saw you." Jason often invited me along whenever he'd hang out with his girlfriend...really. Inviting your six-years-younger-than-you brother to hang out with you and your girlfriend. It's practically unheard of.

"I didn't know you were back in town."

"Yeah...I just, I..." She held her hands out as if not having any control, "I had to get away—"

"Yeah," I said. "Everyone does."

"He could've come to one of us if he was having trouble with Tre," she continued, "or maybe he just didn't trust anyone."

"Well," I said, "Perhaps it wasn't just that he felt guilty and wanted to leave. Maybe someone actually made him feel guilty about it. Maybe someone even—" I gulped—"told him to leave."

Shawna narrowed her eyes. "Are you joking? Of COURSE no one would do that! No one who actually cared about him, at least." I flinched at the words, knowing that's what everyone else thought too.

I shrugged, my head hurting from all the confusion. I didn't want to discuss it any further. "Whatever," I said getting up to leave. "Damage is done."

"Rory, wait," she said, taking my hand into hers, like she used to when we would play around with Jason, back when we were kids and stupid. "I want you to know…it's all Tre's fault. This is what he does. He's a sick, sadistic, messed-up guy. He takes pleasure in putting other people in pain. He knows nothing about love."

I nodded, trying not to let anything show.

***

A terrible storm had washed through the area that day, minutes after my conversation with Shawna. I awoke—finding myself trapped and tangled in destroyed wood and glass, underneath so much debris, I was surprised I could breathe (but barely) and I wasn't crushed. Yet. My head was on the ground, but my body was twisted upward, my legs reaching up and locked somewhere, and my arms…I couldn't even feel them. I tried to move, and I couldn't. The only things I could possibly move were my eyes. I tried to scream, but nothing came about. My whole body went numb, and I thought, *Okay, I'm gonna die.*

I closed my eyes and tried not to cry, and somehow I saw Jason. Upside down. He was walking toward me. Same calm posture, same friendly smile, same greatness. I must've been in heaven.

But how could a person like me have landed in such a good place? Did Jason persuade God to accept me there?

Jason stopped, and his feet were about an inch away from my face. Then he bent down, still looking at me with the eyes I grew up loving, one of the few things that actually made me happy in life. His wispy black hair fell just above his blue eyes. He was still in good shape, a little bigger than me. It was nice to see he still looked the same. Even his flaws were nice to see. His blemished skin never stopped him from being handsome. The familiarity of everything would've been comforting under the most painful circumstances.

"H-help," I choked. I could hardly get the words out. I could no longer see his face, but I heard distant words.

"Then you're going to have to let me use that knife of yours." I knew what he was pointing to. The little switchblade that lay in my pocket.

"Ok-o-k-kay." I really did try to keep my voice steady, but it was just so difficult to get air in my lungs as it was, that just saying 'okay' felt like suffocation.

Since my ongoing sweat made my thick black shirt cling to my body, I felt his wrist brush against my ribs as he pulled for the knife. It was strong and sharp. I felt like a child.

Suddenly, I heard a slitting noise. I closed my eyes and gritted my teeth, afraid. And then my body fell to the ground in one big *PLOP!* and I was able to breathe again. My back was no longer in pain, just a little sore. I didn't know HOW he could've gotten me free so quickly and so easily, especially with nothing but a little knife—but somehow he did it. It was a miracle.

I felt myself being moved—lifted, and it seemed without much effort—into the sunlight. I opened my watery eyes. There he was, staring back down at me, like an angel. I was too weak and exhausted to lift my hand up, and though I tried to utter a 'Thank you', all that came out was a moan. I tried again, but there was a soft "Shhh" and a warm hand placed on my forehead. "It's okay." I closed my eyes and relaxed. When I opened them again, not scared anymore, he was gone.

I lay there for about ten minutes, my entire body sore, shaking from what just took place. Where did he go?

Then I discovered something awful. As I finally sat up, I noticed my fist was clenched really hard. There was a hard, metal thing in it. I looked down, opened up my hand, and to my horror I realized it was the switchblade—I hallucinated the whole thing. Jason had never come. Just like he had never come back since that day.

I stuffed my knife back into my pocket carefully and looked over to where I had been caught up in debris—it turned out that it was a bunch of cloth that was holding me captive, not wood or glass. Still, how did I do that?

"Damn it!" I kicked the ground. I couldn't believe that I was actually naïve enough to think that was really him. I was too ignorant to deny that it was him, because I wanted to believe I was incapable of doing it myself and needing someone to help—who better? I wanted to see him again so badly. That's all I'd ever wished.

I sat there for a while, biting my lip as hard as I could, so hard it started to bleed. I got up and pressed my hands against my head, trying to stay together and keep control. *Jason! Jason, Jason, JASON!!!*

I wandered around, stumbling. I walked over to what was left of my bag. Patches came running up into my arms. Luckily, he didn't seem hurt at all. Just a little shaken.

I kept limping. My knee was bleeding, and I could feel blood rushing out of it. Patches kept quiet as I held him in my arms and looked around. People were rushing around, frantic, crying, fainting. I smelled smoke. There was a fire blazing somewhere nearby, the flames crackling and the heat causing me to cough. I saw the EMTs and flashing lights. I turned around quickly and vomited. Right on the dog. He didn't seem to mind though.

Five minutes later, when I was ready to get back up again, I tripped on a big piece of wood that used to be the door. I saw something sticking out from underneath it—a moving arm. It was a light brown color. It only moved a little, but the watch attached to it looked exactly like the one I saw on someone today.

I put Patches down and began to haul the thing up with so much fatigue, my face grew almost as hot as it had near the fire. I tried several times, but it didn't budge an inch. I tried again. And again. The fourth time was successful. "Aaarrrrgggghhhhhh!" I screamed, letting out all the pain, caring less if anyone heard. I fell backwards on something sharp.

I screamed. Patches yelped and ran over. I got up and realized a piece of glass was stuck in my leg! I was bleeding everywhere.

I quickly wiped away the excess fluid. Then I ripped off a piece of my jacket and wrapped it around the wound. I was panting even more breathlessly than Patches now.

I crawled over to Renee. The tornado tore right through the place, scattering and separating everyone. It hadn't mattered how long we held onto each other, it ripped us apart like an earthquake ripping through two pieces of land. She lay there, battered, but still breathing. I felt her pulse. It was beating kind of fast, but then it slowed down as I wrapped the rest of my jacket around her. I checked all over her body to make sure she wasn't bleeding profusely anywhere. She wasn't.

"Oh God...oh, God...oh..." A tall, middle-aged, blonde man came and wrapped his arms around her gently, but securely. I came around to the front of her, but stood back enough to give her room to breathe. Patches whimpered and buried his face into her hand. She had her eyes closed and leaned her head backwards. I fished through my bag and got a water bottle out. I gently poured some into her mouth. After that, her head fell back onto the blonde man's chest.

"Not my girl, not my little baby girl..." he was saying. I jerked my head up in surprise.

Then I leaned down to her ear. "Everything's gonna be okay," I whispered.

And to think that back in the classroom yesterday, I said that would be the last time I would carry weight for her.

***

I opened my eyes slowly to a bright room. "Mom?" I said quietly. Then I came to realize it wasn't my home. It was Todd's. I was lying on his guest bed, fully clothed, but my shoes were off. The left side of my forehead was all bandaged up, and so were my knee and leg. I took my time sitting up, careful not to agitate anything. It didn't surprise me that I wasn't in a hospital—it was probably packed right now.

I took my shirt off and looked at myself across the room in a mirror—weeks' old bruises covering my shoulders and lifelong scars lay everywhere. I tore my eyes away from the sight.

One of Todd's sweaters was on the chair across the room. As I put it on over my shirt, I noticed Patches sleeping soundly on the floor next to my bag, neatly up against the wall, safe and clean. Todd must've given him a bath.

The doors to his balcony were open. He knew I liked it from the times when I'd stayed here because I'd been kicked out. There wasn't traffic or loud people around. There were just trees and bushes and it was silent. Todd knew I liked this spot the best—which is why he decided to leave a note on the little patio chair for me to see.

I picked it up. It read: *Rory,*

The tornado storm has passed (obviously), but it has left a lot of damage. Your school actually had a little damage (not that it matters to you anymore) but I don't think anyone was hurt. It was just one of the empty trailers outside of it. And your parents' house is fine. After I got you checked out by someone on the scene, I drove you right over. I did briefly recall now being checked out by a paramedic. But I think I fell asleep once Todd and I got in his car. *You're free to go back there if you want to. When I drove you there, no one answered the door when*

I knocked. Maybe they were asleep. You certainly were by the time we got back here. Their car was in the driveway. I called to see if someone can do a wellness check on them. Oh, great. That's going to make my dad thrilled. I silently cursed Todd—he was only trying to help, but could he not? Then again, I always wondered if one day the alcohol would become too much for—

I also was getting a weird vibe from it, a feeling, that there was something he wasn't telling me.

I shoved the thought from my head and continued with the note. *I'm at work right now, but I should be back before two. If you need to go anywhere, Gabriella will be back sooner. There's also some cash and coins in the top drawer in the kitchen. But you need some serious rest. There's eggs in the fridge, bread in the cupboard, and bananas on the counter. I think there may be some cereal too. I'm going to do some grocery shopping tomorrow.*

P.S. You're taking care of the dog.

I read the first line of his letter again. That tornado was really terrible. I was still shivering a little bit. It had been the first tornado I ever encountered, and hopefully the last.

I glanced inside. Patches had now switched his position on the floor, but was still asleep as a rock under water. I went inside, scooped him up in my arms, and placed him gently on the bed. He gave out a muffled yawn, but that was about it. Then I went back out on the balcony.

I took out my notebook and set it on the wooden table that stood in front of the patio chair. I sat down, pulled out a pen, and began to write:

I hide within closets and scurry underneath my bed
I try to save myself, though I wish I were dead
Torn up, trembling, afraid of losing my head
This is my world: cold, fear, and dread.

When the daddy comes home, most kids run up and hug him
But I run to the farthest corner of the house from mine;
It's only the beginning.
Seeing dark discoloration as I stare in the mirror
I wipe away the tears as the vision gets clearer
My heart jumps when the steps come nearer,
And there he is, waiting for me.

I slammed my book shut.

I headed downstairs, my stomach demanding food, especially after all of that forced rhyming. I opened the fridge and cupboard—*DAMN LIAR*, I felt like shouting. Probably not though. Todd could barely keep track of what day of the week it was, let alone what was really in the house or not. There were no eggs, no bread—just some water and bananas. I knew it was petty, but I just really didn't feel like water and bananas right now.

Hey, he takes care of you, I berated myself. *Don't be a spoiled brat.*

I jumped when the phone rang. "Hello?" I answered.

"Hi Rory." Todd. "How are you?" he asked softly.

"I'm fine," I lied. "You?"

"Good. Tired, but good. Would you like me to come home?"

"Oh, no, it's alright...I'm fine on my own."

"I have Gabriella's and Gideon's phone numbers in the drawer somewhere too, if you want to call them to talk to." Gideon. He was one of Jason's close friends. Well, had been, before Jason starting hanging out with Tre. He'd been one of Todd's guitar students as well—that's where Jason and Gideon had met. I wasn't too familiar with him, but I trusted him enough.

"Um, Todd? Did you stop by my parents' house earlier today?"

"Yes. Did you see the note I left you?"

"What did they say?" They always answered the door. He lied in his note.

He paused. Todd never paused. Then he sighed. "Well, your mother *was* asleep. On the couch."

Of course.

"Your dad didn't say anything."

He was still lying. "Todd, *tell me what he said.*"

"He just shrugged."

My stomach dropped. I almost dropped the phone. I bit my lips and the inside of my cheeks.

"Rory, are you okay? Rory?"

"Yeah, yeah, I'm here, I'm fine. Thanks Todd. Take care."

"You know he was probably just hiding how relieved he was, not actually apathetic about it. You know how stubborn and difficult your old man is."

"I know." He was a lot more than that, but I never let Todd—or anyone really—know about those details. It was easy to hide when you had a reputation for fighting.

"You take care. I'll be there sooner than you know it."

I nodded as he hung up, even though he wasn't there to see it. My tongue was stuck on the roof of my mouth. I felt numb. I went in the living room, drew the blinds, sat on the couch, and wrapped a blanket around me. I kept trying to think of funny things, things that made me laugh, instead of the fact that I'd been wrong about the subconscious conclusion I'd come to earlier today—that my father—my FATHER—and I had a moment on that porch. A moment that meant something.

After a while, I couldn't take it anymore. I got up and checked on Patches. He was awake now, and I put some dog food out for him. I decided to head out to the gas station where there was a convenience store. I made a mental note to make a pit stop at the pet store to get some more dog food. I put on my coat and headed out.

***

Inside the store while I walked down the aisles, I heard a little sound. I turned and there she was, looking right at me. She was so small, both in size and in strength. Her face was tear-streaked, her clothes were all wet from the rain and wind outside.

I stepped toward her and hugged her tightly, warming her up. She laid her head on my shoulder.

"Rory," Renee said, "my dad's okay, but my aunt and cousin...they're in the hospital. Critical injuries. The car was smashed. They...I think they were looking for me."

Oh God. I didn't know what to say for the longest time, so I just held her. "Don't worry," I eventually said. "It'll...don't worry." I was going to say "It'll be okay" but I knew that wasn't what people wanted to hear when they were devastated. I looked up and around. "Is your father here?"

"Yeah. He'll be a while." She sniffled. "Do you want to go outside?"

"Sure, just let me pay for this." As soon as I paid for my items, she and I walked out of the store, going around the side where there was more privacy. Not that it was particularly crowded in this barren land right now. We stared at each other for a few long seconds, until I finally followed through with the urge to hug her again. She didn't resist for a second.

Chapter 10: RENEE—A First Smile (Wednesday, December 18, 1996)

After hugging me for a few more seconds he let go, quickly, and I felt the absence of his hands that were on my arms and back seconds before. I looked up, and he was a couple feet away from me, still stepping back, a look of confusion or sadness in his eyes. I couldn't tell which. "I..." he said, "I'm sorry." He turned swiftly and walked away.

***

"I thought the tornado didn't come through here!" I nearly screamed when I entered my room. Or, what was left of it. Clothes were strewn everywhere, all my bureau drawers had been yanked open, and nothing was where it belonged. I heard footsteps coming up behind me and felt a hand squeeze my shoulder.

"It didn't," my dad said. "I did." He walked around to face me.

"*Why?*"

"Because I wanted to make sure I searched every last inch of this room for tools." He cleared his throat. "You know...cutting tools." The way he said *tools* was so infuriatingly calm and casual, as if he was talking about gardening tools rather than something more serious.

A hot anger rose in me. It was all too much. Sheila and Jenny were in the hospital, and would be there for who knew how long. It especially felt weird after the fight we'd had. My dad said we were to go visit them perhaps tomorrow, or a few days. It might take a while for them to recover. Sheila had a broken arm. Jenny hit her head when their car fell over itself several times. It was amazing that either of them were even ALIVE.

And I'd been hearing about casualties on the news all day, everywhere. There were few, but still. Apparently one of them had been a gym teacher at Wilcox High. I shuddered, knowing it was probably someone Rory, Sidney, Sonny, and Jeremiah all knew. And I would've known him too if I'd been there longer.

"That's fine," I shouted, "but couldn't you have put things *back*?"

He came all the way down to my face like a vulture flying down to catch its prey and yelled, "YOU WANT TO TRY TO TALK TO ME LIKE THAT AGAIN?"

I took a step back. I'd never seen my dad so angry before, especially at me. I looked down at my feet. "Sorry," I mumbled.

He sighed and pointed at my bed. "Sit down."

I sat and he paced back and forth in front of me, running his hand through his hair like he normally did when he was frustrated or stressed out. "Now listen, Renee. I'm sorry I messed up your room. But there's something you need to realize. I'm worried about you. And because I am worried about you, I just don't *trust* you anymore."

It was no surprise, and yet it still felt like a kick in the gut. I didn't say anything. He looked like he'd been kicked in the gut saying it too. He didn't look tough or smug. He looked glum. And what was even weirder was that this was the first time my father sounded like an actual parent. Assertive.

He sat down next to me. "That doesn't mean I don't love you. But there needs to be a new set of rules around here."

"So you mean you're not going to send me away to some mental hospital?" I whispered.

Even without looking at his face I could tell he'd gone tense at the question. "No," he replied with conviction. "I'm not. After winter break is over, you'll be going back to school. I'll drive you every morning before I go to work. And pick you up." He paused. "You know...if Sheila or Jenny are unable to—"

"You don't have to worry about me cutting myself—" I said bluntly and irritably.

"I also don't want you wandering off on your own," he said firmly.

"You think I'll do that too because of some stupid punishment for being under the bleachers—"

"Renee, that's the way I want it, that's the way it's going to be."

"Right," I said gruffly.

"You know, there's an art program I found nearby too. At the community college. Usually during the Spring and Summer." He got up, walked over to my small cluttered desk, and picked up a black sketchbook. He opened it to a drawing of a red tank top and a pair of beige slacks. "You have some real talent, Renee."

I managed a tiny smile. "Thanks."

"Maybe we could enroll you during the summertime. And if we somehow can't get you enrolled because all the seats are filled, then we can always try another.

"Also, I think you can wait at the local library near there while waiting for me or the bus. You're not the kind of kid who has a phobia of libraries, so I'm sure you'll be fine."

"Okay."

"I would also like you to do some extra chores around here."

"More than I already do?"

"Do you think the art program will pay for itself? Or that it's cheap?"

"True."

"I will help pay for it, and of course I'm sure Sheila will contribute as well. But, it's still pricey and any help you can give will be greatly appreciated, mostly by you in the end.

"One more thing, Renee." He bit his bottom lip, as though he was nervous about what he was going to say next. "Every day when we get home, I'm going to check your bag and your pockets. Your arms as well. Only your arms. Just to make sure…" He trailed off.

I nodded.

After a couple seconds of silence, my dad said, "What are you thinking about right now?"

"Mom and She—Aunt Sheila and Jenny," I said without thinking. There was so much more, but I couldn't speak.

I was thinking about how mom used to be a big fan of sculpting, how she'd carefully mold the clay together in complicated ways just to make sure it had the perfect shape. I was thinking about how Aunt Sheila had always wanted to open up a crafts store because she liked to piece minerals such as fluorite and diamonds together so that she could create all sorts of jewelry women would love to buy and wear. And Jenny—Jennifer Michelle Jacobs—she didn't even know what she wanted to be. She had the potential to major in a couple of different things, mostly relating to science. She was particularly good at Physics, Chemistry, and Biology. And she was able to pick up on foreign languages pretty quickly once she'd studied them for about two or three months. She'd probably contribute a lot to the world of science or be a translator for someone. I felt myself praying—without even consciously doing it—that she lived to do one or both. Either one was far more valuable than being a fashion designer and just making pretty clothes.

I thought if I didn't speak I could hold it all in. Wrong. My dad enclosed me in his arms, murmuring something about how hopefully they'll pull through, but I hated hearing that. Not knowing was always the worst thing. The stress of it all makes you physically ill. I leaned my head into his shoulder, the tears quickly falling.

***

I kept having Sheila's face in my head yesterday when she found out about my self-destructive habits. It wasn't disgust or judgment like many might have. It was fright. But not the kind of fright one would have for someone they were repulsed by or someone they wanted to stay far, far way from. The kind of fright you had when someone you cared about started doing something that was appallingly careless and dangerous. A huge contrast to the girl she watched grow up in front of her, I now realized, who watched cartoons and huddled with stuffed animals. It must have been surreal for her.

I didn't know if I was allowed to do this or not, but I started down the hall and approached the very end, where the closed door of Aunt Sheila's room lay. Leaning over the stair railing, I saw that my dad was on the couch reading a book, wearing his glasses, and the one table light on in the otherwise entirely dark living room. I placed my hand on the doorknob as if it were an alarm that could potentially go off, turned agonizingly slowly, and pushed it open. To my gratitude, it didn't creak at all. I flipped the light switch on and winced as bright light flooded the room. I shut the door most of the way without clicking it and stood at the entrance, glancing around.

Sheila's room was immaculate. Everything was right in its place, every surface and corner squeaky clean and shiny, not a speck of dust in sight. I didn't know how Sheila always kept things looking perfect, like they should be in one of those commercials advertising cleaning products or furniture brands. It had always seemed like regardless of how much I tried to keep up with wiping down dusty surfaces and vacuuming and the like, it would always be back the next day. How Sheila was able to keep everything exquisite-looking whilst working a job *and* not look exhausted, I would never know.

On her shelf was an assortment of CDs and VHS tapes. She had mostly classical music and old black and white films featuring actresses such as Elizabeth Taylor, Marilyn Monroe, and Audrey Hepburn. At the very end of the shelf she had a photo of herself with her arm wrapped around a friend from work. I didn't know if they were close friends or just acquaintances that never spoke usually. Sheila's face was a little flushed in the photo, probably tired after having worked all day, but looking accomplished, with a smile full of perfect pearly white teeth. Her black hair was parted down the middle, completely straight, with no frizz or flyaways or split ends at all. It always looked as though she'd just come back from a professional hair appointment, looking fresh and new. Behind her were a few straggling customers who also had new hairstyles, each of them looking satisfied. Sheila also had on black onyx earrings and was making a peace sign at the camera. Her nails were perfectly manicured. From her head to her toe, to her bedroom, to her life, everything was perfectly ordered, perfectly symmetrical, perfectly in place. She always has a plan.

A chill went down my spine as my eyes gazed about the room, falling on a wooden fruit bowl with an assortment of fake cherries in it for decoration. It was a little bizarre, but it actually suited the room nicely. Cherries were not only Sheila's favorite fruit, but favorite food overall. She liked anything cherry-flavored—Cherries on ice cream, cherry candy, and even, to my dismay, Cherry Cola.

I didn't know what kind of food Sheila hated. But contrary to her love for cherries, arts, crafts, and hairstyling, she had an intense fear and hatred of bugs. And spiders. She was that person that screamed bloody murder if she so much as saw a cockroach all the way on the other side of the room, even a little one. Which is why I was taken aback when I found an empty jar sitting on her desk that had an important label scribbled on it: *"Use this to capture live bugs"* it said. *"Then take them outside."* I hadn't realized my mouth was hanging open until I looked away from the jar and closed it. Sheila, who was so fearful and repulsed by bugs, wanted to try to spare their lives anyhow. I'd never thought, with how spiteful and dismissive she was to everyone and everything, that she could have that kind of empathy. It was a huge commonality with my mom, actually.

I could feel tears pricking at the backs of my eyes, and before I knew it I was out of there, without having shut off the light or closing the door.

I knew I should've stopped while I was in too deep, but I needed to go to Jenny's room next. It was beckoning to me, some strange invisible force pulling me to it. I couldn't bear, for some reason, to walk right past it. I had to finish this. It was as if it were guaranteed that she wouldn't make it if I didn't do this.

I walked in and saw that, unlike Sheila's room, it was quite messy. She had multiple knit sweaters hanging in her closet of pastel colors. My dad hadn't cleaned anything up yet...did he want to? I wouldn't want to. Were we going to leave it like this? Forever? Just having all their things lying around?

She had a calendar hanging on the wall that had a hot pink border around each of the months. The days were crossed out one by one...the seventeenth, yesterday, was the last day that was crossed out. The eighteenth, today, might not get crossed out. There was something so deeply disturbing about this that I almost ripped the calendar off the wall. But instead I just turned away swiftly and it remained intact.

Perhaps I would do the crossing off for her today. And then she could get back to it when she recovered.

When she recovered.

On her bookcase were a combination of various nonfiction and a collection of works from Shakespeare. She was probably the only kid in school I knew who enjoyed most of the assigned readings in English class. She could have very well majored in English if she wanted. But as she was undecided, she was probably going to go for a Math or Science major, something that would've made a lot more money. She was good at all school subjects. History was usually the hardest for her, but that was only because there were so many different sides and versions being told.

Her sunglasses sat in the top corner of her desk next to tubes of lip gloss, and there was a French book lying open in the middle. Why did she have a French textbook? She already knew how to speak French fluently. The only other things on her desk were a lamp and an unfinished Sudoku puzzle. Perhaps she did these in her spare time to ease the stress and strain and depression and discomforts of life. Perhaps I should start doing something like that as well. Dealing with things in a healthy way. No wonder she always seemed to have it together.

There was a drawer slightly ajar, and for some reason it really hit me in the gut to suddenly acknowledge the mere *possibility* that Jenny would no longer ever be back to close it. Or to open it all the way. What had she been trying to get in there? Feeling a strange urge to somehow "finish" the task, in case it went unfinished forever, I went over and pulled it all the way open. There were little booklets and manuals about different ways to style hair. I assumed she borrowed them for Sheila. We all had been blessed with long thick hair, though theirs were both nicer and stronger than mine, as mine was brittle and broke easily. But certainly Jenny could've pulled off a French braid or two, or perhaps one of those fancy complicated styles that involved flowers or jewelry. She had the hair for it. Hopefully she would keep having the hair for it, because she would keep being.

After flipping through all the images of the hairstyles, I put the booklets back and shut the drawer. When I came to the cracked-opened door and opened it all the way to exit, I gasped and found my dad glaring on the other side. He had his hands on his hips. Under any other given circumstances I was sure this would be deemed inappropriate, rummaging through peoples' things. And perhaps it still was, on the hope that Jenny and Sheila got through this. But he put them down and his face changed when he saw that I'd been crying.

Without saying anything, he put his arms around me and guided me out of the room, shutting the door gently.

***

I had nightmares that night. It was sort of a series of dreams, each either blending into the other, or just happening and having no relevance of any sort to the previous one.

The first was of Sidney shaking me wildly with a frightened look in her eyes. It scared me because she never looked like that. Friendly—most of the time. Angry—sometimes. Afraid or petrified—never. She was screaming something about how close she was to revealing...something. I never found out what that something was until I went on to the next dream. I saw Rory standing outside of the store, late at night, watching happy customers walk out. It was snowing lightly. Delicate snow drops landed on his head and clothes, standing out against his entirely black wardrobe, and then melting. He had his hands shoved deep in his pockets and stood very tightly, as if wanting to fold up and disappear. He looked nervous about something, rubbing his hands together and letting out huge breaths of air, as if that would help him avoid whatever it was.

Then finally, a large, beat up truck arrived right in front of him. Rory bit his lip and started to walk in the other direction when a big man came out of the car, slamming the door. He took such long strides that it took nearly two steps to reach Rory, extending his long, muscular arm and grabbing a handful of Rory's jacket. He must've been the guy I heard yelling the day I saw Rory leave his house. His father.

Rory tried to resist, but could not escape the man's forceful grip. His father put his hand over his mouth, and dragged him to the car, Rory able to do nothing more than squirm as he was trapped in the grip. He was shoved into the passenger side. "Get in," was all the old and lifeless man growled.

From there, it came to a part where it was just Rory and I, standing in an alley, only Rory was not himself—he was angry. Was he often angry? Yes. Was he often so enraged to the point where he lost control completely and became a savage animal? No.

So then why did he lash out and grab me on my shoulder? His fingernails dug into me so hard, I felt the warm flow of blood as it wet my shoulder under his palm. He was looking down at me, with angry red eyes, and I began apologizing. What for? I didn't know. What had I done to get him so angry?

Then he let go really quickly and backed away until I could no longer see him.

I awoke from my dream very suddenly, wondering how I had dreamt so much in just three hours.

I remembered how yesterday when he laughed like a little kid, his smile transformed him completely, from a mean and miserable human being to a kind one.

Despite only getting a couple hours in, I was wide awake, not being able to sleep anymore. Despite feeling dizzy from all the images that just ran through my mind, I managed to stumble to the bathroom outside in the hallway, as my eyes adjusted to the dark. My watch lay on the sink. It was five-fifteen in the morning.

I washed my face and drank some water. When I walked out, I bumped into my dad's shoulder.

Even though my eyes were just adjusting to the dark, I could tell he was startled. "Are you okay?"

"Um, yeah. I just had a bad dream, that's all."

"Okay," he said quietly. "You should go back to sleep."

"Yeah." But as soon as he went back to his room, I went downstairs and watched early morning cartoons that I practically lived in when I was a child. I just couldn't sleep. I curled up on the couch with the blanket. Somewhere after that I fell back to sleep and woke up again around eight.

***

My dad was going out to do last minute gift-shopping later that morning. It felt strange to me. It really didn't feel like Christmas at all. We didn't have a tree, or anything holiday-related honestly. You'd never know it was Christmas just looking at our ordinary house, as if it were any other time of the year. I hoped that Jenny and Sheila could at least be home in time for it. I was sitting on the bottom of the stairs, staring through the railing while he talked on the phone to someone from the hospital, trying to either get information or see if he could speak to Jenny or Sheila. I clutched the small teddy bear in my hands that I'd had since I was a toddler.

I glanced away for just one moment when I heard the phone slam. I jumped and looked up. "Dumb bitch," my dad growled. His teeth were clenched. He looked up at me and quickly said, "Not you."

"I know," I said with a half-laugh, pulling myself up with the railing and walking over. "What happened? Are—are Jenny and Sheila alright?"

"Yes," he replied, his face brightening.

I let out the breath I'd been holding and my heart slowed down. I hadn't even realized it'd been beating so fast. "Are we going to get to go see them today?"

"Well, not exactly." He scratched his head, looking uncomfortable.

"Oh," I said.

He gave me a sympathetic smile. "I'm afraid we'll have to wait until Saturday to see them."

"Saturday!" I exclaimed. It felt so far away.

"Yes," he sighed. "They *are* feeling better, but they need more rest before anyone can visit them. Doctor's orders."

"But we're family!" I said angrily. "Wouldn't they feel even more better if we were there?"

"I'm certain they would. But sometimes people just don't understand that," he said, resigned now. What happened to the anger he'd similarly been feeling a few moments ago? Maybe he was trying to be strong for me. He didn't need to be though. What I wanted was for both of us to march over to that hospital and push our way in to see them.

My dad came over and kissed me on the head. "At least they're okay," he said. "They might even be well enough to come home for Christmas. If not, we'll spend Christmas at the hospital. I hear they at least do a fine job with their decorations." We both attempted a smile. "We do have much more to be thankful for than most people, Renee. Just remember that."

***

Around noon, when I had the house to myself while my dad ran errands, there was a ring at the kitchen door. My stomach flipped. *Who is that?*

My mouth dropped when I saw Rory solemnly standing on the other side, hands shoved into his pockets.

He opened his mouth to say something, then shut it. Then he opened it again and said sheepishly, "I'm sorry. I shouldn't have come to bother you." He took off.

I followed after him quickly, having slammed my front door shut. I caught him in the middle of the sidewalk leading down from my neighborhood. His hands were still jammed into his pockets.

Putting my hand on his shoulder, I said, "Rory! *Rory!*"

He stopped and stood for a couple seconds, reluctantly turning toward me, his eyes facing downward.

"What's wrong?" I asked. "Of course you can come over. You're not bothering me."

"Thank you. Look...I'm the problem here, not you."

"What do you mean?"

"I'm...afraid to get close to people. Uh—you just don't understand."

"I could."

"Please, I—" He let out a sigh, as if giving up on words altogether. He ran his hand through his hair and walked over to the grassy sloping lawn near the woods away from the houses, sitting down.

I tentatively sat next to him. There was a sharp siren sound in the distance. There was a *crack.* Three or four little twigs landed on my thigh from the breeze. It must've blown them from the trees in the nearby woods. Rory's hand came over and wiped them off quickly and they bounced down onto the pavement. The siren sounds from a distance were now getting fainter, until it was so quiet, all you could hear were crickets and the rustling of tree branches.

"Rory, what's wrong?"

"Jason was ashamed of being a part of that gang. But that's NOT why he left." Pause. "I was angry at him for, for not stopping my dad, so I ratted him out, and yelled at him. I said horrible things. Things like, 'I hate you. You're not my brother. I wish you were dead. Go to hell and never come back'."

We sat in silence for another minute.

"I didn't have to do that," he continued.

I put my hand on his shoulder. When Rory finally looked at me, his tired and stressed gaze turned to worry and concern. "Oh, my...Renee, I didn't mean to—"

"It's okay," I said, a little humiliated. "I get overemotional a lot. Rory, your bruises, your father—"

"He's not my father," he said sharply.

"I'm sorry."

"No, I am." He put his arm around me and sighed. "You're the first person I've told this to." A small smile appeared. It may have been a small, tight, even sarcastic smile, but it was still a smile nonetheless. I had never seen him smile before. It made him look like a completely different person. Then he giggled a little. It was unreal. I giggled along with him, the two of us sitting there looking like a pair of idiots.

After a few minutes, I took a deep breath and said, "Well, you should also tell—"

"And the last," Rory said, his smile now a frown.

"Come on, Rory," I began, but trailed off. The look on his face told me not to push it. He'd already been happy, for a brief moment. I didn't want to ruin something rare like that for him.

"Well," he finally said, "I'd better get going. I'm not sure if Todd will call back or not."

"Todd?"

"Jason's former teacher. He lets me stay with him when, well...when my parents don't want me around."

I sighed. "Well, that's good. I better get going too. My dad might call the house. Might." I planned on saying I was in the bathroom if that happened.

"See you later, Ren."

"See you." And for once I didn't mind being called Ren.

***

There was *another* ring at the door a few hours later.

I'd been sitting in the living room on the couch with my head-phones on, listening to "All I Want For Christmas Is You" on repeat by my favorite artist. When my dad and I go visit Jenny and Sheila (which would probably be on Friday or Saturday) perhaps I would see if they were well enough to listen to music. They might want to. It was one of the few things we were completely alike about. There were some people who hated Christmas music, some who were in-different to it, some who liked it moderately, and then us. The ones who *loved* Christmas music of all kinds, all the way up to Christmas day itself and through it.

When I went to answer the door, it was the last people I ever ex-pected to see—Sidney, Sonny, and Jeremiah.

"Hey Renee," Sidney said with an awkward smile. "Sorry to drop by like this. We just wanted to see if you were alright."

"I'm okay," I said with an equally-awkward smile. I glanced at the boys. They either didn't feel uncomfortable like we did, or they were better at hiding it. "You guys want to come in?" I asked.

They glanced at each other and shrugged, stepping in.

"So what happened, Renee?" Jeremiah asked as soon as they got settled down at the kitchen table. He didn't waste any time cutting to the chase.

I recounted what happened over the past couple of days, omitting certain parts, such as the personal stuff I'd learned about Rory. Suspension was such a stupid punishment to dish out over something so small. All they did was extend my winter break. I stopped when I finished about how I'd return in January. Which at this point, everyone would. People probably hardly noticed my absence, especially since I'd been new to begin with.

"I always knew Rory was an asshole," Sonny spat.

"He didn't mean for this to happen," I said, not knowing if the defensive edge in my voice caught him or not. I wished I could tell them about his problem at home, but it wasn't my business or my place to do so.

Sidney leaned forward and asked, "Is your dad home right now?"

"No. I'm here alone."

"THOSE FUCKERS HAVE NO RIGHT!" she shouted, echoing off the walls. The rest of us nearly jumped out of our seats.

Sonny put his hands on her shoulders and started massaging them. "Easy now. Let's just be happy she didn't get expelled. Knowing how absurd they are."

Sidney exhaled and smiled apologetically at me. "I'm sorry. I just get so heated about these things. Hanging out under the bleachers? Really? That's exactly what people do during lunchtime. And it's not like you were skipping class either, it was a *pep rally*. Neither of you—yes, I'm even defending Rory here—neither of you did anything wrong. You *did nothing wrong*."

"Yeah," I agreed glumly. "These zero tolerance policies do more harm than good. You guys want granola bars?"

They nodded their heads solemnly.

Staying for about an hour more, we talked about a bunch of things completely unrelated to school, natural disasters, or family problems. Sidney brought some clothing magazines that she and I browsed, much to the boredom of Jeremiah and Sonny. There were overalls, giant platform wedge sandals, multicolored chokers and bracelets, those strange slap bracelets, scrunchies, butterfly barrettes, etc. Then Jerry and Sonny got revenge by playing "Wonderwall" on repeat for a half hour and singing loudly. At least, it was revenge on Sidney, who covered her ears, while Jerry and Sonny draped their arms over us and swayed to the music.

When the three of them left, I'd been in a happy mood, going around cleaning the house, exercising, and full of energy that wasn't there before. Eventually though, I was on the sofa with a blanket around me, feeling exhausted. I must've fallen asleep sometime around five in the afternoon, because my dad was shaking me awake when he got back.

"What happened?" I asked, yawning. "Why am I so tired?"

"Stress can do that to you," my father said. "And you've been through a lot lately. Along with lack of sleep. Do you feel sick at all?"

"No. I actually feel fine now."

"It's going to be okay," he said, patting me on the shoulder. "You're going to get better soon." He paused. "Renee, you haven't said very much about Jenny or Sheila since—"

Just then, the phone rang. My dad went to answer it, but a few seconds later he came back to me. "It's for you," he said.

I came to the receiver, and said, "Hello?"

"Hey. Renee?"

"Rory? How did you know my number?" I looked around to make sure my dad had left.

"The phone directory. Look, I was at the library today, and I was looking at books and stuff, and information online about...er...cutting." He paused for so long I thought it was my cue to say something, until he said, "I really think you should not try it. And I swear I don't mean that in a patronizing way."

I sighed. "Thank you for the concern, but my dad already found out anyway."

"Oh. Shit."

"It's okay. Really. He's helping me already. Haven't even thought about trying it, honestly. I never much wanted to in the first place." I thought about how even though I'd had the urge Monday night, I couldn't go through with it.

"Well, that's good. Just keep it up, alright?"

"Sure. Hey um...about Sidney...do you still like her?" I blurted out before I could think.

There was silence on the other end.

"I'm sorry," I said. It was such a sudden shift in conversation. I didn't know why I did it.

"No, it's okay. Um. I guess I still do, sort of. But I try not to dwell on it because there's no point. She doesn't want me. She'll never want me again. So I think the best way to deal with it is to just forget about it."

"Oh." It was such a stupid, useless thing to say, but I really didn't know what else to say.

To my relief Rory laughed. "Hey, are you interested in a job?"

I felt more awake now. "Yeah," I said.

"The Winston library, just a few blocks from our school, is hiring people to shelve books. It doesn't pay much, but it seems worth a try. And if you happen to run into a girl—there's a girl I know named Shawna, who will probably be at the library herself. She's always in there, her nose inside of a book. People tend to look twice at her, because she looks more like she should be in a club or a rave, but she's really nice. And real intelligent. She can help you with things. Just tell her you're a friend of Rory's."

"Okay," I said, smiling. "Thanks. Are you doing alright?"

"Yeah, I'm fine now. I'm with Todd. Don't worry about me. I have to go now."

"Take care."

***

Later that night I walked into the kitchen where my dad was sitting at the table, reading a book. "Dad?"

"Yes?" He looked up.

I took a deep breath. "I was wondering if I could get a job. At the local library."

He stared at me for a few seconds. "Why exactly?"

To get experience? To make money? To...get out of this damned quiet, awkward, depressing, and frankly boring house? "To have something to do. Something that can keep me busy."

"I don't know, Renee," he replied, shaking his head.

"I'll go crazy if I don't do *something*," I said, losing it. "I can't just stay in here all day. Don't you want me to be distracted from...you know..."

"There are plenty of things to do here. Read a book. Clean. Go in the backyard for fresh air. Draw. You can also—"

"I need to do something outside of here." I waved my arms around. "I feel holed up in here. I'm not talking about going partying or anything. I need something like *work*. Something that will put pressure on me. It will *make* me do something, as opposed to just sitting around here trying to decide what to do next." *And especially since at the moment, I don't have school to worry about.*

He sighed. "Alright. We'll see what we can do. Tomorrow's Friday and around noon I have an interview. I'll have another one at about three."

"Interviews?" I asked.

"Yes. There are a few jobs I found that I would like to apply for. The bills are stacking up, but I don't want you to get too worried. We can handle them, the medical bills, and everything. Plus, I want us to have a nice Christmas. Now, if I don't get either of these positions, it won't be the end of the world. Though, I shouldn't have much trouble. One is an office clerk position, and the other is as a customer service representative."

"Customer service?" I asked. Now that was the type of job I didn't think I could stomach.

He grinned. "Yes. It's not so bad."

"We'll agree to disagree, dad."

He chuckled. "We can drive over to the library and ask about the hiring there before then."

"Thank you." I exhaled with relief. "Well, I'm going to go up to bed now." I turned to walk away.

"Oh, and Renee?"

"Yeah?" I replied, half-turning back.

"I really appreciate that you took the time today to clean the shelves in the living room and the coffee table. And to vacuum, wash the windows, and take the garbage out."

"Well, it was because of..."

"I know," he said softly. "But you did a good job." He smiled.

I smiled back.

***

The morning wasn't as peaceful as the previous night had been. My dad and I were bickering for a long time before we left. He was complaining about how it was cold outside and I should put on a coat. I thought my long-sleeved sweater would be good enough. In the end, I grudgingly put on the coat.

"Now remember Renee, don't *expect* anything. Don't *expect* to get the job. Usually, they prefer older people with more experience, no matter what the job is."

"I *know* dad," I said for what felt like the millionth time. I was getting irritated. I wanted to be positive about this whole thing, but it was really hard when he had to keep bringing it down for me. Besides, why on earth would you need experience in SHELVING things? I was pretty sure all you needed were two relatively healthy arms and hands, and in my case, some toes to stand on.

"No Renee, you don't." He stopped his car. We were on a deserted road. *Great, not this again.* He always did this when his temper flared. "You're getting your hopes up. I just want you to understand that you might not get a job there. Alright?"

I didn't dare say it aloud, but I was pretty sure he was projecting his own worries about his own interviews later on onto me. "Alright."

He nodded and started the car up again.

We walked into the heated library, and there was a sign that said it would be closed from tomorrow through Wednesday, and again on the Wednesday after that (New Year's Day). So I wasn't surprised that it was pretty empty. The lady from behind the front desk looked up from the book she was reading and smiled. Thankfully, my dad started doing the talking, because I didn't know what to say.

"Do you have any job openings for my daughter?" he asked.

"Yes. We either need someone to shelve, read to the children every Friday afternoon, or be in charge of checking out books for people. Which would you like?" She looked at me.

"I would like shelving," I said.

"Here is an application you can fill out," she said reaching into her drawer. She handed me a clipboard, numerous papers, and a pen. My dad and I went to sit on a couch to fill it out. It took longer than

I thought, but when I finally finished and handed it back to the librarian, she smiled and cheerfully said, "Great! I'll give you a call and let you know, alright?"

My dad nodded and thanked her again and we were on our way. I was glad there were little to no people here. It made me a bit embarrassed that my dad was here with me, but I'd brought it upon myself. But my eyes glanced over the shelves of books and the empty tables and it felt so warm and calming in here.

I turned to my dad, eyes pleading. "Can I please stay here for a while?"

My dad turned to me. "Okay," he said. "If you really want to, but is there a phone here?"

"Yes. Right over there." The librarian pointed to the far right, near the Juvenile section. We hadn't realized how close we still were to the front desk.

"Call me if you need anything. I'll pick you up no later than five," my dad said. He gave me a hug.

"Thanks dad."

***

I spent about two hours reading the blurbs on books, sitting at the tables to read a little bit of one (I needed to get a card to check it out), and rearranging books that were in the wrong areas. As long as these mistakes always existed, they would always need people to fix them. When I finally decided to take a break, I went outside for some fresh air. I walked to the corner of the building, and heard the sound of quick, short breaths. I peeked around the corner to see Rory holding a big black payphone to his ear.

He was shaking all over. I could tell his fingers almost hit the wrong numbers while dialing and he cursed himself out before the phone started ringing, at least I guessed, because now he had his ear listening intently to the receiver. His eyes got wide, like someone had picked up and he wasn't ready. First he just mumbled. Then I heard clear words come out of his mouth. His voice was higher than normal, as though he were being strangled. "I-I-look—I'm sorry..." He took a huge breath, as if he'd lost all air. Rory was sweating, little drops soaring down his forehead, even though it was cold. He whispered something, and hung up quickly. His lips looked like they had whispered the words, *I love you*.

My breath was taken away, literally, as a big black glove slapped down on my mouth. I felt, tasted, and smelled nothing but rough leather push down against it. I was grabbed off my feet and was being flown backwards.

Chapter 11: RORY—Dead by the End of the Night (Friday, December 20, 1996)

"Hey, stop!" I shouted as I ran through the door, making the entire women's bathroom shake. I'd heard someone struggle and when I looked around the corner, Tre was dragging someone toward the deserted bathrooms at the back entrance of a building where the door was propped open—not a very good place to have bathrooms.

I ducked out of it. Luckily there was no one around. The first things I had noticed outside while I was at the phone were the big, HUGE, leather arms tightening her tiny figure in a grip. Tre had held her in place with one leather gloved-hand over her mouth, and another holding a sharp knife, the tip of it pointing right toward her stomach, which had been quickly moving up and down, panicking.

I stopped dead in my tracks as I saw them both outside. "T-Tre?" I breathed, scarcely able to let out a sound. What the hell did he think he was doing?

"Yes, Rory. It's me. And it's true too. If you don't believe I'm going to kill her right in front of you, and that there's nothing you can do about it, this'll be even more difficult for you to watch than you know."

Just as I was about to lunge forward, my arms were caught in the tangle of four other guys, holding me back.

"Why are you doing this?" I shouted, then lowered my voice when he gave me a warning look. Nobody could see us here, but someone was sure to hear, and then he'd definitely kill both of us. "I gave you what you wanted. Now damn it, if you're going to kill somebody, make it be me!" I almost started crying, *almost*. But I hadn't cried for years, and I wasn't going to start up again now, not in front of this bastard.

"I said I'll do it if you don't believe." Tre tapped the end of the knife on Renee's shoulder.

"The hell does that mean?"

"It means YOU," he said, pointing the knife at me, "need to admit it to me."

"Admit what?"

"That you are the cause of Jason's departure." Tre sported a vicious smile that showed off his high cheek bones. He took the knife and held it up at Renee's throat. She whimpered.

I didn't hesitate. I stomped my foot down and said, "Okay."

He stared at me for a few moments, moving the knife away from Renee's face. "What?"

"Okay," I breathed, this time calm and slowly. I glared up at him as he started walking toward me. "It's all my fault that Jason left."

"Louder."

"It's all my—"

"LOUDER!"

"IT'S ALL MY FAULT JASON LEFT!"

Tre nodded. "Good." I felt the weight beneath me fall, and I was down on the hard ground in an instant. "He shouldn't have been influenced by you like that. Jason's a punk. I'd thought he was better than that, better than you. But he showed me his true colors, not being a rider with us like he was supposed to be. Despite being the one to lead us at one point." Renee came tumbling down on top of me, her head landing on my stomach. I lay there, waiting until I knew for sure that it was okay, that the pack of animals were gone. Then I unfroze and sat up, stiffness everywhere, and then pulled her up and wrapped my arms around her, holding her in a tight embrace. She was trembling and shaking. The image of the knife against her stomach was still in my head, and I'd probably never get it out.

***

"I'm going to tell the police," Renee said as soon as we were back in the library, safe and sound.

"What? No, no, you can't do that." She'd started walking over to a different shelf and I walked around her and cut her off. She glared at me.

"The hell I can't," she whispered fiercely.

The librarian shushed us. We both looked at each other and as if on cue, walked outside.

"Do you know what they do to guys like Tre?" I asked, as soon as we were out there. "They keep them locked up for a couple of weeks, months if you're lucky, and then let them out on good behavior!" She opened her mouth to speak, but I cut her off. "Then he'll come after us. He'll *know* it was us."

"That's ridiculous," she snapped. "There could easily be someone else who saw or heard what happened. And at any rate, at least that's a couple weeks of guaranteed safety for us!" Renee retorted. She started to walk away. That's when my temper flared.

"You don't know anything!" I said, spitting on the ground.

She whirled around and glared at me. "*What?*"

I started to apologize but she wouldn't have it. "Is this the *real* reason why you won't get close to anyone? Because you're afraid you won't have the guts to protect them when they need it?"

I flinched.

"That you'll end up doing exactly what you criticized your brother for doing? You don't want to run away because you think you'll look like a coward if you do, and you think it's all up to you, like you've got the ability to control everything?"

My mouth hung open and I had no response. She continued to glare at me.

"Come back to me when you've swallowed your pride." She stormed back into the library.

When I considered the reality in what she'd just said, I had none left.

***

It had been four years since he walked out. Not just out of the house, out of my life. He never wrote or called. He didn't leave any contact info on his note. I searched through all of his leftover belongings, trying to find an answer. I tried thinking of where he might go. Nothing ever came to mind.

So I stood on that cloudy afternoon, behind the caged fence, watching the middle school kids playing baseball. They had asked me to join, but I told them I would just watch.

"Hey Rory," I felt a hard slap on my shoulder. "You okay?"

Jack was a friendly kid I'd met last year. He lived just around the corner, but was going to move soon. I had been over to his house a couple of times because he'd always invited me. His parents were so nice, sitting around the dinner table, just laughing and discussing normal family matters.

I didn't bother moving my hair from my face, and my fingers were still resting on the openings of the caged fence, like it and them were the only things that could hold me up. Rude as it was, I walked away, forgetting he ever existed.

I made my way to the other side of town, down the cement steps of an abandoned underground subway, and pulled on the door. I was always fond of sneaking into places like that, especially with Jason for fun, but now I had to do it by myself, and it was more serious.

I pulled and pulled and it never budged. I banged on it a couple times in frustration, as if that would help. It didn't.

I made my way around to the other side, and broke a window on a door. I crawled in, scraping my exposed knee on a big giant shard of glass. I ignored the bleeding as I went in. There had been worse in my life.

Inside, it was dark, like daylight didn't even exist outside of its walls. I wondered if I could breathe if I lived in here, without the trees and leaves and plants around me. I went to the farthest, darkest, dustiest corner. I saw my little spider friend hanging around, just where he had been the day before.

I looked around the area to make sure the coast was clear. Then I whipped out a can of spray paint.

Hours and hours flew by, until night fell, and I still didn't go home. I didn't care if anyone didn't know where I was. If I wasn't with Jason, it didn't matter. I didn't want to be around anybody else. Forget it. I was on my own.

I stood back to look at my work. Quite sloppy, *I thought. It looked like a rainbow of tiny stick figures stepping on big, giant stick figures. The little ones were Jason and I. The bigger ones were Tre and our dad.*

Just then, I heard sirens outside. There were flashing lights and then heavy stepping sounds, getting closer and closer. They stopped. I turned.

"Hey kid, come out from under there. You're under arrest." However roughly they shoved me toward the car and applied the metal cuffs, it was never close the pain my dad put me through.

Despite not having a job, I still went with Todd today to his music store. He let me clean instruments and rearrange the shelves so I could have things to do. There was nothing to do alone in his house. But it was break now, and I went to *Sonny Morning* where Gabriella was. She smiled at me when I walked in. I nodded in return.

I made my way to the back corner, taking a seat in the semi-empty coffee place. Gabriella strolled over to me. "Is there anything you want?" she asked.

"Oh, no, I'm not really in the mood right now. I had a big breakfast. I hope you don't mind that I'm just in here to relax before I go back to Todd's store again."

"Sure, it's no problem. You're always welcome in here, Rory."

"Thank you."

I sat and recounted the day's events so far. I had been in the back room cleaning up guitars with Gideon.

Gideon was tall and chiseled, at least six-foot six, much bigger than Todd. Bright blond hair, a full beard, wearing a black, short-sleeved shirt and jeans. He'd been Jason's best friend back when they were teenagers. I hadn't seen him for ages. And for most of the time, I avoided his eyes.

Halfway into the silence he finally said, "Hey, Rory."

"What?"

"You know, before Jason left, he came to me with a request."

I narrowed my eyes. "What?"

"His new number. The number of the place he was planning on staying at. I wrote it down."

I looked up at him instantly. I was ecstatic and enraged at the same time. "Why wouldn't you TELL ME about this?"

"Well, I never got a chance frankly," Gideon laughed, but with no flavor of amusement. "You were always either in school, cramped up

in your house, or out somewhere not wanting to be bothered. Now that you're here, I can actually come and talk to you."

"You...I...I..." I was shaking with anger.

"Rory, you can fight me about this later. For now though, focus on what's important."

"Don't you talk down to me." It really took everything to say it rather than shout it.

"I'm not trying to. Just—"

"Give me the number."

Gideon sighed. "Sure," he replied. He ripped off a piece of paper and wrote it quickly and sloppily.

"You sure you memorized that correctly?"

"Yes." Gideon handed me, quite possibly, an answer to my problem in life, lying on a simple scrap of paper. He glanced at the clock. Three-thirty p.m. "Well, break time. I'm going to go across the street to visit Louis real quick." I didn't know who Louis was. Gideon was a social butterfly.

"You can try using the phone in the little office to the left, but it might be jammed," Gideon continued. "That place has been around before the prehistoric times. If no success, there are payphones right down the street. On me," he added, placing coins down on the desk in front of me.

"Thanks," I said through gritted teeth.

As soon as Gideon left, I went to the office he was talking about. But the place I went to for the private life-altering decision was only about four feet on each side of me. I could tell that before I even opened the door, looking from the outside in. There was one little lamp sitting on the scratched up desk, along with a mess of papers that looked as if a tornado had just gone through. There wasn't much else.

I couldn't understand what was holding the door in place, other than maybe it was just a little bigger than its frame. The heat might've *had something to do with it. But it wouldn't budge when I tried to open it, even though it wasn't locked. I tried again, and again. I shoved my whole body against it. Nothing worked.*

I gave the door a final bang and sighed. Then I went outside to the payphones. There I stood outside in the breeze, cringing at the bitter crispness of it. I wanted to run back inside where there was warm heat or go to Sonny Morning *where the sweet smell of cinnamon rolls filled with its aroma. But instead I kept my feet planted on the ground, staring down at the thick black writing of a simple number on a spare white piece of paper clutched in my hand.*

I stared at the phone for two minutes. Finally I worked the nerve to pick up the receiver, and with shaky fingers, punch in the digits.

The phone started ringing. My heartbeat sped up a hundred times faster. I wondered if I would be able to breathe, let alone talk, if he answered. It felt like I had no air, my throat was constricting and closing up on me, and I would gag.

It kept ringing. I began wondering if I even wanted there to be an answer on the other side.

"Hello, it's Jason. Just uh...leave a message. Seriously, leave one."

I gagged, but stopped in time at the beep of the tone. I had to think quick.

"Hi...I-I-look—I'm sorry..." I had to make it quick too. "I love you," I whispered. The phone went slamming down so hard I thought I broke it or my hand.

His voice. *I hadn't heard it in ages. It was surreal, as if hearing a dead person or someone I'd never met before but knew in a past life. All my insides shook. I wanted to scream, and jump for joy, and moan in agony. Why hadn't he been there?* Damn it! *But I felt giddy at the prospect of calling him later.*

I considered calling again right now though. I picked up the cold phone and held it to my ear. I heard the quiet humming sound. I sighed, suddenly weak and tired, and placed the receiver back on the hook. He should be able to tell that it was me. I gave it my all.

I shoved the number back into my pocket, and turned around to see that monster grabbing Renee.

I sat there in *Sonny Morning*, facing the wall and nothing else. I didn't regret it. I didn't regret it at all.

Then I recalled the incident where Tre...*Tre,* that son of a bitch, laid his hands on Renee.

I looked around for a "No Smoking" sign. There were none in sight. I lit a cigarette. It warmed me up, especially since the temperature began to drop more and more.

I took my notebook out of my bag and began to write, starting back from where I had left off:

....he is, waiting for me.
I start apologizing for no reason at all
My only defense against blood splattering the wall,
Stains for years reflecting all the tears
My one and only fear.
Away he goes, with every punch and curse
I want to move away, but if I do, it'll come back worse
Besides, I'm too slow, so here comes the hurt

"Rory?"

The sudden closeness of a voice startled me so much, I almost dropped my pen. I slammed my notebook shut and looked up at Todd. "So uh, how'd you find out I got suspended?"

"Word gets out," Todd said calmly with a sarcastic, tasteless grin. "So uh..." and I could kind of tell he was mocking me a little, because Todd always knew what to say and which words to choose. "You still have that switchblade knife on you?"

"Yes."

"Give it here." He held out his hand.

I looked up at him, mortified. I needed it for protection. What if Tre or his guys decided to attack me again? Or someone else? It wasn't like they didn't intend to kill me, or at least hurt me. Or people around me. I was a liability to everyone.

"I need it."

"No. You don't. What you need is an attitude adjustment, and a little common sense mixed in wouldn't hurt either. I also can give you some pepper spray. But you're not carrying around a knife, one that may be illegal, or one that could possibly get you arrested even if not. If someone's threatening you, Rory, then you tell me about it and we will go to the police. Now Rory, give me the goddamn knife." He still had his hand out, and now he was grinning again, only this time it was sinister, holding something dangerous back. There was nothing amusing about it.

I sighed and stood up, searching my back pockets. When I finally handed it to him, he took it, examined it for a second, then put it in his jacket pocket. Then his hand swung up very quickly. For a split-second, one horrible second, I shielded my face. I didn't know what came over me, I just naturally by instinct raised my hands to my face.

Todd looked confused. "What is your problem?" He had been reaching behind me to push the chair in. He was doing me a polite favor.

Once again, I flushed with embarrassment. "I'm sorry," I stammered. "I don't know why, or..." I swallowed and took a deep breath, "what came over me, I just..." I trailed off, not knowing how to finish the sentence, how to explain.

"Rory?"

"Yeah?"

He leaned a little closer and said in a low voice, "You don't have to be scared of me."

***

Gideon's hands were shaking with the phone in his hand when I got back to the music store. Somehow, he had been able to get the old office door open. His voice was steady, though his face was more contorted than usual. "I, I just called someone who was with him. His body was found, hanging from a dusty chandelier in an abandoned hotel somewhere in New York. The police deemed it a suicide. His alias name was Graham. He had a fake ID made, but not very well. They know. They know it's Jason. They'll probably contact your parents pretty soon."

I stood still for about ten seconds. My heart swelled, my blood froze, and everything inside of me just went numb. I stood, staring at him, and if I took my focus off for one second, I would be down on the ground, in need of being taken to a hospital maybe.

"Rory?" Gideon said, shaking me. He dragged me out of the office, and sat me down on a chair. "Rory, Rory...look at me!" He was shaking me.

I struggled to breathe, my heartrate spiking. I had *just* called him, just heard his voicemail. Just left a message, thinking he'd call me back at Todd's place soon and I'd get to hear his live voice all over again.

Gideon got up to go get some water, after yanking away from my tightening grip on his sleeve.

He came back and I sipped on some water, trying not to cry. Actually, I didn't have to try. My entire mind was too numb. I didn't feel anything.

This must be because of what I did all those years ago. Maybe my message wouldn't have made a difference.

"It's not because of you," Gideon said, as if reading my thoughts. He knelt down beside me. "'Graham', apparently, kept going from job to job, always getting in trouble, and even got evicted from his own house. That's enough to do anybody in."

I wondered how he'd gotten a house. I also felt mixed about there being someone with him, at least for some of his time away. I had no idea he wasn't alone. I was glad he wasn't entirely alone. On the other hand, I wished it would've been me.

I looked down at my hands, as if they would help me erase the news or change back time. I just wanted to know one thing. "Did he ever get my message?"

"I don't know."

I didn't know which would be worse. Assuming he got it and still killed himself despite it, or assuming he had not gotten it at all. Actually, the worst part for me was never knowing which.

***

Before Gideon left, he'd insisted I go home, and even Todd didn't object. I refused though. I kept working throughout the day, distracting myself. Later, I sat there, on the hard and pebbly steps in front of another store across the street from Todd's, pondering over the entire situation. A gust of wind blew my hair in my face and I didn't bother to move it.

I glanced down at my watch. I would go back to Todd in about ten minutes. I'd better get this done quickly.

I stood up and ran my hand through my hair quickly, a poised and confident teen on the outside, a nervous wreck of a boy on the inside, and turned and stepped in.

I walked inside, slowly eyeing different things. I nearly gasped when I saw Gideon behind the counter.

"What are you doing here?" he asked.

"What are *you* doing here?" I countered.

"I'm watching the store while the manager is away. Look, Rory, is there something you want?" He scrutinized me suspiciously. This wasn't your average store.

"No," I said. "There isn't. I'm just looking around for cigarettes." But that's not what I was looking for at all.

I walked around slowly, not looking at anything in particular. Gideon's eyes followed me.

This was not going to be easy. I needed something that would greatly distract him.

I left the shop. I stayed outside for a full ten minutes at least. Then I went back inside and mustered up the most confused and panicked look that I could. "Gideon," I said while carefully picking up a pack of cigarettes, "Your car out there is totaled."

Gideon jerked his head upwards. "No it isn't."

"Yes it is. The driver and passengers windows are cracked. There's something...uh...I think it's spray paint, on the hood. Yes, that's what it is, spray paint. I ought to know what spray paint looks like by now."

I was a good liar. I said all this convincingly, looking him straight in the eye. I didn't waver a bit.

His eyes widened, then narrowed. "Let me just ring up your smokes first," he said.

"NO," I said. "Your windows are cracked open. It's critical. Someone could be trying to steal it, or steal anything inside. I don't suppose you have anything too sensitive in there, but—"

Swearing, Gideon picked up his coat and rushed out the door, flying by the windows I watched him through. I guessed there *was* something sensitive in there. Dropping the cigarettes, I quickly walked to the back of the store and got ahold of a small handgun. I was sure I could find ammo—

Two hands had control of me. One gripping my arm, the other yanking the gun out. I turned to see Gideon glaring down at me with that horrifying wide-eyed stare teachers sometimes do to you when you've pissed them off for the last time.

I gulped.

He stared.

"It's for Tre," I said. How did Gideon get back in so quickly?

"Rory, stop. You're not thinking this through clearly. Jason wouldn't want you to do this. He already felt guilty enough as it was—"

"JASON didn't run away because he felt guilty, now damn it—give me a gun!" I shouted. There was no one else in the store except the two of us. And apparently someone else.

"Rory—"

"Shut up."

"Oh?" Gideon said, his face gone from sympathetic to pissed off.

"Just give me the gun."

"NO, Rory. You don't need it. You're just a child. I won't let you risk mishandling a death device."

"Fine," I snapped. I turned swiftly on my heel and walked out. "But I'll probably be dead by the end of the night anyway," I added, low enough for only me to hear.

Chapter 12: RENEE—A Lost Soul (Friday, December 20, 1996)

Earlier

I sat on the cold stone steps in front of the library, waiting for my dad. The weather was strange this time of year, in the south, nearing winter. It was still a little warm out at times, and then it went all chilly on you at others. The breeze that blew added ice to my bones, so I snuggled right up in my jacket.

"Hi," I said to the figure sitting next to me. Out of the corner of my eye was blowing black hair, pale skin, and that same timid presence.

"Hey...are you about to cry?"

"N-no, I'm...just thinking about my aunt and cousin...they might...and also m-my mother—" My words broke off. The ground blurred.

"Oh Renee..." I felt nice warm arms wrap around me. I leaned my head into his shoulder, and was grateful no one else was around to see me crying. Normally I didn't get this touchy-feely with somebody, but right now I needed it. I would've run to my mommy if she was here.

"Thanks," I whispered softly.

"It's okay. I know, losing someone like that..." HHe sighed, not wanting to continue. "You still mad at me?"

I sighed. "I'm still going to tell the police, Rory."

"That's fine. I'm sorry I tried to tell you not to. But are you still mad at me?"

"No." I looked over at him. His big dark eyes looked sad. I put my arm around him, hoping it wasn't too intimate. "You okay?"

"Me? Oh yeah, I'm always fine." That was bullshit, but I decided not to push him. "When will you tell them, the police?"

I sighed again and looked away. "I...I don't know. I'm kind of scared to, actually."

"Well, you just do whatever feels right to you."

A couple minutes passed by, and he said, "Are you okay now?"

"Yeah."

"Good."

"Rory, you look really pale. What happened?" His eyes were also purple and sagging. Really looking tired.

"I'm always pale."

"You look *much* paler than usual."

Rory looked a bit flustered, but his voice came out calm. "Nothing," he said hesitantly. I looked at him, knowing something was up. "I just," he brought his voice down to a whisper, "I really don't want to talk about it. Not now, at least."

I nodded, understanding and respecting that, and didn't push any further.

Some more silence went by. "Renee? I gotta ask you something else."

"Ask away."

"I know that you had problems with cutting and everything, but how did it feel? Does it really work like people say it does?"

I looked at him. "Oh yes," I said, "I believe it does. But I haven't actually gone through with it. I've only contemplated it several times."

Rory looked surprised. "Oh. I must've misunderstood you. I was under the impression you'd already done it."

I shook my head. I supposed it was easy to mistake that when one knew I had carried sharp objects around with me. "Why did you ask?" I said.

"No reason. I just wanted to know how similar it was to cigarette smoking."

"I'm sure smoking's not quite as bad, although...cutting, I don't reckon, does anything to your lungs." I shrugged. "I guess both are just peoples' ways of coping. No one's perfect."

"It's just hard."

"You can always talk to me if you need to. You know that, right?"

"Yeah. And same here."

A couple more minutes passed by before Rory decided to abruptly leave. I didn't want him to. "It's about to rain," he said, "and I really want to get inside before it hits. You want to come?"

I didn't want to be cold *and* soaking wet, so of course I was coming. He smiled and zipped up my coat for me as the winds grew heavier, carrying dark clouds in their wake.

"Oh. One more thing," I said.

He turned, eyebrows rising in curiosity. I went through my pocket, and carefully pulled it out. It was neatly folded and unwrinkled just like before.

"This dropped out of your pocket at the party," I said.

He looked down and gasped. "Oh! Um, thank you," he mumbled, taking it. "Do—do you like to read poetry?"

I smiled. "Yeah."

He smiled back, sighing with relief. "You want to read it? It's kind of morbid, actually."

"That's okay."

He handed it over to me.

I look through the eyes of a storm

I'm sick of all this anger

It pours rain like tears of pain

And thunder echoes the danger

I try to stay in control

Try to keep it all in

But I can no longer hide

Its shows deep within

The wind blows harder

And I can breathe no longer

Does anything even matter anymore?

***

I waited in the music store for my dad to drive by. By now the wind had picked up a little and the rain splattered across the glass windows. Rory was busy stocking shelves. I'd previously been in the store right next to this one. It was a video game store with an arcade, and had various different games, both older and newer. There was a promotional poster at the front advertising Tomb Raider, a brand new game that showed a lot of promise for popularity. I'd walked around for a little while, gazing at the different titles, getting lost in the interesting-sounding plots of some of them, the graphics, etc. When I'd finished, I'd gone into the music place next door to wait.

"Rory?"

Rory glanced up at a tall, lean man who'd walked over. He was blond and looked to be in his thirties.

"I'm sorry, can I talk to you for a second?" he asked, motioning Rory over. Rory walked over. I could still hear their conversation though. "Look Rory, I'm sorry, okay? I didn't mean to yell at you—"

"I didn't *either.*"

"God, Al-fucking-mighty, what is wrong with you?" the man exploded. I flinched.

"What do you mean, Gideon?"

"You know, I take my time to come here and be as nice as possible, all for what? Disrespect? Attitude, maybe? Why don't you unfold your arms, look up at me, and stop pouting. Stop being a little boy. For someone who wants to be treated like a man, you sure don't act like one. You don't have much confidence, and yet you act cocky all the time. It's a paradox."

I continued looking out the window as though I didn't hear a thing. Why did I always happen to be right there whenever something was happening to Rory?

"I'm not cocky. I know I fail at a lot of things, if not *everything.*"

"You see? This is what I'm talking about." There was silence. I guessed Rory was doing something like rolling his eyes or staring at a shelf, trying to appear more interested in it than he really was. That's what I did whenever I was embarrassed. I returned to pretending like I was interested in a clarinet in a display case near the entrance. I glanced back at the two of them. Gideon was rubbing his head stressfully. When he found his calm again, he spoke in a low voice. I could barely hear it.

"Look, about the gun Rory...if you really want to protect yourself or your friends from Tre, go to the police—"

"It doesn't have to happen again."

I almost gasped out loud, but kept quiet. Rory wanted to get a *gun* to protect me?

"Rory, I think you just need to calm down and *think*. You're in over your head here. Way in. So far in I almost can't pull you out. But I'm trying. You're not exactly making it easy."

Rory grunted.

"Why don't you come with me tonight to Barbecue Bill's. They're sponsoring the grand opening of the store which is on Thursday, after Christmas. A big sale will go on for New Year's."

"I heard Sonny and Jeremiah will be there tonight," Rory said sharply.

"Well, you'll have to get over it."

"Fine. I'll come, I guess."

Before I knew it, Rory was walking over toward me. "Want to come to Barbecue Bill's with me tonight? I, um, I think I'd be more comfortable with someone there with me. I—" He stuttered and looked away from me, embarrassed. "I just find you easy to talk to."

I wished so badly I could say "Yes", so it hurt me when I said, "I'm grounded, so I don't think I'll be able to. But," I added when I saw his face fall, "I'll try to convince my dad. I'll try to."

And that's all I could promise.

***

"Dad!" I groaned. This was worse than I thought.

"Renee, I think it's a fair deal. I want you to be able to interact with your friends, but I can't let you off the hook so easily. Either I go *with* you, or you *don't go at all*."

I thought this through as open-mindedly as possible. It would be a big, crowded area, with plenty of adults as well. He didn't say we had to sit at the same table. And...I *was* technically grounded, and justly so. My dad was awful nice. I could be at a shrink right now.

"Okay," I said through gritted teeth.

"Renee," he said. He had a serious tone to his voice that I couldn't figure out if I liked or not. "We're going to finally get to visit Jenny and Sheila tomorrow. They're going to pull through."

I could feel the corners of my mouth rise, until it had bloomed into a full smile, showing teeth and all. I couldn't remember the last time I'd smiled like that, and without even trying. My dad started to smile too. "They *might* even be able to come home by sometime next week. Perhaps Christmas miracles are a real thing." He came over and hugged me. He whispered in my ear, "I hope that cheered you up."

It did more than cheer me up.

***

Barbecue Bill's was part-store, part-restaurant, with various outdoor equipment to be sold and a small eating area where people could order burgers, hot dogs, sandwiches, and other foods. There was also an outdoor patio area with tables and chairs, but since it was December, everybody sat inside. It was packed.

As soon as we got there, I saw a table with Sonny, Jeremiah, and Sidney. "You can go sit with your friends," my dad said. "Actually, I left my wallet in the car. I'm going back out to get it." I nodded, teeth clenched, hoping no one—especially my friends—would see him. Luckily, for the rest of the night, my dad was away from the drama, all the way on the other side of the store looking at things.

Because what a night it was.

"Renee, you came," Rory said, smiling and giving me a half-hug when I first walked in. We got to talking for a little while. Sidney waved me over at one point. Rory frowned, but turned to me and said, "You should go over. They're your friends too. Go on and talk to them." He didn't even sound angry.

"Really?" I said. "Are you sure?"

"Of course. I can't talk much when I'm eating anyway."

About half an hour into our group gathering, there was a man a few tables over who was laughing loudly, having the time of his life. He seemed slightly drunk. I also spotted Rory walking near the table. It was a loud restaurant with music blaring from the speakers and people constantly up and about as though it were a club instead of solely a place to eat. The man had kept a refilled glass close to the edge of the table, still mostly full. Rory appeared inconspicuous, inching closer and closer to the table.

"Hey!" the man suddenly shouted. I could barely hear the guy past the music hurdling through the speakers, but he was definitely angry.

But Rory was nowhere to be seen. The glass was gone.

A couple of minutes later he came back to our table, something sloshing in a big glass he was carrying.

"How did you get that?" Sonny barked.

"With this," Rory said, flashing a fake-ID. "And the fact that it's more convincing if you already have a drink on you. After all, who would be dumb enough to serve me in the *first* place?" He had a different tone to his voice now. Confidence? No...it was closer to arrogance.

"It's really good," he continued.

Just then the man whose drink had gone missing approached. His face looked beet-red and his fists were clenched. I wanted to look away the way you want to flee when you know a horrific car crash was about to happen.

"You little brat," he spat, shoving Rory. It wasn't a big shove, but it was enough to piss Rory off.

"Hey, fuck off!" he snapped. "It's not my fault you left your shit unattended. You're lucky I only just took it. I could've been a real ass and poisoned it."

I flinched, looking around. People were going to start noticing, be it patrons or workers. I put my eyes back to my plate, trying to shut myself out from the crowd and Rory—both of which I was tempted to keep looking up at, the more I heard.

"You're lucky this isn't the streets, kid," he snarled. "Or I'd have half a mind to squeeze your head dry, if there's anything in there."

"You're older than my dad," Rory scoffed. "Try it, grandpa."

Why was he doing this? We were supposed to be having a good time.

Sidney, Jeremiah, and Sonny were oblivious to it for the first few minutes but soon started to notice. At one point, Jeremiah finally got up and stood between Rory and the stocky, well-built man that was probably capable of flipping a table any minute. "Stop it. Rory, stop it. This is stupid."

"Tell your friend to stop taking what's not his!" the man shouted, pointed at Rory with wide, crazed eyes."

"He's not my friend—"

"He's right, you know," Rory said in a slightly slurred voice, as if it were lost somewhere in his throat. His eyes were red and his skin was a pale pasty white. And still, he was able to move and walk alright. Slowly, at least.

"Jeremiah, sit down," Sidney said, not daring to look in Rory's direction. "It's not your job to take care of this." Sonny and I just sat uncomfortably, trying to act like we didn't hear or see what was going on.

"I know it isn't, but..." He reluctantly sat down.

Rory rolled his eyes and took another sip. "It's fine," he claimed, shrugging and handing the drink back over to the man, who took it with a look of disgust, and stomped off. I let out a breath of relief I hadn't realized I was holding. Rory walked over to us, a little wobbly with each step. "It's fine."

"The hell it is," Jeremiah growled. "Rory, *what* are you *doing?*"

"Yeah, I..." Rory's whole frame now seemed unstable and he dropped in a chair beside Sonny, who inched away from him.

"Don't come here if you're going to draw more attention or start more fights," Sonny growled. "That guy thought you were with us. He probably thought we were all in on it."

"In on what?" Rory asked stupidly.

"YOU, stealing things!"

Rory's eyes narrowed and his voice got very low. So low I had to lean in to hear it. "He left it unattended."

"*That's still stealing,* you moronic twit."

"Sonny, Rory, just drop it," Sidney said in a nervous voice. "Let's all talk about something else."

"No." Rory picked up Jeremiah's glass and took a sip. Jeremiah snatched it back from him. "You all think you're better than me. You've always thought that."

"We *are* all better than you," said Sonny.

"SONNY."

"You're actually defending him?" Sonny asked incredulously, looking at Sidney with a 'you've-got-to-be-joking' face.

"NO Sonny, I'm just trying to calm him down, that's all," Sidney snapped.

Just then a younger man in a white work shirt and black slacks, wiping his hands with a towel, came walking quickly over. He had a huge, disapproving frown on his face. "Hey," he said, "what is the deal over here? You're making a lot of noise over here."

"What are you talking about?" Rory asked, waving his arm around. "There's noise all over the place."

He got in Rory's face immediately. "Are you TRYING to wake the other side of town? This is still a public establishment, not your outdoor patio. You are disturbing the rest of the customers, especially ones with children. You almost got into a physical altercation, because I hear you've been taking things off of other peoples' tables. Now, I don't have proof, but I can very well check the cameras—"

"Not 'other peoples' tables'," Rory said. "Just one."

I put my face in my hand.

The worker did not look amused in the slightest. "KEEP IT DOWN OVER HERE."

Rory didn't flinch, but he blinked his eyes once. The guy turned his back and Rory gritted his teeth in anger. He spat, "Don't you try telling me what to do."

"Oh boy," Sidney mumbled.

The guy turned back around in a split second before Rory even finished his sentence, a dangerous look in his eyes. We were all holding our breaths at this point. The guy walked back over to Rory, looking angry enough to crush his foot by just stepping on it. Rory glared up at him.

Just as Rory started to get up and walk away, the guy hissed "What kind of influence does your man have on you?"

Rory spun around. "What?" he shouted so loudly, Jeremiah almost dropped his glass. Getting in his new enemy's face, Rory said, "You got a problem—" He stopped, frozen in mid-sentence, as he noticed the guy pointing at his lower arm where a scar had been born long ago. Both of them stared down at it. This was a rare occasion Rory had taken his jacket off, wearing short sleeves.

The music died down, ready to put on another song.

People all over were staring at us, some with curious fascination, some with annoyance.

The guy lightly tapped Rory on the arm, and he yanked his arm away, and looked back up, disgusted. "Don't you touch me," he growled. "You understand that? DON'T TOUCH ME. *Ever.*" By now he was so close to the worker's face they were practically touching. The man had his hands up, as if he wanted to give this job up right now.

Jeremiah got up. "This is getting out of hand," he muttered as he walked over toward Rory. Sonny groaned, repeatedly saying, "Why are you trying to help him, *it's none of our business...*"

"Who do you think you are?" Rory asked, an inch away from the worker's face. The worker pushed Rory back, separating them about a foot apart. "You need to leave," he said in a cold voice.

Rory stood there, hardly breathing, shocked. "What the...I thought I told you not to touch me, you asshole!"

The worker just looked at Rory with a bored expression, as if he'd seen this before. "You'd better watch your mouth kid. You're going to land in much more trouble one day than just getting kicked out of somewhere. OUT!" He looked at the other four of us sitting down, not doing anything wrong. "Take these four with you."

I opened my mouth ready to inform him that we weren't a part of this, but Sidney silenced me with a hand on my shoulder. She shook her head, as if it wasn't worth it.

Rory took a step forward with his mouth clenched shut, and I didn't know what he was about to do.

Jeremiah stepped between the two, just as he'd done with Rory's previous altercation with someone. He grabbed him around his waist and started pushing a struggling Rory away. The three of us got up and followed Jeremiah, Sonny cursing under his breath. Rory, though being dragged out, was still glaring at the man, now walking away shaking his head. He was probably getting ready to make an announcement to everyone in the restaurant saying, *'It's okay folks, the troublemakers are gone.'*

When we got outside, Rory shoved Jeremiah away. He also tried looking up and around, searching around for the guy again. He looked like he was ready to rush back into the front doors of the restaurant. "Funny, I didn't take that first guy as the 'can-I-speak-to-the-manager' type."

"You're not going back in there, Rory," Jeremiah warned.

"Jerry, fuck it!" Sonny said. "Let him! If he wants to embarrass himself, fine! Let's all go somewhere else."

"My dad is still in there," I muttered.

Rory headed over toward Gideon's truck and opened the passenger door.

"You've made a complete fool of yourself tonight," Jeremiah yelled. "You're an embarrassment!"

"Why do you care?" Rory snarled. "You're not my friends!"

"Damn straight," Sonny spat.

Rory looked like he was going to let loose an angry string of retorts when Jeremiah grabbed him by the shirt and thrust him roughly into the back seat of the car.

"Give him a bucket, damn it, I don't want him throwing up back there," Gideon growled bitterly, making all of us jump as he came walking up behind us. "What in tarnation brought this on?"

All of us stood silently. We really didn't know what to tell him. Had he seen the whole thing? Had he heard some of it? Was he in the restaurant when it happened?

Gideon shook his head and got into the front seat of his truck, zooming out of the parking lot.

***

My dad took me home and we had a loud fight about me supposedly "getting involved." Getting involved in what? "You never listen to me!" I shouted. "And for the record, I never cut *once.*" I rolled up my sleeves and showed him my forearms. "See? So you can stop worrying...or *judging.*" I slammed my door in his shocked face. We went to bed enraged that night. I lay wide awake on my bed.

The car ride was so long, and my headphones weren't helping, as I'd found myself listening to the same song over and over again. "Dad," I finally said, "Why did you do it?" I tried to make my voice sound firm.

He didn't answer.

"Answer me."

"Don't take that tone with me."

He had some real nerve. "I deserve to KNOW!" I could've thrown my headphones at him.

My dad stopped the car.

I stared at him, anticipating rage.

But instead he sighed. "Okay...you want to know the truth?"

"Yes."

"I do love your mother. It's just, I can't stand to hear you weep every night in your sleep. I'm sick of lying to you and saying it'll be okay. You know it won't, and you're mature enough to handle the truth." He paused, squeezing the steering wheel. "It was Sheila who did it—"

"You went along."

"Yes," he replied. "Yes, you're right. But Renee, I'm not opening the door for another woman to come in. No one will ever replace your mother. There will be no step-mother. Just you and me, okay? I've vowed never to date again."

"You don't have to do that," I said. "You don't know what will happen. You might very well find someone else you like." It stung for me to admit it, but it was true. And I had no right to get in the way of that. I vowed to myself right then and there that should it happen, I wouldn't be that bratty child of the man some woman was dating who didn't want to even try to get along. But I still prayed he wouldn't find anyone else. Ever. I didn't care how selfish that was.

Even though people say there's always tomorrow, tomorrow's never guaranteed. It was hard not to think of such a thing when you didn't go through a loss like I did my mom and Rory did his brother.

I tried to be quiet as possible, but I heard some footsteps outside my door, heavy footsteps I knew were my dad's. Through the crack of light at the bottom of my door, I saw them stop. I held my breath for a moment, and they carried on.

***

My dad and I went to the hospital the next day. Both of us had seemed to have forgotten our spat the previous night. Now the only thing on our minds was Jenny and Sheila. It was a weird mix of positive and negative energies—the positive from the fact that they were alive, after all, and they were healing pretty well, according to doctors—the negative being how stressful it was going to be, being in a hospital again. Not to mention, how awkward this might be. I hoped nobody got teary-eyed, that was not going to go over well with me. I felt fine being that way around friends, but emotional *family* gatherings was not my thing. At all.

The silent car ride didn't take long, which was good, because you could feel the nervous vibes emanating from both of us strongly. We parked, got out, and made our way to the frosted glass double doors up the steps. Inside, stepping on the linoleum tiles, it smelled of cleaning agents, disinfectant wipes, etc. It had a very sterile smell to it as well. Many people hated these smells, which may have been why many hated being in hospitals (along with the washed-out white walls, ceiling, and floor), but I didn't mind them much. Then again, maybe I would've felt entirely different if my situation was more tragic, rather than fortunate.

It seemed more crowded than I expected. I didn't know why I was surprised, it was Saturday after all. And it was close to the holidays. There was a small Christmas tree with lights wrapped around the foliage in one corner we passed. I could vaguely smell the fresh scent of pine needles and balsam, and would've gladly stayed to smell this Christmas smell and marvel at the glittery ornaments forever.

When we finally arrived to the room, in which both Jenny and Sheila were sharing, I held my breath. Both of them looked asleep. Sheila had her right arm in a sling, and she was facing upwards toward the ceiling. Either she liked resting on her back or she was in a deep sleep. Jenny was lying on her side, burrowed under the white cover, with a big white bandage on the left side of her forehead, facing away. She didn't appear to be moving, but I could just see the slight up-and-down motion of her breathing. Her dark hair looked greasy and uncombed, not the way it normally was. I briefly imagined what it would be like to be in a car, and, due to a tornado or an accident or anything else, start tumbling around in it, the entire world flying about around you, not being able to keep up with anything with your eyes and ears, and having absolutely no control of the situation whatsoever. It'd probably be impossible to even *think.* I shuddered.

My dad leaned down toward me while also looking at her, and whispered, "Usually a concussion lasts about a week, although sometimes longer. Hers isn't too severe."

Suddenly Sheila's eyes flew open. They widened when she saw us both standing there. "James. Renee. You both came."

My dad, looking surprised as well, gestured for me to sit in the chair beside her bed.

Sheila turned to me. "I'm really okay. Just really tired. It also doesn't help that these hospital beds aren't that comfortable."

I smiled at her familiar critical tone.

She turned her head slightly downward, looking at my bag at my side. "What have you got there, Renee?"

I'd recently purchased a few gifts for them at a gift shop not too far from this hospital. For Sheila, I'd gotten three notebooks, since she likes to write things down a lot. She writes lists, little notes, things to remember, etc. She doesn't use a regular agenda book, just pretty notebooks with fancy covers. I used those a lot too, but while mine were full of drawings or doodles, hers were filled with words and reminders and important stuff.

One notebook was a deep red with an extra cover of black filigree over it. Another one of the notebooks had a cheetah print design, since I noticed Sheila wearing that type of print sometimes. I figured it's one of her favorite prints in general. The last notebook was fake snake skin with a small picture animation of pens in the top corner and in gold fancy writing said, *'Here's to your future works.'*

"These are beautiful," Sheila said as I went through them. She held the hand of her good arm out, and I didn't know if I should hand one to her because her other arm was in a sling. But they were skinny, light notebooks, and my dad nodded when I looked at him. I reluctantly handed her the one with the faux-snake skin and writing on it, and she held it in her hand, turning it back and forth from its front and back. "You should keep this one," she said, handing it back to me. "I don't have 'works' in the making. Unless my grocery lists are works. You do."

My mouth opened but I didn't know what to say. I took the book. Sheila said, "Did Jenny get anything?"

Jenny's gift was two things that came together—a snowman-theme necklace and bracelet. The necklace had a little snowman in the center, while the rest was made up of little snowflakes all around, encrusted with sparkling jewels. The bracelet was designed pretty much the same way. I'd seen them in a shop and thought they were awfully pretty for a cheap price. It was a good deal.

"I don't know," I said, "maybe snowmen are kind of cliché for the winter and Christmas."

"Snowmen are good," I heard a groggy voice say. My dad and I glanced over in surprise—Jenny hadn't turned around, hadn't changed position, and for that matter hadn't even moved. But that had definitely been her voice, hoarse as it was.

Sheila turned back to us and grinned. "Frosty was playing earlier. She's in a snowman mood.

"Well, you guys had better be getting back now. It may very well be a white Christmas this year, which is rare for Texas. Or at the very least, it will be colder than ever. Goodness, and we just went through a blizzard *last* winter where we lived. There were areas that had gotten four feet of snow due to wind drifts—and I think one in Virginia got TEN feet!"

My dad nodded. "I remember that. You guys were lucky to have gotten out of that alive," he said, only half-joking.

She was so talkative again, it was like she'd never been injured. I liked having things go back to normal like that. I didn't like when people got dramatic and dwelled on everything and blew them up even more. She could talk about snow storms forever if she wanted to.

Sheila and my dad got into a conversation about the Blizzard of 1996—the one that happened up on the east coast, in Virginia, D.C., Maryland, and other areas. It had been a few feet that we got, power loss, whiteout conditions, the whole thing. After experiencing that, I supposed moving to Texas had its upsides. I highly doubted we'd ever experience anything like that here, but who knew?

And at the very end, my dad kissed Sheila goodbye, and she briefly took my hand. "Jenny and I were planning on doing some shopping for your Christmas gift. It was going to be a surprise, and we're still going to get it for you. But since we might not get it by

Christmas day itself, I'll just tell you: It's a sketchbook with several different types of pencils, and also a tutorial booklet to go with it. Although, you might already know that stuff, so maybe I should get something a little more advanced."

"Oh," I said. "You don't have to do that!"

"Nonsense. And…I put a picture of Nicole on the front cover."

I gaped. I was NOT going to cry, so instead I opted for looking surprised.

"And there are a few other things too," she continued, taking the cue that I didn't want this to be emotional, "but that's the only one I'll tell you about for now."

I didn't think me and Sheila were going to fight as much anymore. Maybe bicker some, maybe bicker a lot. Maybe Jenny and I wouldn't be braiding each other's hair or doing each other's nails anytime soon, but we actually made an effort to get each other something nice on occasion. And I knew more than ever now that there were families out there a lot worse off than that.

When we got back in the car, my dad turned and said to me, "Looks like it'll be a good Christmas after all."

I nodded in agreement, and shivered at how cold it was.

He smiled, put the heat on, and said, "Let's go get warmed up."

Chapter 13: Rory—Four a.m.
(Friday, December 20, 1996)

"Rory, don't do that again," Gideon said.

"What the hell kind of bullshit were you trying to pull tonight?" Todd asked, coming into the kitchen as I sat down, exhausted. Great. So Gideon told him, of course. "You're sending your life down the drain, second after second, because you want to do what RORY wants to do, huh? This is why I have to babysit you constantly."

I got up, fists clenched. My posture was better now, but Gideon still rushed to my side in case I fell again. "I never asked you to babysit me," I said indignantly.

Todd started to walk toward me and opened his mouth, but before he could say anything, Gideon held up a hand. "Let's wait for this Todd, okay? Let's all just settle down first before anyone does anything rash."

Todd stomped out of the kitchen.

Fine. I would've rather had someone's hatred than pity anyway. If I needed a shoulder to lean on, I leaned on my own. A hand to massage aching muscles, my own. An arm to touch, *my own.*

"Let's go get you cleaned up," Gideon said absently, taking my arm. "Come on." He jerked his head in the direction of the bathroom.

Gideon aided an open wound on my left shoulder. It reopened when I tripped on the pavement outside walking in when we got back. Then Gideon pointed to the sink where I began to wash my face gently.

A couple minutes passed by. "Rory...what are you doing?!" I heard Gideon scream, horrified. The sink had filled up with water and I had kept my face in the water a little too long. I still didn't know if I just sort of passed out there or if I'd done it on purpose.

Gideon pulled me out immediately, water splashing everywhere. I started coughing and sputtering. It finally died down after he hit me on the back a couple of times.

"What were you *doing*?"

"Washing my face," I replied. He stared at me, wide-eyed, before he threw the wash cloth down in the sink and walked out.

***

Though I was still in recovery mode, I called Renee. I was sleepy and exhausted, but I'd calmed down quite a bit. I hoped it wasn't too late. "Sure, one moment," he father said gruffly. I guessed it was. I hoped she hadn't told him very much about me.

Renee's voice came into my ear. "Hello?" She sounded pissed.

"I'm sorry Renee," I said. "I um...for everything."

"Don't mind me, my dad and I just had a fight," she responded. "Rory, are you okay right now? What *happened* tonight?"

"I'm a little better, still kind of queasy. I got...out of control."

"You think?"

"Sorry. For being mean to you, for being an ass to you...for getting you all kicked out, for embarrassing you...I'm sorry. I'll understand if you don't want to talk to me anymore."

There was a long silence. Such a long silence that I was afraid she'd hung up on me, even though I could still hear her breath.

Then I heard her let out a huge sigh. "Rory, I don't think you're a bad person. I think you need help though." She paused. "*Let* people help you. Don't just keep pushing them away. It'll just get worse and worse. I probably sound like a hypocrite right now, because my dad and I aren't always on the same page ourselves, but yeah. I have to work on it too."

"Renee, I want to tell you why I did it," I whispered.

"Sure. I'm listening."

I bit my lip. "I found out that my brother died today."

I heard a gasp. There was a long silence. "Rory," she said, "I..."

"It's okay. My dad thinks it's my fault, I'm sure."

"He's a vile—"

"I love my dad," I blurted. I slapped my hand over my mouth. Had I really just said that? I'd heard being drunk could sometimes cause people to be more open about things, but still. All along it was there, and I kept trying to deny it, denying that he was even my father.

"I know," Renee said softly. "It's hard to hate a parent. And I'm not going to try to pretend I understand what you're going through.

"Thank you, Renee. I don't know what I'd...you're...you're easy to talk to."

I could hear a hint of a smile in her voice. "You are too. I have to go now. I'm really tired."

"Sorry. You go get some rest. Do you think that maybe I could call you again?"

"Sure Rory. And I also like to go to the library too, so you could always drop by."

"Thanks Renee. Goodnight."

"Goodnight."

***

It was hours later that I awoke.

I was lying on a bed in the same clothes. Despite the nasty smell that consumed them, I felt very different. When I breathed and sat up I felt so much better. More clear-headed. Like a bunch of heavy weights had just been lifted off my chest.

I was horrified when all the events came rushing back.

I swung my legs around and got up. I felt so alive. After I changed out of my damp clothes into a warm sweatshirt and black jeans, I started pacing around the room, trying to remember things. *How did I black out? Did I collapse? Where was the last place...the restaurant? No.* I remembered the kitchen. *Crashing plates.* I was scared for a moment. *No,* I convinced myself. *No, it wasn't out of anger like him. It was an accident. I was drunk, and couldn't even hold myself together, let alone an object.*

Then I recalled the weird dream I had while dozing off into another world. A dream of a little girl, holding on to me tightly, begging me not to let go. And Jason. He said something, but I couldn't remember what. It *must*'ve been a dream. Jason didn't exist anymore.

I pushed this painful thought out of my head and went back to figuring out what exactly took place between when I left consciousness and now. Someone must've brought me up here. Maybe Todd. *Todd.*

My heart sunk, and despite the fact that it was cold outside, I knew that wasn't what caused the shiver to go down my spine.

He was not going to be happy. He'd probably heard all about it by now. Hell, probably the whole town had. Different versions. I almost wished that he *would* hear a different version instead. Gideon probably told him the correct version, he'd probably heard it from Sidney and Jeremiah and Renee, or probably had seen it, or spoken to a worker there. Todd probably had an account by now of all the ugliest parts.

I glanced over at the clock. 12:15. Todd would still be up right now. *Better to confront him about it now than to wait until tomorrow,* I thought miserably. I slowly opened my door and made my way downstairs, careful to not be too loud. The only light that glowed in the dark house was the dim one from the kitchen. I heard low, distant voices, but couldn't hear what they were saying. One of them was Todd's for sure. His voice was higher than usual, clearly upset. The other one was too low to recognize.

I tip-toed toward the dining room. My stomach was doing somersaults the closer and closer I got. I forced myself forward, running a hand through my hair, and peaked inside. Todd was sitting at the table, head in his hands. No one else was in sight. Maybe I was imagining the other voice.

I gently pushed opened the door, trying my best not to let it creak, but it did anyway. Todd alertly raised his head. "Sorry," I muttered.

He smiled and stood up. It wasn't a happy smile though. "Awake at last, huh?" His tone sounded like it was whispering in my ear, *About damn time.* He sauntered over to me and set both of his hands in his pockets. "Heard you got into a couple of fights last night."

He started tossing his keys up and down in the air numerous times, a habit of his I knew all too well. My eyes went up and down, following them, as if being hypnotized. I took a deep breath, trying to keep it steady. "Where are we going?"

"You got into two fights last night," he said again, ignoring my question. It was immediate, dismissing what I had just asked, and a little louder this time. His face was now blank.

"They weren't really fights...but...I guess I did act stupid and cause a bunch of disruption." I cleared my throat. "Publicly." I swallowed. "And got myself and others kicked out."

His expression turned from amusement to confusion. He raised his eyebrows and held out a hand, as if urging me to continue.

"I'm...sorry."

Todd scoffed, looking at me incredulously as if he actually found it amusing. He placed his hand on the table beside him, harder than anyone needed to. "No. No. Don't tell me you're sorry."

"What do want to hear then?"

Now he was just staring at me. I could see the red veins pushing through his eyes. I realized then that Todd usually went to bed earlier than most *kids*. He always woke up early—like around five. He always had somewhere to go, even if it wasn't work. He was the biggest morning person I knew. And I knew for a fact that he was exhausted, every day, after work.

"So help me," he scoffed again, "you'd better have an explanation. It's not about 'what I want to hear'. Otherwise, there'd be no point in having this discussion."

"Honestly, I don't know what happened. I didn't mean to, I just..." My voice trailed off. I sounded pathetic. There was a moment of silence indicating that he wanted me to go on. "I was depressed. I wanted to get my mind off of things, so I started with one bottle, and from there..." Again, my voice trailed off. "By the time I knew what was happening, it was too late."

Todd nodded at me for a couple seconds, looking amused. Then in the blink of an eye that expression of amusement was gone, and his jaw clenched and his face hardened. I was afraid he'd scoff again, but instead he nodded his head and yelled, "I don't EVER want to hear about you doing shit like this again, Rory. You hear me? And don't blame the beer, which you should NOT have been drinking anyway." His voice began to rise until he was shouting at the top of his lungs. "You are so *fortunate* to not have been arrested for a *number* violations last night. The world has been very kind to you."

Anger was starting to boil in my stomach.

Gabriella came up quietly behind me and put her hands on my shoulders.

Todd went on, "I know what it's like first hand to lose someone. I've experienced losing many people. But I wasn't a victim. I wasn't weak. I despise weak people. I got through it, and I'm alive today. And I don't go around making a complete FOOL of myself over it. It's all about decisions, Rory."

"It's not that easy for some—"

"SHUT UP, I'm not done talking yet," he snapped.

I looked at the ground, shaking in rage.

"I mean, yeah, I'm a little pissed at the fact that I can't exactly get more than three hours of sleep at this point, due to your self-ishness, but that's no big deal. I'm SHOCKED at how selfish you were to your friends though. And yourself. *You're* not being fair to yourself. You say you're depressed? Well, I guess just dulling and numbing everything so that you can avoid it makes everything bet-ter, right? And then antagonizing people and getting thrown out of establishments, because you can't control yourself *AT ALL*. I guess that cheers things right up, doesn't it?"

I didn't say anything. I didn't have anything to say.

"Huh, Rory? Someone dies and that's just going to make every-thing okay again? Is that going to take away all the pain? Is it going to bring them back, right by your side?"

"Stop it," I said quietly.

"Does fighting take all the pain away too?" he pressed. "You know for your sake, I wish I could say it did." Now Todd's blood-shot eyes were so close to me, I could see my reflection in them. "You seem to do that quite often." He was torturing me with questions I myself didn't have the answers to. "You want to keep going down this route, getting into trouble, getting into fights, possibly landing yourself into jail, then *fine*. I'm not going to try to stop you anymore. I'm not going to try to bail your ass out of anything anymore. I'm not going to try to save you when those mean cops show up"—he said this mockingly—"who deal with misbehaving disrespectful kids like you. Because one day, Rory, one day they won't see you as a kid anymore. They'll see you as an adult. An adult who can't control himself and who is a danger to others, who can't follow the law or take responsibility for himself. And then there'll come a day when you won't come *out* of jail."

He fell silent for a couple seconds and stared at my trembling self, and then continued. "You're not making anybody proud here. Whatever happened to Rory who went to school, played guitar, the way you were before getting involved with Tre and his gang? I thought you'd be smarter than that."

I looked up at him, my eyes narrowed, fiercely protecting them from tears. "You guessed wrong then." My voice came out in a raspy tone.

"Clearly."

"I don't have to take this from you—"

"You're here, so you'll take it. Otherwise, there's the front door—"

"You think you know everything—"

"I know a great deal more than you—"

"I don't need to hear anymore, I get it—"

"Rory, BE QUIET—"

"Don't—"

"DAMN IT, WHAT IS WRONG WITH YOU? *SHUT UP.*"
There was silence.

"I'm not going to lie to you. You're throwing yourself away little by little. At the rate you're going, you'll be in jail before you reach adulthood and then life will be nothing but one big steel cell."

After a few heartbeats I said, "I'm not going to do anything bad enough for *that*."

"Do you want to leave? Do you want to get kicked out of mom and dad's house again, and then be on the streets? You have NO IDEA what it's like to live on the streets, Rory. You wouldn't survive, trust me. Sometimes it's worse than jail."

"No, I don't want to leave."

Todd stared at me for one last time that night. "Then go to bed," he replied in a low growl. He walked up the stairs. A door slammed.

"Is everything alright in here?" A tall, old man with an Eastern European accent—I think it was Russian—came walking in. I had never seen him before.

"Who is that?" I asked, alarmed.

"Some strange old man who followed Todd home one day," Gabriella replied, trying to lighten the mood.

"NO!" Todd yelled from upstairs. Gabriella jumped. "It's Alexei."

Alexei, one of Todd's neighbors. He sometimes joined Todd for breakfast. I'd never seen him here so late though. But I'd oftentimes heard of him sleeping in one of Todd's guestrooms. I never knew if it was because he was having money trouble or family trouble. In my case, it was both.

"Everything's just fine," Gabriella told Alexei. "Nothing to worry about." She went over and led him back to his room, their voices fading out. I stood in the middle of the dining room, wishing what Gabriella had just said was true.

***

There was a loud thunderstorm that night. I didn't blame Patches for jumping up on my lap when I got up to my room. I sat there petting him for a while, rubbing his tummy when he turned over.

I couldn't sleep that night. First it was too cold. Then it got too hot. I nearly tore my shirt off, I was burning up so badly. I didn't understand. Did I have a fever? All I knew was that I was really sick because I threw up in the bathroom twice.

I'd had it. I threw on an undershirt along with some jeans, and headed downstairs in silence. I went to the kitchen and sloshed some cold water down my throat.

Patches followed me downstairs. I put some water out for him and he drank away. It was burning up; the power went out and so I had to use a flashlight. This would mean the air-conditioning was gone.

I sat at the kitchen table staring out the window of the side door that led to the garage. I wanted so badly to go out and be in the rain that pounded against the ceiling, but I'd probably catch something else.

I sighed, and felt two cold hands touch my shoulders. I spun around and almost dropped the flashlight. "Hello, kid," came a deep Russian accent.

I yelped for a second, and then remembered the old man's voice. It was only Alexei. "Oh, um, hi."

"You look troubled. And so does your shoulder. Let me have a look."

He was right. One of the bruises on my shoulder had started to turn blue and purple, and it was very sore.

I let out a huge breath. "Oh. Alright," I said reluctantly.

For the next ten minutes, Alexei gave me some ice for my shoulder, speaking most of the time. "It broke my heart when I learned my father passed away."

"I'm sorry."

"Yes, it was quite painful." We sat there in silence for a while, staring out the window at the rain beating down on the glass, and eventually Alexei started speaking again. "Did you know, Rory, that at one point Todd tried to kill himself?"

I almost dropped what I was drinking. "Wha—he—what?"

"He was only a teen. His father came to help him before it was too late. But it was ultimately Todd's choice. The kid had a lighter in one hand, and love in another. He couldn't do it, and at the last minute, called for help. It paid off. If he hadn't, he surely wouldn't be here today. You know Rory, Todd *really* does care about you."

"I don't know," I said. "He used to. Not anymore."

"Yes, he does. Only love could justify that kind of anger. Only love."

"Or disappointment."

"Perhaps. But disappointment to that extremity makes a person fight harder, or hope further. You still have a chance to prove yourself." He pat me on the shoulder and got ready to leave for bed.

"Why was Todd going to kill himself?"

Alexei sighed. "Everything. Because of everything. There was not one specific reason. Everything wasn't going his way. His grades dropped, he was losing more and more confidence every day, and felt ashamed at what he had become...temporarily." He glanced back at me, his hand on the door. "But it *is* just a temporary feeling, Rory. Remember that."

Chapter 14: RORY-Aftermath
(Saturday, December 21, 1996)

I woke up the next morning feeling very, very exhausted. I must've only gotten four hours of sleep, and even that had some to subtract, for I was up half the time vomiting, being downstairs, and tossing all over the sheets like a possessed person. It was the most miserable night of my life. No matter how tired I was, I couldn't get to sleep. So despite me wanting badly to stay in bed when Gabriella came to tap my shoulder lightly, I figured it'd be best just to get up since it was doing me no good anyway.

Four a.m. came, still dark out, and I was lying awake, staring at the photograph of Jason I'd put on the desk beside me. Sometimes it helped me sleep at night, other times it haunted me. Or, like now, it tore me apart, but was still an addiction.

"Hey Rory," she said softly, "It's time to get up."

I pushed myself up and turned around. Gabriella looked worried. "Oh Rory..." her voice trailed off. "Have you been crying? Is it because of last night?"

I glanced at the photograph. It was all I could do not to fall back down on the bed. It just felt wrong to get up and work another day without him in the world, knowing that the last bit of himself that existed in this world was concealed to a photograph.

Gabriella stroked my shoulder and arm. "No," I said quietly, "I'll be okay."

Patches jumped up on the bed and rested his head on my thigh. Gabriella giggled. "He seems to like you."

I attempted a smile. "Thanks," I said quietly. "He followed me home one day."

Gabriella gave me a hug and as soon as I'd gotten out of bed, I headed straight for the bathroom and washed my face. I got changed into a clean shirt and pants.

When I walked downstairs, I was about to pass the kitchen quietly without being seen, when Todd beckoned me to come in. It could not be avoided. I took a deep breath and walked in.

Both of us acted like last night never happened, which was fine by me. "You hardly ate or drank anything yesterday," he stated. "You need at least something in your system before you go, even if it's little."

I nodded absently and walked over to the fridge.

"I'm going to drop you off so you'll be there alone at first, but I should get back there sometime before we close up at noon. Okay with that?"

"Noon?" I asked, confused.

"It's Saturday and it's almost Christmas. We won't be back open until New Year's."

"Oh." I yawned and then sighed. "Why is it so hot in here now? It was cold last night."

"Because the air-conditioner itself still doesn't work."

"No I mean...it's almost Christmas."

"Because this is Texas, not New York."

I groaned and sat down to drink my orange juice.

"I'll try to have it fixed as soon as possible. All the same, please bring a coat."

"A coat? Why?"

"Temperatures are supposed to drop sharply today. It *is* December, after all."

I nodded. "Okay. I'll bring a coat."

Todd sat down at the table, across from me. He leaned back, still struggling to get his eyes open from the early hour. He looked as young as a teenager with his black messy hair hanging down his face. He abruptly looked in my direction with a scowl on his face, but not at me. Or at least, not at my *face.*

"Rory, come over here. Let me see your shoulder." He lazily motioned me to come over, so I sat down beside him. He lifted the sleeve of my shirt up further, and examined it without touching it. He kept sighing and rubbing his eyes.

"I think it goes further than that. Like up to my neck," I said quietly.

"Yes, I know that," he replied impatiently. Finally he let go and sighed again, pushing his hair back with his hand. "Rory, do you guys have medical insurance?"

"I'm not sure..." My parents never talked to me about that stuff.

"I'm going to have a word with your mother." Seeing the look of panic on my face, he quickly added, "Either that, or I'll pay for an appointment for you to get looked at, right out of my pocket."

I didn't want either to happen. "Todd, you don't *have* to."

"Yes I do, and I will."

"It's not that serious—"

"It *is* serious, Rory. One day, you'll realize that all of this is serious, and not something you should brush off."

Muttering to myself, I got up. The rest of the morning was awkward. It mostly consisted of me getting ready, waiting for him out on the porch steps, riding beside him in the passenger seat, and him dropping me off. I was always afraid to look him in the eye, but then again he never really looked at me all that much either.

We said nothing as he pulled up near the store, the parking lot looking deserted. I looked at him and tried to smile, but he was too busy going through his wallet to look at me. But it wouldn't have mattered anyway. I wasn't able to crack anything on my face.

"If the door in the back is locked, get Gwen to open it up when she arrives. She should be there soon. She's managing for today and has access to a set of keys. But I need you," he said, handing me some keys of his own, "to lock the door behind you when you go in. It's supposed to be closed today. Please, see to it that you lock the door right after you step foot in."

With a jolt of horror, I remembered I'd given a set of keys to Tre. Had he been around? *Would* he come around? I hadn't heard about anything like that yet, no reports from Todd...at any rate, having another set of keys should deter them. I put it to the back of my mind, not even entertaining the idea.

"Okay," I muttered, taking the keys.

I got out of the car and as I was walking up the steps I stole one last glance back. But he had already driven away.

Quickly locking the door behind me, I stepped in. The store looked fine, everything seemed to be in its right place. I stood in one spot for a while looking around. Nothing seemed amiss—no mess, no vandalism, no person creeping around the corner. I didn't know what I'd expected—maybe for it to be in shreds or something, like from a tornado.

I heard the door being unlocked and open behind me. It was Gwen. She was a little older than Todd, with light brown skin, dark brown eyes, and long curly black hair. Usually there would be a "Hello," and a warm smile from her when she saw me. But today she looked like her mood had taken a hit.

"Good morning," I said. When she didn't say anything in return, I turned to walk to the room in the back to start my usual tasks of cleaning guitars and stacking books.

"There are three guitars missing," she said.

I spun around. "What?"

"You heard me. A black Gibson, a red Fender, and a black Behringer."

"I..."

She had her hands on her hips.

"What are you looking at me like that for?" I asked, getting angry. "You don't think I took them, do you?"

She didn't say anything.

"Why the hell would I? I already have one anyway."

"To sell for money," she said.

"That's ridiculous," I spat. "I don't know who took the guitars, but I'm going to go do some work now. Why don't you and Todd look at the cameras or something?" Before she could respond, I walked off to the back room in a huff. But I knew darn well who took those guitars and Gwen wasn't far off with the selling illegally claim.

***

I had been working for about a half hour before I heard a scream towards the front of the store.

I rushed out of the room. They weren't robbers. They weren't even grown men. What kind of teenager gets up this early for anything but school? The guy was much bigger and stronger than Gwen. He had a big strong grip on Gwen's arm, his other hand holding a knife. The chains on his leather jacket seemed to glint in the light. The long strands of dirty blonde fell over his eyes.

"Hello Rory. You're looking a little tired this morning, no?"

I froze. The way he looked up, it was like hell had frozen over. I stupidly realized it didn't matter that I'd locked the door. He had a set of keys, he could come and go as he pleased.

My voice sounded far away. "Let go of her...I swear. And give me those keys," I added, eyeing them sticking out of his pants pocket.

"You'll swear what, Rory? That you'll kill me? You were barely anything even when you had Jason to protect your sorry little ass. How weak will you be now—"

"Fuck you!" I snatched the keys from his pocket and jumped back, expecting to get jumped by a couple of the other guys there. They looked like they wanted to, but Tre stopped them with just a look.

"That's fine. I don't need them anymore," he shrugged. "But Rory...that language...that's not very nice." Tre smiled, and I never thought there was a legitimately evil way someone could smile before. He nodded toward the cash register, near the hook where the keys usually hung from on the wall behind the desk. "Hand me all the money that's in there."

"No."

"Do it, Rory," he said in a quiet voice.

"*No.*"

Tre narrowed his eyes. He glanced down at Gwen casually. "Well, well...this won't end well for the lady, now will it? Tsk tsk, Rory. I'm used to you not caring about yourself, but you would sacrifice someone else? How selfish," he said mockingly.

"I'm not sacrificing anyone," I said, starting to panic. "I..."

Tre's head busted open as it greeted the corner of the desk. Then his entire posture was shattered as he was sent against the glass door. It was the first time I threw a swing at him.

Several other pairs of hands gripped my shoulders, arms, and around my stomach. Tre whipped around, rubbing where I had punched him, his cheek turning purple. His eyes rose up to mine with a hatred in them, all amusement gone. He made his way toward me.

Gwen stumbled backward, barely able to breath. I ducked my head from Tre's winding hand.

I jumped up and kicked Tre as hard as I possibly could. He shouted. There was lots of shouting. My body was automatically released, and I almost fell to the ground.

"Tre, we've got to leave man."

"Leave? Did you see what that son-of-a-bitch just *did?*" he cried. His face was red, and his teeth were bigger than I thought.

"But he's coming!" one of them yelled, pointing out the window. I assumed he was talking about Todd.

"What are you so afraid of?" Tre snarled. "He's one person."

"I think he's got a gun."

"That's ridiculous," Tre said. For once, I thought I might've agreed with him. That comment had gotten my attention. I was never aware that Todd had a gun, but maybe he did.

"His friend owns that gun shop, Tre. And I could've sworn I saw him go inside it a few times. I'm not taking any chances." This obviously alerted the others and made them look flustered and uneasy. They started heading out, until it would just be Tre standing there. And he was a coward on his own. Maybe not while facing me or Gwen, or even most people, but he certainly wouldn't be willing to face Todd on his own.

"Let's *GO!*" the same guy shouted, the last one remaining, his hand on the doorknob, looking back at Tre frantically and impatiently.

Swearing, Tre threw one last scathing look at me, and was off. Every last one of them exited through the glass door and their footsteps became quieter and more distant as they became little dots sailing off into the sun.

I heard someone rush into the store, heavy breathing.

"Rory, are you crazy?" Todd almost screamed, staring at some of the glass cracked in the door while helping Gwen up. "WHAT gave you the nerve to do that?"

"I was trying to help her," I explained. Todd was examining the bits of glass that littered the floor of the empty store. He stood up with a shaking Gwen, his gaze traveling from the door to me.

"Helping her would've been to lock the door, LIKE I TOLD YOU TO DO!" he shouted. He lowered his voice, realizing it shook Gwen even more. But it still came out hardened. "I'll speak to her about it as well. Come on, Rory. Use your brain every once and a while. It's not like it'll hurt your head that much."

"I *did* lock the door, Todd!" I yelled, angry that he was assuming it was all my fault. At this point I was pretty sure an asteroid could hit, and he'd find a way to pin it on me. I was shaking with fury. He'll 'speak to her about it', but just yell at me. He was always giving me shit, telling me different things, giving me bits of different information, confusing me, and it was always my fault.

"How did he get in then, Rory? Huh? How did they get in?"

"I don't know." But I did know. I hoped the answer wasn't written on my face. Without thinking, I glanced at the keys I'd taken back from Tre. At least he wouldn't be able to try this again.

Todd glanced at the keys too, and back at me. He and Gwen looked like they believed me about as much as they'd believe a four-foot snowstorm happening here. His nostrils flared as he gazed down at me, the source of all his problems.

He couldn't prove that I was lying though, so he switched back to the same topic of argument he always did.

"Always fights. Yes. That's it. Fighting is always the main solution to the problem—"

"It was out of *self-defense*," I murmured through my teeth. I wanted to start shouting about how they would've broken in anyway, how locked doors didn't stop people from going where they wanted, they just served as a temporary obstacle. But I was too exhausted to say anything else.

Todd's eyes went back to the door. He led Gwen to the backroom and stayed in there talking to her for a while along with calling the police to report what happened. I only heard their quiet murmurs here and there. I went into the room, going to the other side, away from them.

After getting off the phone and making sure Gwen was okay, Todd came back over to me, where I was basically hiding behind a shelf pretending to be interested in the equipment there, and I heard a loud sigh. I turned to see him staring down at me, exasperated, arms folded. As if he was waiting for me to say something.

"Look, I'm sorry," I said. "But you don't need to go off on me like that—"

"Don't you start with me today Rory," he said. "Not this morning."

I didn't say anything. I thought if I even breathed too loudly it would piss him off. We were both a jumble of nerves right now, both on edge.

"Go back and finish cleaning the guitars over there."

***

The cops had arrived and had taken a look at some of the damage done, asked each of us questions, and told us to call them if anything else happened or if we remembered any additional details. They said they would look for them. I wasn't so sure they would. For some reason in this town, cops didn't take much seriously, especially early morning break-ins to small privately-owned businesses like this one. I didn't know if there were any working cameras in here, but if there were, they were probably blurry and low quality. I gritted my teeth when they left. I never liked cops, and that's probably my own fault for always having small brushes with the law. But they always made me feel uneasy, even when I hadn't been the one who did anything wrong.

I was allowed a break around ten o'clock, which was when I realized that I'd forgotten something at my house. Not Todd's house. My dad's. Since the day I left, I had taken most of what I wanted and needed with me, such as clothing and my notebook. But there was something else. Something really important.

I entered my house, which was so quiet it seemed deserted, abandoned, and forgotten. For all purposes, it was, now that Jason was gone forever. As I walked by the living room, I saw my dad lying passed out on the couch as usual. He was sweating up a storm. In the kitchen I could hear the soft clinging and clattering of plates and silverware as my mom washed the dishes. How peaceful and calm the eye of the storm always was before the wind and rain and thunder.

Perfect time to seize the opportunity.

I scurried up the stairs and stood at the door of my old room which reeked of memories. It held so much, yet there wasn't much in it. Small, with a bed in the corner and an old desk shoved up against the wall where there were still carvings engraved of when Jason and I would stay inside during rainy days, bored, creating our initials and leaving our mark. Just like we did on the bark of the tree. Just like we did on the wet pavement of still-wet cement on the sidewalk. I remembered the times we did that and how we laughed until it brought tears to our eyes, and when some unthreatening guy would come chasing after us and we'd run home.

Instead of just standing there living in the past, I tore myself away from the gripping pain that lingered in my throat and set back to getting what I came for. I turned my gaze toward my closet. It never occurred to me how badly I needed this. It had been stashed in there once upon a time. It once belonged to Jason. I felt sick for not figuring that out earlier and for the way I had been treating it, this inhuman object, so carelessly rejecting it.

I opened my closet door, looked through a bunch of old clothing and shelves, and there it was. I grabbed it, put it in my bag, and walked out the door as quickly as possible.

I sat in the kitchen and put my headphones on. I turned the volume down low so as not to disturb my mom. But something uneasy was in the atmosphere with her, and I didn't exactly know what.

That's when I saw her toss a beloved shirt of hers, one she hardly even wore, into a box. It was one Jason had given her as a birthday gift.

"Mom?" I asked. "What are you doing?"

"We're leaving."

I choked on the water I was drinking. "What?"

"We have to, Rory." She swallowed, and I could tell she was trying not to cry. "You're coming with me."

I winced. "But...where though?"

"I have a friend who'll let us stay with them up north for a while until I can get a job."

"And...we're...you want us to leave...today?"

"Yes. Today, or tomorrow at the latest."

"SO WHY DIDN'T YOU TELL ME ABOUT THIS? Don't you think I would've wanted to know? *SOONER?*"

She gave me a strange look. "I thought you'd *want* to leave. I thought you hated it here."

"Well..." I swallowed, thinking about Sidney. Thinking about Todd. Thinking about Renee. Hell, even Sonny was sometimes funny. An asshole, but sometimes funny. "There are some things here that I like...and, it's where I grew up. Did you ever think that regardless of how hard it's been, I want to stay here? I mean, maybe not *here* here," I said, waving my hand around at the house, "but here in this area? I mean, when you say up north, do you even still mean Texas, or a different state entirely?"

"A...different state."

My mouth dropped. "NO! Mom, no! I'm staying here. I can put up with dad, and all of the idiots around here. But, it's still my home and where I grew up. And it's where I'll graduate. I am not leaving."

"Rory, if you're doing this just because of that girl—"

"I am *not* doing this for any girl!" I shouted. I didn't know if she'd been talking about Renee or Sidney, but it didn't matter. I took a deep breath and said, "I'm not doing it for any particular person. Except myself. I can't just be yanked out of here and dropped down somewhere else. I don't want to start anew." I almost slammed my walkman down on the counter.

"Maybe starting anew would be a good thing."

"No. I already made my decision. Why can't you see any of this my way?!"

"I'm sorry, goddamn it! You know Rory, everyone makes mistakes. It's not just you who's not perfect."

"I know, I know," I said. "I'm sorry." I got up and started to wrap my arms around her for a hug, but she slapped me. It was so hard, my head turned. The side of my cheek stung. I then heard a gasp and a breaking sob. Soon I felt her arms around me, her apologizing rapidly into my ear, and hands rubbing my back, messaging it soothingly.

"It's okay," I said quietly. "And it's okay if you want to go up north. I just..."

She said something in my ear. I lifted my head, which had been resting on her shoulder. "What's that?"

"Rory," she said fiercely, gripping my shoulders, looking up at me as though she might slap me again. "You need to promise me that you will call me every day. *Every single day.* Here, I have her number right here. If you lose it, I still have our home number and Todd's number. If you're not at either of those places, I'll know something went wrong, and I'm coming right back. Don't make me do that, please?" She bent down at the table, scribbling the number on a post-it, the pencil scratching angrily. She stood up and handed it to me. "Not your pocket," she said. "Put it in your bag." She took a deep breath and gazed at me again. "I don't want you to live here. I want you to go straight to Todd. If anything there goes south, I want you to call me. Do you understand? I don't want you to try to live it out here. I've reached my threshold, and so have you." She looked around, knowing this was the last time she'd ever see this house. Somehow though, I knew she didn't have to look at all, because these surroundings would be etched in her memories forever.

She stepped back and looked at me. "If you really want to stay here..." She looked out the kitchen window above the sink, into the bright sunny day. "I know it means much more to you than it does to me. I think you're old enough now—with the help of Todd, he seems like a good man, even if I don't know him very well—I know Jason liked him so much. And he liked Jason. You will be able to stick it out here. At least for your last two years of high school. I won't try to make you come with me. But remember, what I said about calling me every day," she said in a sterner tone, pointing at me. Then she took a deep, shaky breath. "And, I'm very, very sorry I slapped you Rory."

"It's okay."

"I'm becoming like him."

"*No you're not.*" I kissed her on the head. I managed to keep calm, even though my jaw trembled a bit. I hugged her as tightly as I possibly could. How could one of the best mothers out there have ended up with someone like my dad? I knew one thing, he was not my dad. Because he wasn't *a* dad. Maybe at one point he was, but he was gone. Replaced by something else.

"I got two tickets," she whispered into my ear. "You can still change your mind. Anytime you want."

I shook my head. "No," I said. "You go. You go and live somewhere safe. I have to stay here. I can handle myself."

She started up protesting several times, and at one point I thought she might slap me again. I wouldn't have cared if she did. I knew this was the right decision. I knew I'd regret it severely and it would eat me up inside if I went, without telling anyone, just got up and left. All of their faces flashed through my mind—Todd, Gabriella, Renee, Sidney, even Sonny and Jeremiah. I would regret such a permanent, irreversible decision. And that was the last thing I needed right now. I wanted things to start going *right* again, not wrong.

***

I thought my dad was going to be gone the rest of the day, getting more beer, like he usually does. I was wrong. Or at least with the "rest of the day" part.

He came a couple minutes after my mom disappeared past the corner that ended our neighborhood. I didn't know how long until I would get to see her again.

When he found out of my mom's departing, he was more than livid. I tried screaming as loud as I could, but sometimes my words were choked back or cut off.

First he grasped a handful of my shirt before I could realize what was going on. He yanked my shirt back until the hole was digging into my throat, cutting off air supply. I couldn't breathe. With his other hand, he punched me hard in the mouth, causing me to stumble back against the wall. He charged at me and slammed me back up against the wall again, just as I'd been falling over. If he hadn't pinned me in place, I would've sunk to my knees. I tried to breathe, to get air back into my lungs, but it was doing no good.

He kept yelling such weird things to me, things that didn't even have anything to do with what he was so up in a rage about, things like, "Get your fat ass up! Goddamn, you take up all the food in the house, now your mother's space too? You are spoiled beyond rotten, you fucking *pig!*"

I was five-foot six, and one-hundred twenty-five pounds. Definitely not overweight.

Then he hit me over the head with a large pan. I hadn't known when or where he'd gotten it. While I lay there on the floor in pain, holding my throbbing head with one hand, he'd been filling the sink with water. He wrapped both of his hands around my head and yanked me upwards. He then shoved me forward and my face got colder and colder.

I was the water. It was *cold*. I was lifted up abruptly, and heard water splashing in all different directions carelessly. I was forced under again and then back up. It was then that I found my voice. "HELP!" I screamed as loud as I could. "Somebody, *HELP*! Stop it!" I screamed, my voice so tired. "Stop..."

Suddenly I fell to the ground. I *fell*, as if he simply dropped me, not as if he threw me. I sat there on my knees, staring at the wooden cabinet beneath the sink. I turned, and backed up against it. I could feel another presence beside me.

I looked up at my dad. He stood, glaring down at me, his jaw hard, his mouth a straight line. The only people he ever touched or shouted at was me and mom. And he never cared to do it in front of another human being, for fear of being reported and thrown in jail for the rest of his life.

I reached out to the standing leg beside me and wrapped my arm around it for protection, like it was a tree limb during a hurricane. Like a *child*. I didn't even care anymore; for looking like a child, for whimpering like one, or even screaming and begging; at that moment, it didn't matter. All that mattered was safety. That's what I needed, and I didn't care who it was from.

I heard Jeremiah's whisper travel to Sidney and Renee's ears, something about waiting in the car, and both left without question. After they were gone, Jeremiah continued to stare down my dad, and the ever-going silence was getting to be too much to carry on with.

Jeremiah took his eyes off my dad. He bent down and put his arm underneath mine, supporting my weight. I leaned on him. Jeremiah gazed back once more at my dad, then carefully walked me out of the house. The bright sunlight felt great, despite the cold. He opened his car door and using both arms, sat me down inside. He pressed a warm, wet cloth against my mouth, which was bleeding from the earlier blow. He closed the door, got in the front driver's seat, and started driving away.

I was humiliated. There I was lying in the back of Jeremiah's car, bleeding. I could feel everyone else's panic from up front, their skin crawling, their hearts beating.

I looked at my reflection in the car window. It was like when I was looking at myself in the lake. I wanted to break it like the mirror. I shuddered, and turned away.

The brakes slammed. "Damn it!" I heard Jeremiah bang the steering wheel in frustration. "The road's blocked!"

Sidney murmured something to him, and he calmed down. "I'll just take a turn off here," he said.

He parked his car in the same neighborhood I had unknowingly walked into a couple days ago. We shouldn't have been able to get here this soon. Jeremiah could've gotten a ticket for speeding.

Jeremiah whispered something to the girls. As he was whispering, Renee reached her hand out from behind her, around the seat toward me, and took hold of my hand. It sent a little tingle up and down my spine. Whatever was said, they did not hesitate. Renee gave my palm a little squeeze, and both immediately took off and zipped inside the house, not wanting to keep waiting to do what was ordered for a single second. I *really* wanted to keep holding her hand.

Now it was just me and Jeremiah sitting in the quiet car. The only other sound was birds. Jeremiah got out of the car, slammed his door, and opened the door to the backseat. I felt a cold breeze.

Jeremiah sat down next to me. I played like I didn't notice. I leaned against the car door with my elbow propped up, and just stared down at my fingernails, observing the chipped black polish. But the entire time I could feel Jeremiah's eyes on me. He put his hand on my head and gently turned it, leaned over me with his minty breath, and held up another clean and fresh wet cloth to my broken skin. It was warm and soothing. He sat there holding it, his other hand resting on my shoulder keeping me still. Jeremiah led me inside, walking very closely to me. Neither of us said a word.

He took me into the bathroom where he cleaned me up some more. I didn't see Renee or Sidney as we went in. I stared longingly at the closed door and bit my lip.

Jeremiah lifted the wet cloth from my wound and turned to see what I was looking at. He glanced back. "You miss her, don't you."

"What? I mean...well, um..."

"It's okay, I know you do."

"She hates me," I said quietly, closing my eyes with a fake smile on my face, looking back down at my nails.

"Oh c'mon."

"She *does*, Jeremiah. She can't stand me." I motioned over to the door and then let my hand fall. "I can't even talk to her without her wanting to punch me in the gut or something—"

"Don't say that." Jeremiah was shaking his head. "You know it's not true. Look, I won't claim anything for Sidney here, 'cause I don't truly know how she feels. But I doubt she hates you as much as you think she does. People like her don't hate people. Sidney doesn't have a hatred for anyone."

I nodded, trying to take in everything he just said, every little drop of it. "Okay," I said, giving up, so tired I was barely audible. I hadn't noticed up until then just how worn out I really was. I wanted to lie down or go home and sleep. I wanted to rest. My body just couldn't function and the more I was up, the more heavy my eyes grew.

"Rory, let me tell you a secret, okay? And you have to promise not to tell anyone, not even Sidney."

"Okay."

"I was drunk once too."

"So?"

"No, no. I...was driving while intoxicated."

I winced. "So what happened?"

"Well, I hit a tree. Totaled the car. No one died." He swallowed. "Thankfully. My parents screamed at me when they found out what happened. They not only took my car and license away for almost a year, but also wouldn't let me do anything other than have people over. I couldn't really go anywhere, I was grounded. Which especially sucked around Halloween. And every night at the dinner table I had to hear my dad yell about it...he's got quite a yell, that guy. I didn't hear the end of it for a while." He grimaced. "At any rate, this was all a while ago, and what I will always admit to is that I *could* have killed someone. It would've been manslaughter. It would've been...pretty much the end of my life too. I was lucky."

"Wow I..." My voice trailed off. I didn't know if he meant because of the law or because of his parents. Probably both. And Sidney...her and Sonny would never look at him the same way again.

"It's okay." He smiled sincerely, putting his hand up. "I sure as fuck am never trying that ever again." He paused for a moment. "Though I do still speed sometimes if I need to."

I cracked a grin. "Yeah, thanks for that."

I could've gone back to Todd's where Alexei was watching Patches. He was really nice, but was the type that really wanted to hold a conversation. I didn't want to talk to anyone right now.

"Do you want to stay here for a while?" Jeremiah asked.

"I don't want to be in the way."

"You're not in the way. You need to rest. My mom is downstairs and she knows I have friends over. She won't bother you."

"You sure she...won't just come into the room or anything?"

Jeremiah laughed. "The only times she's done that were when she still did my laundry, but I do my own laundry now." He winked. "If she finds something to yell at me about, I'll be in the living room, downstairs."

"Okay," I said with a small smile.

He even gave me an extra set of his clothes since mine were a mess. They were a little big on me, but it didn't matter. It was getting colder out by the minute. He let me sleep in his bed for a little while. He drew the curtains so that it was completely dark in the room, then left shutting the door all the way, leaving me completely undisturbed. I slept for a good hour or so, but when I woke up I felt so energized, it felt a lot longer than that. I must've fallen asleep almost immediately.

When I came downstairs, I saw the sight of what I had always known a family should be, but never really experienced myself. I saw Jeremiah, Sidney, Brooke, and their fluffy golden retriever all lying around side by side on a big floral couch watching TV. Or at least, attempting to find something to watch on TV. Glancing around the rest of the living room, I saw a glass sliding door leading out to a patio, some potted plants and hanging plants here and there, and a big pine bookshelf with glass cabinets, holding books, figurines, and more plants. I heard Jeremiah's parents talking in the kitchen. From where I stood near the stairs, I could just start to see the beginning of an ivy wallpaper design bordering the ceiling in there. They must've come home early. From the smell, they were making something *good*. Jeremiah sighed and put the remote down after he finally flipped it off. He turned to Sidney. "You hungry?" he asked. "There's a TGI Friday's just down the road." He gestured toward the kitchen. "This won't be done until tonight. My mom will cut off your fingers if they go anywhere near the pot in there." He said this so seriously I wondered if it was really a joke.

"Actually," Sidney responded, "I was just thinking of heading over to *Sonny Morning*, not just to stop by and say hello to Sonny and Gabriella, but also, I've been dying for some pancakes."

"Anything for the pancake queen," Jeremiah laughed, and Brooke agreed upon it as well, insisting on some chocolate milk they had on the menu there. "Alright," Jeremiah surrendered. "I'll get my wings later. I'll be right back—" and as he got up and turned, he blinked in surprise. "Oh! Rory. We were just going to get you. Feeling better?"

I jumped. I hadn't known that he could see me behind the stair bars. "Uh, yeah. Where's Renee?" I knew someone was missing from the picture.

"She had to go home," Jeremiah responded sadly. "She'd been at the library, and we met up there, but...she called her dad to ask, and yeah. Got a little ugly." His face looked grim.

"That sucks."

"Okay, so shall we get going?" Jeremiah asked cheerfully grabbing his coat, and I couldn't help but to smile back. Even though I really wished Renee were here.

Jeremiah insisted that I eat something. Earlier that day, Todd had insisted that I bring a coat. Both of them were right. It was freezing out now and I snuggled warmly into my jacket. And up until then, I hadn't realized how empty my stomach felt. I'd hardly had anything the day before, and all I had today was some orange juice early in the morning.

When we got there, Sidney said, "You guys go right on in. I have something I need to look for in the trunk."

"Sure, okay," Jeremiah responded quickly. I thought they were both acting weird. Each of them had strange, insincere smiles on their faces. And they each made an obvious effort not to look in my direction.

I could see through the glass window of the restaurant Sonny working behind the counter in Todd's place with Gabriella. I didn't know he worked here. Then I saw the "Now Hiring" sign. I planned to ask Gabriella later if I could get a spot. Although, it might be uncomfortable having Sonny and I in the same room.

The two of us entered. Jeremiah sensed my nerves. "Hey, don't worry," he whispered. "He's busy. If you don't bother him, he won't bother you."

Gabriella was behind the counter leaning inward toward Jeremiah, listening intently, a look of concern growing on her face. It occurred to me then how much Jason and I used to play around on the bright red stools when we were little. Images of my mom still laughing and smiling while she had been sitting there with her friends watching us, and the regular color of her face, brought back memories that almost made me smile for a second.

Jeremiah walked over and I lifted my head, escaping my thoughts. "Rory," he sighed, "I have to go and get my car fixed. But I can stay here for a while if you want me to."

"Oh no, that's okay," I replied. "I don't want to hold you behind."

"Thank you, I just don't want to leave you all alone."

"He has me," Gabriella said walking up behind him.

Just then, I noticed someone else coming up from behind Jeremiah. Long dark hair, pretty light brown skin, soft face. "Renee," I spoke softly.

Chapter 15: RORY—What Do You Do When You Look in the Mirror, and All You See is the Reason You're Alone? (Saturday, December 21, 1996)

BANG!

The kid hit the ground hard and his face was smothered in sand. He was a little older than me, but a lot smaller. It was two years since the incident with my brother had happened. I was only fourteen. I wished it hadn't. I really wished I did everything differently.

It was a major overreaction. He hadn't meant any harm when joking about Jason. "Hey, your brother ran from home to get away from you" he'd said.

I stepped on his back really hard. The kid let out a sharp yelp. I felt sweat dampening the maroon bandana Tre had given me. He was behind me, plus a few others. I could hear him laughing.

I heard sirens. They were arriving now. I would not bother trying to run. Tre was my friend—he'd get me out of this predicament. Besides, it wouldn't work. It never did.

My arms were pinned behind my back within seconds. The kid went running off before anyone could help him. I was shoved up against the hood of the car and metal greeted my wrists. The officer was like the Hulk. There was another officer beside him assisting. Suddenly, the one who had my wrists locked up kicked me so hard in the back of my leg, I yelped out involuntarily.

"Officer!" the second one said sharply. "That's enough. There'll be none of that." He was black and I recognized his voice instantly. That was Sidney and Sonny's father. I didn't know if he recognized me or not. I'd only met him a few times whenever Sidney brought me over. I looked away, hoping he wouldn't see me, just in case he did remember me. I didn't want to be the scornful topic of conversation at the dinner table that night.

I heard somebody coming. I looked up. Todd stood there, looking in at me. I hid my disappointment. I didn't know him that well, but I knew he was no Tre. He'd been Jason's guitar teacher and mentor, someone I'd only met a handful of times. I think he'd tried to encourage Jason to leave the gang, but I don't imagine he meant like this. *Tre often claimed he was just some cowardly guy who ran a music store. But the man standing at the bars and staring in between them at me didn't fit much the description of a coward.*

"Rory," he said. It didn't surprise me. He vaguely knew me and I vaguely knew him out of association. I didn't know what to make of him yet. You couldn't read him. He was calm. You could never tell what emotion he had raging inside of him. He never looked happy, angry, sad, or frightened. Just focused. Just aware.

"Yeah?"

"I thought you were better than this. Don't disappoint your brother."

"Of course I won't disappoint my brother," I hissed in anger. Then I banged the bars with my hands, but Todd didn't flinch an inch.

Sidney's dad gasped, almost dropping his coffee. "Hey!" he yelled, turning toward us. "What's going on in there?"

"Nothing officer," Todd called, "just a little tantrum, that's all."

He pursed his lips as though he didn't believe that was all it was, but went back to the papers on his desk.

"You are wrong if you think you can do both," Todd growled back. "Be loyal to Jason and run with those pack of hyenas?"

"They said they'd help me find him," I responded through clenched teeth.

Todd laughed. I stared up at him, pressing my face against the cold, thick, slippery bars. "Mhm, right," he said. "You're a bottled-up naïve fool who doesn't know anything." Then he started to walk away.

"Wait!" I called.

He turned, a question mark on his face. It irritated me to no end.

"Aren't you going to get me out of here?"

He cocked his head to the side. "Explain to me why I should do that. Give me every reason you can think of."

My mouth hung open, and I looked down, defeated. Because there was *no reason why* he should. If I were in his place, I wouldn't let me out either.

He walked over to Sidney's dad, who was supervising the place for the night. I couldn't hear what he was saying, but both of them walked over, and Officer Wilcox unlocked the door and let me out. Was he even allowed to do that? Was this proper protocol? I didn't question it. I looked up at Todd, no words in my mouth.

"You need to start backing up the stuff you do and say if you want people to take you seriously."

***

"Where were you guys when I needed you?" I yelled. "And why are you all just sitting around? You promised to help me find my brother!" I was all out of breath, but not out of memory, remembering what Tre had said the night before while sitting on his front porch. "We'll find him Rory," he'd said in a truly sincere voice, friendlier than I'd ever *heard him.* "I know I saw him in town yesterday, so he's returned. He had a car and everything. It's okay, baby; I will reunite you two brothers."

Tre just ignored me and started writing all over their next victim of property with colored chalk while blasting up their stereo so loud, I couldn't tell my own voice from the recorded screaming ones anymore. I charged up to Tre. "ANSWER ME!" I shouted at the top of my lungs.

The music cut off and the others guys just stood around staring, waiting to see what would happen next. Nobody talked to Tre like that.

"Excuse me?" he said, glaring down into my face. But I wasn't afraid. There were just times when I was stupid, maybe, but didn't care. This was one of those times.

"Your brother was weak," he finally said. He had the audacity, and that's when I was pulled to the ground, my back scraping up against the pebbles.

These lying TRAITORS! *I thought.* HOW? How could this happen? *I had fallen right into his clutches in both senses.*

Then there was running and commotion everywhere. I could breathe again, because I didn't feel hands or knees propped against my chest, strands of hair in my eyes, or Tre's cologne suffocating my breath. I sat up and breathed in.

Soon all was silent. I felt a hand nudge my shoulder, but nothing more. I turned, and saw Todd sitting down by my side. "See?" he said. "I told you. I told you, you were a bottled-up naïve fool."

I had been sitting there with Renee for a while. I heard Sidney's faint sobs outside. I turned and looked out the window. Her head was cradled up on Jeremiah's chest. The window was cracked open. I heard her murmur, "Why does he do that to him?" Jeremiah shushed softly and caressed her head some more.

A couple minutes after she left, I could hear Jeremiah mumbling into a pay phone. Though he was distant, from the way he sounded, I could tell he was speaking with Todd. Maybe he was telling him what happened so that when I came in with extra décor on my face, he wouldn't have to wonder.

No matter what, everyone you love in life and make a connection to will die one day. Why risk all the pain? If there's one thing in my life I had learned, it was that.

Sonny arrived with our soda. I tried to smile and failed.

"Do you want anything else?" he asked quietly.

I shook my head. I felt lousy for not speaking to him, but I know if I had my voice would've cracked. I could tell Sonny sensed the flicker of pain that went across my face. I hoped he didn't take it as an implication that I was annoyed or anything like that. I hoped that Renee wouldn't take it as an implication that I wanted to be alone. I *needed* someone right now.

Sonny left. After that, Renee dented the silence and spoke for the first time. "You seem...calm," Renee said to me. "And yet, upset, at the same time. And I understand. Are you going to be alright?"

I looked up at her. "Aren't you grounded?"

She flinched. "I snuck out again."

"Your dad's really going to kill you this time." I knew he wasn't actually going to though.

Her face went a little red and she turned away. So I answered her question. "I'll be fine," I lied. "I will." There was more silence. "I just," I sighed, "tend to contain things a lot now because I don't want to cry but I'm so sick of being angry all the time." This was why I lacked so much emotion now. I was becoming like Todd. Complete apathy. I used to think it was from being around him so much, but now I realized that it had to come with your own experiences that you didn't want to talk about. Maybe that's what had happened to him.

Being angry hurt almost as much as being miserable, maybe worse. They could be considered synonyms, for all I knew, and I wouldn't be able to tell the difference.

"But you're nicer to be around now," Renee continued, keeping the conversation steady.

"Yeah," I said, barely above a whisper. I didn't know what to say to that. "Sorry. About—before I mean."

"I forgive you."

"My dad thinks I need to lose weight," I said with a sarcastic smile.

"That's so weird...my dad always says I need to gain weight. But I eat just like everyone else, so I dunno."

"You're fine the way you are."

"You too."

I suddenly remember her saying how her aunt and cousin were hospitalized after the tornado. I didn't know if it was appropriate territory to approach yet, but I took a plunge. "How...uh, how are your folks?"

To my relief, a calm and genuine smile spread across her face. "They're going to be okay," she said.

"Good," I said, smiling back. At least one of us was getting a break.

She had to know the truth.

"Renee," I started out slowly, "I, uh, I can't..." *Tell her.* "I, I can't..." *C'mon, you can do it, just tell her.* "I can't talk to you any-more." There it was. It was out. And it hurt so badly, but I would accomplish this one painful task if it was the last thing I ever did.

Renee's mouth dropped, and I wanted to punch myself. "Why?" she asked. She was so innocent. "Did I do something wrong?"

"No, no, you didn't. It's me. It's so hard to explain, but, well, Renee, I...I just end up messing up and making mistakes when this sort of thing happens. I wish I could learn from them, but I never seem to. And I just want you to be safe." *From my wrath.* I paused for a moment. *No. No, I never was like my father, so I never will be. It won't get to that point.*

But still.

"Okay," Renee said slowly, "maybe we can talk later, Rory." She seemed confused now.

"I just, I can't do this," I stated again, quicker this time, and finally stood up. I didn't look back at her. "I have to go." I clumsily picked up my bag and murmured a small, "Thanks for listening", then hastily walked out. I felt numb, not really able to feel anything. This is not how I planned it to be. I felt like I was sitting up inside my head, watching at what went on outside of it through my eyes, as an outsider.

On my way back to *Todd's Music Store* (it was almost noon), I stopped to rest. At one point I stopped to heave in random bushes, and sat down on the grass. Some woman offered me a ride. I politely declined. I couldn't stop for five seconds and not cough.

As I made my way around the corner, almost back at the music store, I stopped and took out the crumbled piece of paper Jason had left me on my bedroom desk four years ago. I unfolded it, and for the first time in four years, I read it to myself:

Rory,

I am sorry about this, Rory, I really am. I love you so much and you know it. I don't want you to become tangled up in this group, I don't want you to think it's okay doing the shit that I've done. I think you'll be better off without me. I think you'll have less problems if I'm not there to stress you out with any of this. You're too young. Frankly, I'm too young too, but I can tough it out. With me out of the picture, you'll be able to live a (somewhat) more normal life. And with one less mouth to feed, this should take a load off of mom and the old man's backs. I know it always seemed like they loved me more, but it wasn't true. He just saw you as an easier target. He'll be a little less cruel now that I'm gone.

Well, that turned out to be wrong.

This was my problem. So don't feel guilty. Stay strong, lil' bro.

I love you,

Jason

I sniffed and wiped at tears that hadn't yet fallen. I COULD NOT let Todd see me crying. Or anyone, for that matter. I couldn't.

Dark storm clouds had gathered by the time I got back. Twelve-ten. Ten minutes late. *Ten.* My stomach was nervously doing somersaults. Before I entered Todd's store, I took one final glance at my reflection in the store window. A dead image of Jason was pounding in my head. It would never go away. He was hanging from a rope in an old and dark, filthy place with rats and dripping blood from the ceiling. I was one of the rats crawling around.

I walked into the store and to the back room. "You're late," he said without looking up.

"I know. I'm sorry."

I didn't realize my voice was so flat and drained.

He looked up. "Rory, what—"

"I'm fine." I staggered into the room as my stomach gave a lurch in nauseated pain.

"I should drive you home. I'm only doing some extra work here. You sound like you're catching a cold—"

"I'm *fine.*" I went out back towards the shed right behind the store, away from everything else, isolated on its own. It held old or used instruments, in need of repair, broken down parts waiting to be recycled, thrown away, or used for a different purpose, and other items that could be sold if they just got some better attention and handling to them. Empty jars were scattered here and there and some of the shelves were broken down. It looked ancient, just like the office, and I wondered why no one bothered to fix it.

It took all my might to pull open the big wooden door. When I stepped in, the place felt like a cave. It was already starting to freeze outside, but inside, it felt even colder. When I took my first breath, I sneezed immediately. The dust had filled my nostrils faster than it had begun to rain, and by now, it was pouring out. It was dark, damp, and dirty. It looked as though it hadn't been cleaned for ages.

I went rummaging around through the different materials, at times my curiosity getting the best of me and leading off in another direction to explore something unknown, until that little voice in my head finally came back and reminded me to just keep looking for what I came for, don't keep Todd waiting. This reminded me of how often I'd scurry off on my own as a child, in stores, streets, and out of our own back yard. Back then I hadn't realized how danger-ous it was, and couldn't grasp or understand why my mom or Jason were angry when I'd come back after five minutes later. *Rory, you can't do that*, Jason would scold, steaming. *We could lose you. I don't ever want that to happen.* These words of that very real memory came back to me clearly, as if they were yesterday. I shuddered and finally shut my mind off completely.

Okay, so where is it? Todd said he wanted a can of blue paint. Let's see, there's green, yellow, red...red. Red was the color of Jason's face when he'd found me alone in the street corner. So was my mom's. But what about dad's? What color was his face again? It was usually al-ways red, but this time it was...almost purple. "Where's daddy?" *I re-membered asking. When I saw him, he went from purple back to his normal-looking color again, like nothing was wrong at all. Like noth-*

ing had happened. Quite unusual. My mother had been furious to-ward him for that.

Stop! I was furious with myself now. Why couldn't I just let the past go and move on? Why couldn't I focus?

I continued moving along the shelves, examining each of the cans. Where was *blue*?!

My eyes spotted the can of paint, and my arms lifted toward it, as if I were a robot. I wrapped my fingers around it tightly, held it up in front of my face: **BLUE.**

When I got back to the store I knocked, holding the can underneath one arm. Todd looked up, rolled his eyes, and came walking over. "Rory, I thought I told you to leave this door open," Todd said, as soon as I came back in. "It's not like a little cold air in here will kill anybody."

"It's RAINING. And I did leave it open, but why didn't you just leave it unlocked?" The door always shut on its own, it wasn't my fault.

Todd sighed. "Alright, whatever, it doesn't matter."

"Todd, I—I'm sorry," I said.

Todd was just as confused, maybe even more. "For what?" he asked, looking at me for the first time in a while.

"I..." I shrugged, wordless. "I don't know. I'm just really tired." I shook my head and looked away from him, because now I knew I was rambling.

He nodded. "I know. Is that your excuse for not leaving the door open? Also, the door to the shed was left open. I shouldn't have been able to just walk right through. It's just like earlier this morning," he added quickly without letting me answer. "You know, it's a good thing you don't live by yourself and that you don't have my keys."

"I wasn't looking to make an excuse," I growled. "Sorry for saying sorry. Damn."

"Rory—"

"Don't you ever get tired and fed up with being in a bad mood?"

"Do you want me to sugarcoat things for you?"

"*No*, Todd, but why do you always have to be biting my head off? I'm sorry I'm not perfect and make mistakes."

"It really doesn't take a perfect person to not make mistakes like the ones you have. You think *I'm* perfect? Not by a long shot."

I sighed. There was just no use in arguing with him. He stood over me, dangling the keys in my face. His last words before he walked away were, "Go lock it."

When I came back, surprisingly the door was unlocked this time. I came in thinking, for once, I could avoid a confrontation since Todd was busy and I had work of my own to finish doing.

"Rory?"

"Yeah?"

"I found this in your bag." Todd took out a bottle of beer. "Where and how did you get this?"

"I got it at the bar two blocks from where I live. I..."

"Fake ID?" he said.

"Yeah." It was incredible how much people fell for those.

"And you thought you were going to drink it, get drunk again, and I wouldn't notice?"

"I wasn't going to get drunk—"

"You thought you were going to lug this around and I wouldn't notice?" he said between gritted teeth.

"Fine," I snapped. "I'll throw it out." He took it out of reach before I could grab it.

"You look way too tired to be working," Todd said. "And your injuries haven't healed. Maybe you need to sit today out and go home."

"I told you, I'm fine," I snapped again. "I've had worse."

Before we could continue, someone walked in the door and needed their guitar string replaced.

I turned to Todd questioningly. "I thought it was closed today."

He COMPLETELY ignored this, and instead said, "There's one of your first customers," Todd said. "Go for it."

***

"God *darn* it, will you hurry up!" screamed the middle-aged man. He sat beside me the whole time, a little less than considerate about personal space (if he had ever even heard of such a concept), and I had spent quite some time now attempting to fix up his old, beaten guitar, but I had never tried something like this before, and even for skilled people, it took time. Why couldn't he understand that? Plus, this thing looked to be in worse shape than *me*. I was now losing my own patience and was through with being polite.

"If you would stop yelling and complaining and let me just *do* this, you might be out of here by now!" I snapped, as he just stared up at me, eyes widened in disbelief, anger flashing about them. "*Don't* yell at me." I said these words, with all my might, as calmly as I possibly could.

Todd looked over from the other side of the room. His expression told me I'd be in big trouble when the customer left. Gideon, who had entered a couple minutes earlier, and who had been sitting on the other side of me watching uncomfortably, finally stepped in. "It's okay Rory, I'll take it from here. You can go back to Todd now." He tried to smile, but I could tell there was annoyance on his face as well. I did as he said without argument.

Todd was past livid by that point. "Rory," he said exasperated, "you can't just yell at the customers like that. It's disrespectful and disruptive."

"But *he's* allowed to disrespect *me*?" I pushed passed him. "I'd say that's just as bad, considering he's in *your* store and I'm trying to do something for him. He could at least be a little more grateful. And trust me, Todd," cutting him off before he could reply, "he was being way more 'disruptive' than I was, I can assure you." Todd walked around to see me face-to-face. I put down the guitar I was working on and looked at him. I swallowed. "I've been disrespected like no one else has before, and have taken a lot of crap. I will NOT take it from anyone, much less some 'customer'." I walked to the back of the room, and turned the corner, into the tiny little space that was about six feet on each side, almost as small as the office. It was an isolated storage room, I guessed, but there were all sorts of materials in there that just couldn't go anywhere else.

"Stop acting like you're the ONLY one, you don't know what goes on in other peoples' lives," Todd nearly shouted. I spun around, glaring. He let out a frustrated sigh and closed his eyes for a second. I think he wanted to scream at me, but he was in a public place, even if it was nearly empty.

I rolled my eyes, turned back, and reached for something on the top shelf. Except I couldn't reach it. Todd grabbed it for me, and dropped it in my hand. I could feel the tension rising unsteadily in him, and he walked out. He must've stood out there for a few minutes, pinching the bridge of his nose, pondering over my weird (to say the least) behavior when he heard the crashing sound, followed by a spill.

Todd came rushing in, only to find me on the ground, blue paint gushing down my pants and beads of it dribbling down my arms. I sat there gritting my teeth in pain. Why had he left an open can of paint right there on the edge?! And I got scolded at for not locking a door. The aches in my side returned when I slipped and hit the ground, and I slowly rose, reaching up for the wooden counter to pull with one hand, and wrapping my other arm around my waist. I tried to breathe deeply, but my breaths came short and quick. There were a thousand knives running through that area.

"Rory, what the hell were you looking at when you were walking?" Todd exclaimed. He lay a hand on my side for one moment, and I flinched, so he immediately pulled a mop out from the closet and started to clean up the mess—at least he tried. All he did was smear it across the ground more. Todd growled.

"Maybe you should just get someone else to clean it," I said slowly. "With water."

"Mhm, thanks."

"I'm just trying to help—"

"Oh yeah, this helps a WHOLE lot—"

"Sorry," I scoffed. "It was an accident. Maybe if you hadn't left it—"

"Rory, I'm not perfect, BUT NEITHER ARE YOU!"

Todd turned swiftly and picked something up, as if to escape the situation bluntly by switching the topic of conversation. "Here," he said, handing me the box of matches. "Take these out, and I never want to see them again."

It's my fault, it's all my fault, was all I kept thinking. I don't know when my mind shifted over to Jason. Then again it had been on him all day. Every little thing reminded me of him. I couldn't let this eat me alive and devour me whole. Hey, if I was going to die of lung cancer, someone else had to know.

I was surprised and sick at how apathetic and careless I felt when I thought about it. Maybe I was just so numb by that point that I didn't feel anymore.

It's all my fault, and I at least want someone else to help me carry the secret. But it would no longer be a secret. I had to let it out, so I wouldn't be lying anymore. Just being honest with myself wasn't enough. Now I had to be honest with someone else too. It was time to let it out.

It's my fault that Jason's dead.

"Um...Todd? Todd...uh, it's, it's my—it's my fault—"

"Rory," he cut in sharply. "Take this outside, if you don't mind." He handed me a half-filled trashcan, intending me to dump it in the dumpster out back. I didn't know why this was so necessary when it was only half-filled.

I took the trashcan outside and dumped it. I didn't dump it in the dumpster. I did it on the ground. Not only did I turn it over and drop everything—papers, Styrofoam coffee cups, paper clips, and other things—but I also stepped on them, burying them, if not beneath the earth, then beneath the ice at least. I would've loved to set everything on fire, and watch it rise into the sky until it died out. None of it would ever exist, ever again. They were buried beneath me, in the past.

I turned to go back in, but I saw the shed in my periphery. I turned on my heel and took my time to tip-toe toward it. I wrapped my hand around the handle and tugged. The door creaked open. I stepped inside, and this time, it was different. It felt warm, but something cold still lingered in the air. What was I in here searching for?

I noticed a slight piece of paper sticking out from an untidy row of thick dusty books. And the dust was so thick here, there were large pieces of it that fell off if you so much as walked by them too fast. Why did it look so familiar?

In the silence, all I could hear was my heart beat. A screeching sound cut through the air, a telephone. I hadn't known there was one in here. It was vibrating so hard and violently, I could almost feel it. It was probably a wrong number, but I decided to answer it anyway.

"Rory?" My stomach dropped at the sound of her voice.

"Hey mom," I said in a high, thin tone, like a little kid on his first day at camp or kindergarten. Or getting caught doing something wrong. "Are you there already?"

"Yes. It was a quick flight. You sound like you've been crying. Are you alright?"

"I haven't been crying, I'm only tired. I'm fine," I said, trying to sound confident. "It's just...are you okay?"

"Yes," she said, and she sounded it. "You will need to visit me several times too. I forgot to mention that." I could practically hear her slapping a hand on her head. "It's so nice here. And I'm not just saying that, it really is beautiful. Quaint little shops, a pond in the park where ducklings gather...it's gorgeous."

"You could, um, visit me and Todd too," I said, not knowing if she'd ever want to come back to even this town ever again. "And Patches."

"Patches? Oh, oh that's right!" she said excitedly. "I remember, you told me about him once. I've always loved dogs, Rory. I'll have to see him sometime." I could tell by her voice that she was beaming, and for the first time in a while, my mother's color had probably come back and she was her normal, beautiful, outgoing self again. She was happy. Bold. She was never like that around my father.

I put my head in my hands. "Oh mom, I should've asked you this first—where exactly are you?"

"I'm in a little town north called New Haven. I want you to see it soon." She breathed in. "I wish you were here with me right now, you and Jason." I felt a knife in my gut, but I forced a smile. "He would've loved it. I mean, it's a nice town with friendly people, but it especially has nice nature as well. He always loved nature. Rory...you know his death isn't your fault, don't you?"

The words 'his death' were not something I was ready for. "I know, I know," I said quickly. "Let's wait until later to talk about him." *Much later.*

"Rory, would you like to come up here right now?" There was concern written all over her voice. "I can fly you out. But, what about Todd? Has he been treating you well?"

"Oh no mom, you don't have to do that for me. I'll pay for it myself when I come to see you. But yeah, he is, he's amazing...we have no problems at all," I lied. But it was a small lie. This would clear up, once both of us were a lot less stressed. "Just a couple of—disagreements—that's all." I tried to smile while saying this.

"Listen, Rory. I know you miss Jason. Terribly. I do too. And honestly, don't you think we should talk about it?"

"No." I paused for a moment, sorry for my quick response. "Well, yeah, but—but, maybe later. I can't now, because I have to go back to Todd in a second, and if I think about it too much, I...I might...I don't feel like getting all emotional." I sounded calm when I said that, but I was very certain it was the truth. I was even afraid to think too much about it. There was a roadblock in my mind I'd deliberately set up in front of the very real image of Jason, hanging from the—

"Okay," she responded warmly, "it's okay, I understand. I want you to be comfortable. You're right. But maybe I can...talk to you later?"

"That would be great," I said. "Please do. You have Todd's number, right?"

"Absolutely. Todd's number, the store's number, and of course...our number." I had a feeling she might not be calling that last one anytime soon.

"Okay mom. Please call again. I mean it."

"Yes, I will. I love you. Goodbye." She hung up. Even though she was no longer on the line, I murmured "Bye" into the air, and did the same.

I turned back to the dark corner of the shed I had been staring at before. In the very back of my head, some voice was trying to tell me that it wasn't really my fault—but it was. I knew it was, I wouldn't let it fool me.

I got a firm grip on the edge of the paper, and very gently pulled it out of its place. A picture of Jason and I on Christmas morning, way back in the days when nothing went wrong. I was hugging a stuffed lion, from Jason. I remembered it. Somehow it had gotten torn though, and we had to throw it out. But I looked incredibly happy in that picture.

This photo must've fallen out of Jason's bag here at some point. Maybe Todd kept it, maybe it'd gotten swept up in the chaos of things. Or, maybe Jason's spirit was taunting me.

Then, it hit me. Now I realized why that sick feeling had been in my stomach for so long. Looking at all the memories staring back at me like a mirror was a reflection of what I had become. I knew why I hated myself so much. It wasn't because of the anger I always felt. It wasn't because of the lies I told. It wasn't even because of the fights I got into, have been to jail before, lost Sidney's trust, or got suspended. And most of all, it DEFINITELY wasn't because of all the beatings I repeatedly received.

I killed my chances of ever having a great brotherly bond so many would die for. I hurt the ones who loved me the most. Not out of hate. Out of selfishness. Out of stupidity. Out of impulsiveness. The way I'd yelled at Jason that very day... I *hated* myself so much. How could I have told him that I wished he was dead and that I didn't want him to be my brother anymore?

My eyes fell to a mirror shard on the ground. What I saw staring back made me devastated, knowing that I wanted to punch it. I wanted to love myself—but what did you do when you looked in the mirror and all you saw was the reason why you lost something dear and precious?

I held the photo close to my chest and thought about saying a quick prayer. Hoping that God existed, and that if he did, that he was as forgiving as everyone said he was. Then I turned and walked out into the vengeful sleet.

As I was making my way down the second step, my heel slipped, and I lost balance. At this point, I was becoming a horror movie character. I was on my bottom in an instant. My hands flew up and the photo went out of reach.

I sat up. When I tried to *get* up, my body wouldn't allow me. There was a searing pain going up and down my shin. I lifted my pants leg a bit and saw a bruise forming. Just what I needed, another to add to my collection.

Todd stood before me, flustered. He pointed and his eyebrows flew up. He started to say something but waved it off, and instead bent down so that he was at my level.

I turned toward the place behind me where the picture had fallen and tried to reach. But it was too far. All I could grasp was air.

"Todd...get it." I felt the same way I did that day when I was caught up in the rubble left behind by that deadly storm—just as helpless. Lost. However, this time I knew this was no illusion or hallucination.

Chapter 16: RORY—On My Own
(Saturday, December 21, 1996)

Todd brought me back inside. Most of the time I had to lean on his shoulder or lean all my weight on one leg. Once inside, I was embraced by the warmth. It felt so good.

Todd took me to a nearby restroom and sat me down in a chair. I grimaced at the pain I endured just from bending my muscles. Todd said he'd be right back and to stay where I was. He wouldn't be long.

I took out my journal, and began to write:

As the heart beat fails one dreary and lonely evening
Searching and searching for what once was gleaming
It always falls out of reach, whatever he tries to chase
Never returning for more than a glimpse, a kid tossed out of place.

I hoped I would improve when I got older. It wasn't like I could get worse.

Suddenly realizing a presence looming over me, I turned and jumped. "Todd!" I exclaimed, slamming my notebook shut.

"Nice try," he said sarcastically. "You know, you have potential. If you keep practicing, or even go to school for that, you could improve over time. And really become great."

"Oh, um…" I was embarrassed by the delayed response. "Thank you." I could feel my face burning. It wasn't often Todd gave someone a compliment, much less to me.

"Seriously," he said again, this time with a little more enthusiasm. "Getting your emotions down on paper is healthy."

"Mhm." I felt lousy for giving a quick, short response, but I didn't know what else to say.

"But lying about them isn't."

There was silence. I scrutinized him for a second. "Excuse me?"

"Bottling them up isn't, either. Concealing yourself just to a mere composition book…Rory, I can see it all in your eyes. Talk to me."

"Ummm," I stammered, "nothing's wrong." *My brother's dead.*

"Nothing's wrong?"

"Well, everything's wrong, now that Jason's…but I'm fine."

"Don't lie."

"I don't want to talk about it."

"Okay," he said casually, shrugging it off. But I knew this wasn't over. Todd just had a way with bringing things back up and out of people. I was already starting to feel an overwhelming vulnerability.

Todd held a damp warm wash cloth near my shin. "This is going to sting a little."

Slowly he rested it against my leg. I hissed at the slight but sudden pain. Todd held back for a second, and looked at me. I nodded for him to continue.

My leg burned a little when he pressed the cloth to it, but something inside of me overflowed by now as well. My stomach felt that raw stab of pain it gets when you try so hard for so long to keep something locked away, and it just bursts out. I looked away hurriedly, covering my mouth with my hand, but it was too late. Much too late. I knew Todd had seen it. "It's not supposed to sting *that* much," he said.

"It doesn't sting, it *burns*," I responded, trying to wipe away the alarming tears as they came. *NO!* I screamed in my head. *Why are you doing this?*

He put a hand on my shoulder. "Rory—"

"Back off," I said way more aggressively than I should have.

Todd sighed and rested his hands behind his neck. "I'll give you a moment. When you're ready and better again, you know where to find me."

"Kay," I said, not quick enough to reach his ears. The unintentional slam of the door interrupted it.

***

When I came back to the room, Todd was nowhere in sight. I decided to quietly roam around, browsing different parts of the store. There were guitars of many colors and types: Fenders, Gibsons, Rickenbackers, Jacksons, in blues, reds, whites, blacks, black with fire hugging it, the list went on. There were some old acoustic ones sitting near the very top of the shelves, electric ones beneath it. There were amps of various sizes, posters gracing the walls, drum sets, clarinets, flutes, trumpets, violins, pianos. It was strangely calming standing around all of these things.

It was mostly the right side of the room that held the instruments. The left side shelved music books, Beginner's, Standard Levels, Intermediate, and Expert.

My memories started to run through my brain, anything that didn't involve Jason. Or my mom or dad. Or Tre. Suddenly one with a very different person hit. It was on the second month of the year, February, and at around four p.m. That's when it had happened—Sidney and I had our first date. Only about two more months to go and it would be exactly one year.

"Deep in thought?" Todd asked, making me jump. *How does he do that?*

"Todd, I really don't want to argue—"

"Let me take you home."

"For the LAST TIME, I don't need to go home just yet."

"Rory, don't take that tone with me."

I sighed, giving up. I didn't look into his eyes. In the quietest voice, so that he had to lean downwards, I whispered, "My brother's *dead*." That's what was wrong.

I walked around him and turned the corner, into another messy and cramped workspace where things were waiting, I guessed, to get shipped out. As I was doing so, the chain on my pocket got caught on the corner of a desk, and I fell forth, crashing into a pile of stacked paper, some drum sticks, and big metal paint jars, which luckily were sealed shut this time. But it still hurt like hell.

I heard Todd's running footsteps before he came in and I hadn't even gotten up yet. He stared down at the mess I'd made, his mouth agape.

"I'm sorry," I started quickly, "I'm so sorry—"

Todd pulled me up by the arm. He started picking things up, exhaling harshly. As soon as he was finished thrusting the papers and materials back onto what looked to be an old school desk shoved in the corner, he turned back to me.

"Are you okay?" he asked. I detected a hint of concern somewhere in his tone, or maybe it was just my imagination.

"Yeah, but Todd, I'm sorry—"

"It's okay, ARE YOU ALRIGHT?"

"Yes."

Todd nodded and walked out of the room. I followed. He went over toward the book shelves. "Alright. Your eyes are red, and I know you haven't been drinking alcohol or smoking. I'm taking you home right now, and there'll be NO argument about it."

I looked to the ground, not saying anything.

Todd had had it. "Get your coat, Rory."

"I'm okay—"

"Rory. You're not. You're going to have to face that sometime, sooner than later. Whether you like it or don't. I'm not a therapist or anything, but I can tell you're not doing well."

"I already told you why," I growled. I wanted to scream. "And my mom's gone. She left, and I still talk to her, but it's not the same. My dad beats me, all because he too had a shit life, and I don't want to become like him. And I, I—" my voice melted embarrassingly into a slight sob, I was going too fast, but couldn't stop. "Sometimes I'm afraid he'll kill me," I whispered.

"Rory, he's your father."

"No, he's *not*, Todd. At least not anymore." I took in a sharp, quivering breath, and continued, "You have *no idea*. I'm sorry if that sounds arrogant. But you had parents who cared about you. A father who came and—" There was a long pause. "When I see families and friends outside, laughing, joking around, and having a good time, it kills me. I see people celebrating and decorating their house for the holiday season. I see dads teaching their daughters how to ride a bicycle for the first time, and not yelling at them when they fall down. I hear people singing. I see people shopping and hanging out, or little kids playing in the snow. It *kills* me. I am happy for them, but sad for myself. Which I know is selfish and pathetic and unproductive, that I'm wallowing here in my self-pity, but I can't help it."

Todd was silent for a while. "Well I'll be damned." I glanced up at him. "For the first time in YEARS, you give up on holding it in. But you're still giving up on *you*." He paused. "You just about carry the weight of the world on your shoulders, now don't you?" It was not sarcastic, but I knew more was coming. "But are you still under the impression that everyone has it the opposite? Look at me, Rory. Nobody could ever tell that I'd ever been to a point where I wanted to die. To never be again. To never breathe, speak, to not be here talking to you right now." He took in a deep, even breath, clearly disgusted by the memory. I felt chills on my bones, imagining him just evaporating into thin air right now. "Rory, my point is...I mean, you carry a lot of weight, but you need to know that there are people who can help you to carry it too. Either because they know what it feels like to carry weight, or because they want to help, even if they haven't gone through the same things you have."

"Sometimes it feels literal."

"You need to let go of some of that weight, and start over fresh."

"I know." I wiped my eyes with the back of my arm.

"If not, at least let *me* carry some of it for you," he said quietly.

"Yeah," I whispered.

***

I sat on the bushy balcony that evening, Patches spread out across my lap, rubbing his back. Todd and Gabriella were below me on the back porch. Their mumbles were too low for me to hear exactly what they were saying, but every now and then I caught snippets of their conversation. It was mostly bills and stuff.

I made my way downstairs, tip-toeing quietly so as not to disturb Todd and Gabriella. As soon as I got to the back door, and I slightly lifted the curtain, I spotted them. I took my time opening the door. They both glanced back at me, which was slightly awkward. "Oh hi. Sorry, I'll just—"

"Hi Rory," Gabriella said, smiling. "How are you?"

"Hi Gabriella," I replied. "Um, I was wondering..." I looked at Todd, thinking I'd need his permission more than Gabriella's. "Can I take a short walk outside?" It was around four in the evening.

He turned away, face looking anxious for a moment. "Okay. But be back soon, it's going to get dark out."

"I will."

I decided to take a short cut through the woods. Straying off toward the edges of it, I was now away from the noisy rush hour traffic and on my own. It was peaceful and calming when I was alone physically, surrounded by beautiful nature rather than crowds of happiness and joy.

My peaceful mood abruptly came to a halt when my mind went to Tre. There was an ungodly pounding in my head. I hoped I wasn't going to run into that thug again. I could barely handle him on a good day.

Thinking about Tre, with his blackened eyes drained of any color and shape, made me think of a bird of prey soaring down for a visit. And I was the worm. Shuddering, I walked on trying to block out the thoughts that seemed to bombard me one after another—my father, Jason, Sidney, Jason, my mother—all these things were in the order of the people I'd lost, in one way or another, and my father was the first thing listed because it seemed I'd lost him well before he was even my father.

I leaned my head downward so I could fight back the tears in private, despite the fact that there was no one around. It was like I didn't even want the squirrels to see my face.

As I made my way further down the hill, moving low-hanging branches out of my way, I saw a figure in the distance sitting on a rock near a small lake. Even though it was just her silhouette, with the sun setting opposite her, I could already tell it was Sidney. She was alone.

She usually always looked quite happy a lot of the time, even when she was alone. It had always seemed like she'd had a small permanent smile on her face, which is probably a big part of what initially attracted me to her. She was so friendly and approachable. I suddenly had a memory spark up in me of her and I watching a movie together last summer, one that I'd first seen in theaters in 1993, when I'd only been thirteen. It was a feel-good movie that we'd both enjoyed, and I remembered walking out of the theater with her, my arm around her, both of us smiling and continuing to sip on our drinks. Times were so simple then. But like hell if she looked it today. At least when I approached her.

She glanced up quickly, then glanced back to the lake again, staring straight ahead. Her mouth was set in a straight line. "I'll be damned if you ever sneak up on me like that again."

"Sorry," I muttered. "I didn't think I did." Even though the rock was big enough for the both of us to sit on, I sat down on the grass. I was sure when I got back up my pants would have sticks and twigs stuck to them, but oh well. I was a bundle of nerves the size of boulders ready to crash anyway, so that was the least of my worries.

Guilt clawed at my insides because the last time I saw her she was crying outside of *Sonny Morning* in Jeremiah's arms, all because of what she witnessed in my house. *But you don't know that's the sole reason she was crying,* I berated myself. *How selfish. Maybe there are other things going on in her life right now too. It might not be as squeaky clean as it looks on the surface. Quit assuming it's all about you.* Great, now I was feeling guilty for feeling guilty.

The pink ends of her black hair would sometimes flow up with the occasional breeze that came to visit. They were beginning to fade. She sat calmly with her knees to her chest, arms wrapped around them.

For the longest time I had been meaning to tell Sidney that I still cared about her. I was done lying. Everything else seemed to push its way to the surface—why not this? It was my turn to confront the situation myself.

She didn't look directly at me. "Let's start over," I said casually. "Good evening, Sidney."

"Hey," she said back.

"So..." The phrase "What's up" sounded too awkward. "Where's Jerry?" I was surprised I felt comfortable enough to call him by his nickname.

"At home, cleaning and stuff."

"Why aren't you with him? Or at home with Sonny?" I felt rude the moment it came out.

"I just thought I'd sit out here for a while. Do you want me to leave?"

"No, no don't go." I felt clingy, like I'd felt in elementary school. How I would be friends with people, and then they'd be closer to each other than I had ever been with either one of them. Some people just drifted apart. I remembered seeing it before that dark and dreadful day I had inadvertently ended things with Sidney—before I screwed things up. I couldn't lift her up in my arms like every other guy did for his girl, even though she was light, because they were too sore. I'd leave her hanging on an empty phone line whenever my dad would bust in the room, or I'd make up excuses for why she could never come over to my house, never meet my family. That's what Jeremiah was for. *It's not my fault,* I would silently tell myself. Then why, why did I feel so guilty and crappy when she started hanging around Jeremiah? He could give her everything she needed: fun, warmth, and attention. The things I had trouble with on a regular basis. I never felt comfortable with admitting that to her, because I knew she could do so much better. I always felt like I saw the judgment in other peoples' eyes—Sidney's, Todd's, Gabriella's, Jason's, my mom's—but I was probably projecting a lot of that.

"It's cold," Sidney said.

"Yeah, it's December."

Sidney giggled half-heartedly. I almost couldn't believe it. For the longest time it seemed as though she would never crack a smile around me ever again. Maybe I wasn't an annoying bug that needed to be stepped on over and over again after all. And it felt amazing.

I giggled in return. Then I carefully placed my hand on top of hers. "So, you want to—"

"Rory, don't start this," Sidney said, yanking her hand away quickly. I was taken aback by her sudden harshness. "You know we ended it a long time ago, and for good reason."

"Well, can't you just let the past go? Besides, I was just going to ask if you wanted to take a walk around the neighborhood. To warm you up a little. As friends."

"As friends?" She gave me a skeptical look, as if to say, *You sure that's even possible?*

"Yes," I said firmly. "As friends."

Sidney got up and briskly walked away from me, further down the hill and toward the street.

"Sidney, LISTEN to me!" I almost screamed, grabbing her and turning her around so we were face to face. "Okay. I know I messed up. You think I don't know that? You have a great boyfriend now. And I'm happy for you, because you deserve it. But it tears me apart inside to know that I'm around you all the time and I can't even talk to you. I'm *sorry*." I was practically begging. "I'm so sorry, Sid—please."

I didn't know whether the look in her eyes was of disbelief, displeasure, or neither. For the fraction of a second, I thought it might've been fear. She turned away too quickly for me to tell, and started heading across the street.

A bus was headed straight for Sidney. "SIDNEY, WATCH OUT!" I ran as fast as I could.

Her body was slammed so hard, the wind was probably knocked right through her. She was down on the ground in an instant, on the opposite side of the road. With me bent over her. I had pushed her out of the way. The bus continued onward, its monster engine roaring loudly, clean in the front. Never knowing that it almost killed someone.

She was breathless and panting, but not injured. I lifted her shirt. Even though she hadn't been hit by the bus, it was still quite a fall and impact, me having come at her at a full run and knocking her to the ground. I turned her around to check for blood, marks, bruises, scratches—anything. There was nothing. She didn't seem to know what was going on.

She looked down the road then glanced at me. Her panting was uneven, and her wrists shook violently in my hands. I stared back at her, not knowing what to say.

"Thank you," she whispered. Her voice was echoed by the wind and her hair was dancing in her face.

"You're welcome," I murmured, combing her hair out of her eyes.

***

It was close to dark now, and I knew I should start to get going. Sidney and I had been walking around on random sidewalks and paths for about an hour now. It was almost like the way it was when we first started going out—we preferred sidewalks, parks, and benches to parties, concerts, and movies. Except we would talk more, and fool around with each other, and laugh until we cried our eyes out. There was even one time when we went back to her place and almost did it. But I chickened out at the last minute. And I was ashamed of my body and the bruises. She didn't know the full extent of what I went through. She knew I got into fights sometimes, but she didn't know the severity of what my father did. But she was understanding and never pushed me. Maybe she just figured I wasn't ready.

"Rory, there's something I have to tell you." Her voice became shaky. She sounded like she was ready to cry. "I, I was at the Safeway earlier today. I overheard two men talking on the other side of the aisle. I don't know who one of them was. The other was your father."

I cut back a sharp hiss. "And just what did he have to say?"

Sidney clenched her teeth together in nervousness and shifted her balance over to one foot. "He said he launched a plan to go and fly up to New York yesterday."

Jason hadn't killed himself.

Every particle of energy that ever existed in me flew around and my legs almost gave way, feeling like strings. Or like I was being held *up* by a mere string. My head began to pound. "That asshole," I growled.

"Rory, it couldn't have been him. Hasn't he been here this entire time?"

"Yeah, but..."

"I bet it was Tre. He seems to know how to find people," she said bitterly.

"But why?"

"Maybe Tre hired someone to do it." She thought about it some more. "They're doing it for the money. That's what Tre's all about, remember? Not drugs, not alcohol, not sex—money. That's his language." She bit her lip. "And...Jason sometimes got involved with bad people, even though he himself wasn't bad," she finished quickly.

All I could do was shake my head. I was conscious now that I hadn't taken in air for a while, so I began to gasp for breath fiercely, and when I took my final jittery breath, I turned and began to walk the other direction. My pace got faster and faster with each step.

"Rory!" Sidney yelled after me. By now she was at least ten yards behind, trying to keep up. "Where are you going?"

I called back in a blunt monotone, "Business to take care of."

Chapter 17: RENEE—A Shot At Redemption (Saturday evening, December 21, 1996)

There was an urgent knocking on my door that could've awoken a bear out of hibernation. My stomach jumped before I could say, "Dad?"

"It's Sidney! Renee, something's happened. We need to talk."

I hated it so much when people started conversations like this.

I swung the door open to come face to face with a panicked Sidney. "It's about Rory."

That too. Even more, actually. What had he done now? Had he gone out looking for more trouble with more people? Had he bitten off more than he could chew, sip more than he could swallow? Take enough pills that were hard to swallow?

"Out with it," I said quickly. I hadn't meant to sound impatient, but I couldn't help it.

Sidney ran her mouth like a marathon. By the time she was finished, she was panting as though she actually had run one. "He just took off running," she added.

Now I was REALLY afraid. What if Rory was going crazy and planned to commit suicide? Or murder? I couldn't stand the possibilities. "We have to stop him," I ordered. "Where's Todd?"

"At home. I think. I don't remember the number or directions..."

Numbers. I dashed toward the phone in the hallway, Sidney following behind, trying to keep up with my pace.

"You have it memorized?" Sidney asked. I hoped she wasn't bothered by that, but I was too frantic to pay attention to her tone.

"No..." I dashed to the kitchen. What was I thinking trying to use a phone when I had no number?

I began opening different drawers, finding nothing but coupons, keys, and silverware. *Where is it?!* I began tossing things around, trying to find it.

Sidney looked confused. "Renee, what are you doing?"

"Hey," my dad said, entering the kitchen. Oh great. "What's going on?"

"Found it." I seized the yellow phone book and began flipping furiously through the pages. "Last name?" I asked.

"Z-Zimmerman," Sidney stuttered. "Todd Zimmerman."

My dad was glancing back and forth at us now, clearly confused and suspicious, but luckily decided to save the interrogation for after this was done. Clearly my girl friend hadn't just come here to talk about movies or lip gloss.

I was at the phone in the kitchen in the decimal of a second. I punched in the numbers. A ringing sound started humming in my ear. *Come on, Rory, come on...be there. Answer. Tell me you went back there and decided to back out of whatever crazy thing you were going to do.*

"Hello?"

I gulped. "Rory, S-STOP!" I sputtered. "Uh, it's Renee, now listen. You can't do this, it's going to hurt you. Whatever it is, it's not worth it. Please, it's okay, just come home, we can talk, and I'll make you feel better, and—and—"

"Renee?"

I realized in horrifying embarrassment that this wasn't Rory I had been talking to. This was Todd.

"Renee? What is going on? *What* is he doing?" Todd bellowed through the phone. So loudly, Sidney stared at me with expanding eyes, and I knew she could hear him too.

"He's—"

He hung up.

I grabbed my jacket, and Sidney reached for hers, both of us hustling in unison to throw our shoes on at the same time, multitasking. "Dad, it's an emergency!" I exclaimed, as he stood in front of us, blocking us from the front door with his hands on his hips. His eyes were hard. "Oh no you don't," he said. "Tell me where you want to go and I'll drive you there. You're not going out by yourselves this late in the evening." None of us said a word as we rushed out the door. Our motives were equal—we had to stop Rory.

***

Sidney managed to convince my dad to drop us off at her place. We were going to tell Sonny and her parents about what had happened (when we didn't even know what ourselves), and perhaps have them drive around in search of Rory, she told my dad. Todd already knew Rory was out somewhere too, and had likely called the police. My dad kept giving us the side eyes, like he didn't really trust us. But he reluctantly dropped us off anyway and didn't leave until, naturally, we were inside the house. It drove me crazy and made me want to scream, but I shoved it down and tried to remember he was just worried about me.

We weren't completely lying—we *were* going to tell Sonny, who had his license, and call Jeremiah and make sure he knew too. Jeremiah's parents luckily trusted him to stay out late at night with the car, probably because he was a little older than us. I was about to ask Sidney as we stood awkwardly in the entryway of her house, what the plan would be. Or where Sonny would look. Or if her own parents were home, and would they be okay with me just waltzing in like this, and would they allow Sonny to drive after dark, without them coming along.

"Uh, yeah, they're home," she said, only answering the first part of the question. She had that mixed-up panicky look on her face where she was trying to figure out what to do next. We'd succeeded in getting away from my dad, but now there were her parents to deal with. "Maybe we could ask Jeremiah to come pick us up—"

"SIDNEY EVELYN WILCOX, you are *late!*" shouted what I could only assume was her mother, coming down the stairs. She was a tall woman with light-brown hair and skin lighter than Sidney's as well. But she definitely had the same features, same sharp nose, and same sharp glittering eyes that I'd recognized on Sidney's face whenever she got angry. Her voice had bounced off the walls and made both of us cringe.

"Sorry mom," Sidney said. "This is Renee. I told you about her."

"Oh," her mother faltered, now looking embarrassed. "I didn't know we'd be having company." She smiled, an edge to it that said she was still pissed at Sidney for just bringing me here without having told her, but would play the part for now for the guest. "Hello Renee," she said, holding out her hand. I shook it. "Would you like any—"

"Actually mom," Sidney said, trying to rush this along as politely as possible, "Renee was helping me to look for something I'd lost. It's my history notebook from school. I think I may have left it in my locker. If we could just have Sonny drive us back to the school, I'm sure it's still open—"

"A notebook?" Her mother put one hand on her hip, exasperated. "Do you really need that notebook tonight, Sidney?"

"*Yes*," Sidney said, feigning desperation. "I still need to look over a few notes for that test after break. And it's first thing in the morning." I would never have been able to come up with a sensible story so quickly, nor would I be able to act it out so well. I only hoped her mother would believe it and allow the three of us to go.

Sonny entered with his headphones on, when his face fell in confusion as he saw me. Taking them off, he said, "Renee, did you get kicked out?"

"*Sonny!*" his mother said, horrified.

"Oh no, no," I said, forcing a giggle and trying to play along. "I uh...we're looking for Sidney's notebook. My dad knows I'm with her." I sounded so hysterical, it was obvious I was talking about something more important than a notebook. I would never make it as an actress, I could cross that off my bucket list right now.

Luckily other than appearing a little suspicious, Sidney's mother assented and allowed Sonny to drive us back to the school. Or so she thought.

"But be very quick," she said. "And be very careful. I want you all back in this house by eight o'clock sharp. Is that understood?"

We all nodded and went out, Sonny jingling his keys and looking across at us with narrowed eyes. "So what's this *really* about?" he asked when we were all in the car.

We quickly ran through all that had happened, his eyes going wider and his eyebrows rising more by the minute, until his face seemed frozen like that. It would've been comical had it not been for the circumstances. He let out a long exhale and said, "Okay. So...where do we start?"

"We start by you driving us down this road," Sidney said, "and then dropping us off. We have to continue on foot, onto the path in the woods."

Sonny tried to protest, but Sidney kept arguing her case, until it practically became a screaming match. "I have to start where I last saw him!" she cried. Sonny finally conceded and dropped us off on the side of the road, where he insisted on coming with us. "No!" Sidney said. "You can't just leave the car here. We'll go, you drive around and search for Rory. In fact, maybe go to Jeremiah or Todd's place and see what's going on with them." Sonny stomped back to the car, fuming.

Sidney led me down the path she had last seen her troubled ex rush down. "He got down here," Sidney panted, "and I don't know which way he took then." The path led to a road in town, an opening in the trees showing the cineplex and a couple of stores.

"What are we going to do?" Sidney bit her lip, and I knew she would start crying.

I spoke quickly, but forcefully. "Sidney, maybe you and I should take different routes. This place is more crowded, I think we'll be okay." It was a flat-out lie and she knew it, but I still thought we'd have more of a chance of finding Rory if we split up. If I could've sent everyone in the world out to look for Rory at the moment, I would've.

"Are y—" Sidney took a quivering breath and wiped her eyes. "You sure this will work?"

"No, I'm not sure it will work Sidney." I put my hands on her shoulders and tried to console. "But it's the best solution I can come up with."

I gave her some coins for a payphone. We parted ways.

Hopefully, for his sake, we won't need *a solution.*

***

I stood in horror. "Rory," I breathed, "what are you *doing*?" I'd found him at a deserted bus station, about a block from Wilcox

High. There was a lone shop here and there, closed, no sign of activity nearby. Well out of the way of where I was supposed to be.

"Oh," he spoke quietly. "So you found me." His voice was eerie. He looked and sounded dead. Gone was the ivory skin. Now it was gray, with darker splotches of it in some areas, bruises. His voice was a monotone, careless, apathetic. His body was as stiff as a skeleton in a closet. Even though he was trying to look tough, he looked so frail, like it pained him to stand. Given the fresh bruises on his face, which shown even more starkly in the streetlight, it was not a shock. His eyes looked more bruised than they had earlier this afternoon, one of them black and almost shut. I could only imagine what his body must've looked like, under his layers of warm clothes. Had he encountered his dad again since I last saw him?

Tre stood in the black, wet, distant corner, hardly visible, though I could see his snow white grin.

There was only one light shining down, creating a circle on the floor, and Rory stood in the center. He held a gun in one hand, black, heavy, metal, pointing in Tre's direction. *I thought Gideon hadn't given him a gun though.* Then it hit me and I realized Rory must've stolen it. *Business to take care of,* as Sidney had quoted.

"Rory, STOP IT!" I screamed, grabbing onto his arm. The look he gave me told me it wasn't a smart thing to do. Where there were guns and struggling, there were accidents too. I let go immediately.

"You know, Rory," Tre said in mock concern, "your brother *died* yesterday."

Rory's fist clenched and went completely white. His face whitened as well. For a moment I wondered if his heart had stopped pumping blood.

"The mail usually comes on Saturday afternoons, no?" Tre continued. "Because Jason reportedly was seen rushing to his mailbox at his current address about an hour before the 'suicide'."

"S-suicide?" Rory muttered in disbelief, noticing how Tre put it in air quotes.

"Oh yeah, he *was* hung. Right after he was knocked out." Rory's face fell and the gun slipped in his hand, but he held onto it firmly. "Hey," Tre said, holding his hands out like it was no big deal, "it was at least quick, little buddy. Haha, 'little buddy'...is that what your cuddly, older, warm, and protective brother used to call you?"

Rory's finger went to the trigger. I took half a step forward. "Rory...don't—"

"No, Renee, YOU don't. You shouldn't be here. This is not your fight." His eyes shifted over to me.

"So tell me Rory," Tre went on. "Have you checked *your* mail today?"

Tre walked up to Rory, his shoes echoing hollowly on the pavement, and I flinched, thinking Rory would shoot him. He didn't, steadily holding the gun and his breath, as Tre came up and dug his hand into Rory's pocket in his pants. Rory held the gun, the tip of it pushed against Tre's chest. By now I had backed up several feet, nearly hiding behind the trashcan, ready to duck if anything happened.

Tre yanked out an envelope and threw it on the ground a few feet away. Rory's eyes expanded and flickered over to it, but went straight back to Tre, still holding the gun and not moving a muscle in his body. The only thing that gave away his nerves was the slight movement in his throat.

The envelope was right near my feet. I stood, frozen in time. For just a moment the world seemed still and cold, like I was the only one left alive, the sound of my heart beating off in every direction. An unknown force crept inside me, and I dashed for it.

I remembered the only other time I'd felt this sort of thing. It was a day when I'd ran across my neighborhood back in Maryland when

Jenny came to get me to tell me mom had had an accident. I had never ran so fast in my life. It had begun to get to the point where my feet were no longer lifting up and coming down, but dragging across the rough pavement. I'd had to use the little strength left to jump out of the way so that I didn't end up smashing into our mailbox when I'd finally arrived back.

I pick up the envelope with small, midnight blue, capitalized ink. It was addressed to Rory, but the return address said *Graham*. Graham? Who the hell was Graham? I didn't know why, but for some reason I got a strong feeling that even though it wasn't from Jason, it was important anyway.

My body did all the rest of the work. I was watching myself in a movie. I was involuntarily breathing and moving. In a mere second I'd gotten the letter out. Sweat broke out on my neck. I unfolded the small paper before me. It read, *You are one of the only good things that was ever in my life. Don't feel bad or responsible for anything. Love you, little brother.*

Ever since I met Rory, I longed to see him smile, longed to see him laugh, longed to see more than just that sad, lonely, miserable figure. He had proven it a couple times. I'd known there was someone fun and playful and loving in there. But I wanted *see it*. And could the rest of the world see it too? This would do it. This would heal a great deal of his past emotional scars. Now he could live free of the guilt that bottled him up all these years. If he allowed himself to.

I heard some shouting and a loud scuffle, someone getting knocked to the ground. I looked up again. The pistol was still shaking in his hand. Quietly, I hissed, "DON'T."

Except this time, it was Rory's *father* he was pointing at instead. Tre lay in an unconscious red and purple heap on the ground. What just happened? Did Rory do that to Tre? No, it was his dad, who had a much more capable hand for that kind of thing than Rory.

Rory's father walked up to his son, chin almost pressed against the weapon, looking down at him. The sky was rumbling and I thought I heard thunder. I wondered where Sidney, Jeremiah, and Sonny were. I wondered where Todd and Gabriella were. I wondered if any of our parents had called the police on us already. I wondered if the police were now looking for us.

His father spoke, "I'm going to tell you exactly what I told your brother. You're foolishly lying to yourself. You're not a murderer. You're just a weak little victim. Like me."

Against my better judgment, I took a step closer to Rory. I could see anger, fear, and defeat all dance around in his eyes at once.

Don't do it, I thought. *Don't do it.* It was silent for what seemed an eternity. Rory tried to keep a straight face, struggling to keep his mouth still, but I could tell his teeth were clicking on the inside. For one awful moment, when he sucked in his breath, I really thought he'd changed his mind and was going to pull the trigger.

But he lowered it. Lower and lower. His eyebrows that had been arched were starting to straighten out considerably. There was no more anger in the eyes. He was losing the urge now, the urge to kill. *Yes.* He backed up two steps, and dropped the gun. A prompt *thud* sounded. It echoed loudly. He was staring at his father now, face neutral. He was visibly starting to quiver more.

Then he slowly turned toward me, until he was facing me and his back was toward his father. The depressing world he had been trapped in for years, struggling to break free, he put behind himself. He tried to keep himself under control but his emotions burst loose. His eyes disappeared behind shiny, abundant pools, and I had him in my arms. My body wrapped around him so tightly, I thought I would break him. I held him close and stroked his head.

My ear picked up the quick scraping of metal on the ground. An explosive shot fired. I could feel the warmth of it against my face. Someone screamed. I hid my face deeper into Rory's jacket.

Another shot sounded momentarily, and I felt Rory's weight fall on top of me. My head hit the pavement with a loud bang, the last known sound I heard before I blacked out.

Chapter 18: RENEE—Life and Death (Sunday, December 22, 1996, midnight)

One week. I had known him for almost a full week, and now he was gone. Or about to be, I was certain. Amazing how time flies by and yet that week I'd known him felt like two, three, maybe even four years. Gabriella had her arms around me, and I could tell from the movements they were making, that she too was crying.

There was a Christmas tree in the corner with lights wrapped around it so tightly the tree looked like it was choking. Jeremiah and Sonny were huddled together a couple of seats down from us, both paler than I imagined possible. Sidney was in the bathroom, crying. She blamed herself for this mess. I promised myself to make her see that it wasn't, no matter how much talking I was going to have to do. My dad was sitting on the other side of me, squeezing my hand. Partly out of love, partly out of anger. The latter wasn't for me though. And Sidney, Sonny, and Jeremiah's parents were all sitting around too, waiting it out.

The police had been looking for Tre after I reported that he'd followed me around and assaulted me twice. It was mortifying having to tell my dad that.

Rory got the first shot—his father got the second, and didn't make it. *Tre...you fucking bastard.* I hoped the police squeezed the sharp metal upon his wrists as hard as they could and never let him out of them. Tre also confessed to arranging Jason's murder, and making it look like a suicide as a way to cover it up.

He was transported to the emergency room via helicopter. I shuddered. That was only for the dire cases.

I refused to think about the fact that he was shot in his back, to think about the possibilities. The silence of the hospital, with the exception of the humming vent, was so mind-numbing it made me want to shut the door and never walk back in again.

Gideon was pacing around, back and forth, clearly a nervous wreck. He went to a vending machine downstairs and got a soda. But then he only drank one sip before tossing it in the trash. On the contrary, I wanted one so badly, but I gagged every time I even thought about drinking something. Todd sat closest to the room Rory was in, his hands folded, staring at a magazine table diagonal from him, a couple feet to the right of my dad. There was an image in my mind of a graveyard and tombstones and a small group of people. Everyone stood around wearing dark cloaks as they carried out a long, wooden coffin...

I heard someone step out toward my right, the door closest to me. The light came sprinting out and splattering across the floor and walls. I glanced over and knew it was the doctor once the first foot came out.

"He'll survive," the doctor said. "But if he's able to walk again—and that's a big if—it will take close to year."

***

It was 6:06 p.m. exactly as I lay on my bed, exhausted from everything. It was now Monday the twenty-third, the eve of Christmas Eve. Even though my dad was still angry at me for stupidly running off in such a dangerous situation and almost getting shot, he'd cooled off a little, and was even in a festive mood. I heard the sounds of Christmas songs on the TV downstairs.

Rory's mother returned. Todd and Gabriella were helping them out with arranging the funeral. The funerals. There were two. In the course of a week, they'd lost two family members. Somehow, they both still felt extreme sadness at the loss of Rory's father, even though he'd been abusive to them most of their lives. But Rory had sworn that his father got shot because he was trying to protect him. That in that one last moment of life, he used it to put himself in the line of fire for his last remaining son, who he'd all but destroyed before. And he didn't kill Jason. Even with all of the anger and toxicity that had filled Rory's father over the years, that was a level of evil even he couldn't have ever stepped into.

Once Rory recovered, he would be off with his mom. They were going to help move stuff out of that house, it being a hollow place of past ghosts. I wondered who would move in after that, and if they would be haunted by those ghosts too.

I had just gotten finished mailing my Christmas letter to Jasmine. It would be a little late when it arrived, but I knew she'd be delighted. I'd written it with a gold gel pen, her favorite out of my batch. Now I was sketching some patterns in a notepad when the phone range. "Renee!" my dad called. "It's for you."

Thinking it was Sidney, Sonny, or Jeremiah (I was pretty sure Rory wasn't in any shape to talk on the hospital phone just now), I said, "Hello?"

"Hello, Renee?"

It took me a full second before recognizing the voice. "Oh, hi Todd."

"Rory would like for you to visit him tomorrow night. Perhaps after you visit Sidney's family."

I gaped, forgetting for a moment that I was on the phone.

"I told him it would be better to rest for a while. I don't think he has the energy for anyone right now." His voice was hard. "He insisted that you come and see him tomorrow night. As long as it was okay with you. Said it would be one of the best Christmas Eves he's had in ages. I eventually gave in."

"Oh, uh...I would really like to." Would Rory be alright though? Was he be in any shape to see anyone right now?

"I should speak to your father about this before we get off the phone."

"Yeah, okay. That would be a good idea."

There was a long moment of pause, but somehow I knew he still had something to say. "Maybe it's the seriousness of the situation, or the holidays, but no way would any of us have been allowed to even wait for him the other night. No one except his mother. That's normally not allowed for anyone except immediate family." He paused again. "He'll be moved from the Critical Care Unit soon, now that he is awake and able to speak, and now that it's apparent he won't...he will live."

I swallowed. "I can get my dad now, if you'd like."

"Thank you, Renee."

***

Christmas Eve, 1996

Before we went to the Wilcox house, we went to the hospital where Jenny and Sheila were staying. They weren't going to be released for another two-to-three days, but that didn't mean we couldn't still celebrate Christmas.

"This is beautiful!" Jenny cried when she held out her necklace. She leaned over and gave me a hug. She was sitting up and looked like her regular old self again. And we actually looked like one of those families on TV.

"You may tire of it come summertime."

"I have stuff for every season. And, I'll get sick of heat real fast. So the snowman will keep me good company."

When we got to the front door of the Wilcox residence, everything looked dark outside by now. But the windows were bright with warm, orange light. When the door opened, the Wilcoxes' golden retriever pawed at the screen and barked at us. Sidney's mother stepped out.

"Good evening," she greeted us with a sincere smile. I briefly wondered if she remembered me at all or knew my involvement of the horrific events of the past week, if or how much Sidney had told her. But if she did, it didn't appear she remembered or cared.

Sidney was standing in the hallway between the living and dining rooms. She had on her usual jeans and hoodie combination, but also seemed a little more accessorized tonight than on a normal day. She wore a choker, had her hair pulled back in a bun, and her nails were professionally done up, perfectly manicured with different Christmas designs on each one.

Her younger sister, Brooke, was in the living room watching Christmas cartoons, curled up with the family dog who'd come to join her. It got up and pit-pattered over to us, letting all of us pet him. He loved the attention. There was a whole stack of VHS tapes on the shelf beside the TV. Winnie the Pooh, Little Bear, Disney movies, *The Land Before Time*, and many others. She wore a pair of overalls and she had a beanie baby hanging out of one of the pockets. I imagined she probably had the entire gang of them in her room somewhere.

Jeremiah and Sonny entered the hallway and greeted us. I noticed my dad and their mom walking into the kitchen with each other, talking. This was their first time meeting, but they seemed to be getting on well. With us, there was an awkward elephant hanging over the room we all steered clear from. Especially now that we knew the miraculous outcome of it.

"It's starting to snow out!" Sonny squealed, glancing at the window.

"It is not—" Then Sidney gasped. "It is!"

Jeremiah and I rushed forward and stared incredulously out the window. This was TEXAS. I hadn't thought it was possible.

Just then, Mrs. Wilcox came out of the kitchen, clapped her hands, and said, "Okay everyone, dinner is ready."

They had an extremely long table, one that the Wilcoxes only used for special times of the year, when they had several guests. Jeremiah's parents were there, a few close neighbors of Sidney and Sonny, and there were some extended family members of the Wilcoxes as well. The dog sat on the ground, eating excitedly out of his bowl. Everyone was really friendly. I could tell my dad was surprised by it all too. Neither of us ever experienced this type of Christmas before, even though it was probably normal for many other families.

We said Grace. Sidney and Sonny's father added, "May this night give us the strength to remember what to be grateful for, all year round." We all said "Amen" and dug in.

I remembered Sidney once telling me that the Christmas dinner at her house had not only ham, roast beef, cranberry sauce (her personal favorite), and stuffing, but they also went out of their way to provide everybody's special favorite food. She wasn't kidding—there was banana bread, s'mores, shrimp, pizza, little tacos, etc.

After dinner was over and everyone went their separate ways, I saw Sonny through the screened back door, sitting on the porch with the golden, admiring the snow. He was wearing Sidney's pink frilly gloves, and I suppressed a laugh. Sidney and Jeremiah had gone upstairs to play on her PlayStation. The kitchen was empty and silent, nothing but a sink full of loads of dishes to do the next day.

Over the next hour, I'd gone up to Sidney's room and played some of her game, talked to her about school and TV shows and family stories, watched her and Sonny quarrel over her gloves, and sat with all of them as we watched *A Christmas Story* downstairs on the TV. The subject of Rory never came up, but I was more than relieved about it. It felt wrong somehow, almost disrespectful, to bring him up when we knew he was lying in a hospital and we were all here having a good time. It would be like pitying him. Which he would never, ever, want.

When I got back to the car, my dad hugged me and whispered in my ear, "Merry Christmas."

***

"I'll pick you up in about half an hour," my dad said, looking at his watch. He hadn't been keen on letting me come. Not because it was late. Not because he didn't like having me out of his sight. But because this was the second trip to a hospital I'd made tonight. Nonetheless, he waved at Todd and nodded at me to go on.

Todd stood waiting outside of the hospital, his hands jammed in his pockets, and gave me a curt nod when I got out of the car and approached the steps. He turned to lead me inside.

Unlike the hospital I'd visited Jenny and Aunt Sheila in, this one had barely any Christmas decorations at all. I could hear the distant sounds of carol singing on the radio in some areas, but otherwise, it could've been any time of the year. Any cold, quiet time.

"He's going to need surgery," Todd said, not looking at me. I had to walk fast to keep up with him as he strode down the corridor.

"Oh." I didn't know what to say at all.

"I'm not sure when exactly, but they'll be moving him to the operation room sometime. I'm glad you're here. Rory needs more friends. Especially people his own age."

I hadn't realized how apprehensive I'd been of Todd until how taken aback I was at these kind and appreciative words.

"Blood is important, but certainly people can be family without being blood."

Before I had time to become nervous about what I would see, Todd swiftly and sharply turned into a room. I followed close behind.

Rory was propped up against some pillows, his face whiter than I'd ever seen it, some grayish-blue color under his eyes. He managed a small smile and even lifted his hand in an effort to wave. I nodded and sat on the small, uncomfortable, metal chair with a single thin cushion coming off of it, next to his bed.

Todd turned from one of us to the other, then seemed to take the hint and left the room.

When he left us alone, Rory turned to me. His voice was quiet so that I had to lean in, and it was a bit raspy. "My mom's been fussing over me a lot. She's probably going to wheel me around everywhere after this." He grimaced. "And Todd and I argued for about ten minutes about bringing you here. But as far as I'm concerned, you're just as much family as him and mom." He took a deep breath. "Anyway, I...I'm sorry about everything. I've caused you a lot of trouble." He bit his lip. "Oh Renee...if you'd been shot—"

"It's not your fault. What I did were my own actions, and what Tre did were his—"

"Is it okay if I keep calling you?" he whispered fiercely. "I can't stand the thought of never seeing or hearing from you again after this."

There was a lump tightening the back of my throat. "Yeah," I said. "Of course, Rory." I couldn't stand the thought either. "What about Sidney, Sonny, and Jeremiah? Are you going to keep contact with them?"

Rory opened his mouth and hesitated. "I don't know," he finally said. "I don't know if they want to."

"You'll never know if you don't try." I glanced around, trying to find another conversation topic to grasp. "How's uh...how's the food here?" Ugh. It was like talking about the weather.

"Actually, not half-bad. I guess Christmas is a good time to get put in the hospital."

I glared at him.

"I hear they might even be serving s'mores tonight. But even for Christmas, that's probably cutting it close."

There was a whole two seconds of silence before I burst out laughing.

"Sonny chows those things down like it's an eating contest or something."

"I'm sure he does."

I suddenly felt another presence nearby. I turned and saw Todd returning.

Rory didn't seem surprised to glance over and see Todd. He tried to smile but the pain was visible beneath it. It was as if the silly conversation we'd just had erased itself from the past. He looked down at his bedsheets, but somehow Todd and I both seemed to sense that he was about to say something. "I know it's my fault what happened last night...and the same goes with what happened with Jason and stuff."

"Rory—" To hell with Todd seeing me yell at him—"don't say stupid stuff like that," I said.

Rory turned to me and his voice lowered. "Why not, Renee? It makes sense. You would agree with me, ANYBODY would have if they saw the whole thing and was actually *there*, like me. You should've heard what I yelled at him, guys, and seen the way he reacted." Rory turned back to Todd. He kept glancing from one of us to the other, eyes pleading. Either for us to understand or to tell him he was wrong, I wasn't sure which. "I *destroyed* him, Todd."

"Rory, Jason was a really smart guy," Todd said. "He knew you were only angry, he knew you didn't mean any of it. He knew you were only a kid. And, he knew that he screwed up." I started to say something but was interrupted. "He felt guilty for the way he'd let everybody else down, and *that's* why he left. Bottom line, Rory."

"Don't say that. He was a good person."

"I didn't say he wasn't a good person, Rory. But people tend to not be as truthful as they should be once someone dies. We can still acknowledge that he had problems which remained unresolved."

I reckoned Rory would've started walking away from us by now if he'd been able to. His voice was strained, like he was trying to hold back. "It's...always going to feel like it's my fault."

"Then you're always going to be wrong about that." Todd gritted his teeth and as the light shone in his eyes, I could tell from the angle that he was on the verge of tears himself.

"It's...you don't understand. You don't understand..." Rory's voice trailed off. He was exhausted. He was overflowing and being drained at the same time, of energy and oxygen, drowning him. He could no longer talk and breathe at the same time now. He had to at least have enough unfailing senses to know it was better to just relax first.

"Okay, just breathe, breathe..." Todd hushed, rubbing the back of Rory's neck. When Rory finally regained his thoughts, he mumbled in a rough and uneven tone, "Every...every relationship in my life…always ends badly. I don't even know what I did until after it's too late." He paused, and took a glance upward toward me.

"Rory," I finally said, "you almost got yourself *killed* again. You could've died."

Rory lowered his head. "Yeah, I know," he whispered.

"Rory," Todd quickly sighed, and again tried recompose himself to sound calm and casual. "If you're really sorry, *believe* that it's going to be okay."

Rory stared at him. "I can't," he said quietly. "I never could."

"Well, you need to. The more you keep thinking like this, the worse it's just going to get. You need to start thinking on more positive terms. Otherwise it does things to you. It makes you more depressed than you really need to be. Go out for some fresh air—especially when the weather is warmer and sunnier—or speak with somebody, or read a book, or play with Patches, or whatever. Do what you love to do the most. Express yourself. Get all the heat out. Do whatever you have to do Rory, but DON'T just sit up in your room all day and feel miserable, because if you don't believe it's going to get better, then it won't. BELIEVE me when I tell you this Rory—it WILL get better. Things WILL be okay in the end. I would know, and look! You and I are still alive, that's already better right there!"

"Yeah," I sighed, remembering that awful experience that would never go forgotten or forgiven. "That's a given."

"Don't you think it's a miracle, Rory, that you got shot in your *back* and you're still alive? You could be DEAD right now, but you're alive. There's even a chance that you'll walk again. And you're here, surrounded by Renee and I, and we both care about you very much. You should've seen everybody at the hospital that night."

Rory stared at Todd. "Everybody?"

"Sidney, Sonny, Jeremiah—yes, them," he added, at the incredulous look on Rory's face. "You know, there were several points where I ought to have given up on you," Todd said bluntly. "And I did, at some point or another. But it's kind of impossible to do that with somebody you care about."

It was silent for about a minute afterward. Then Todd finally said, "I'll be right back. I want to show you something." He turned and walked out the door. I assumed he was going back to his car. Rory and I looked at each other curiously. In the meantime, Rory's mother came in and hugged me, then asked Rory about four times if he'd eaten, had plenty to drink, knew how to contact the nurses, in case he needed help getting up to use the bathroom (at which point he turned a scarlet shade and practically shoo'd her out of the room). She gave him a big hug and planted a kiss on his head, before giving us time alone again.

"This is the most energy I've seen her have in *years*," he commented.

When Todd came back, he was holding a big shirt up. Rory's mouth hung open in disbelief, and his eyes widened in recognition. It looked like he was waking up for the first time. "Todd, that...uh..." He couldn't quite get the words out, but he held up a finger, and narrowed his eyes, confused.

Todd nodded understandingly. "I take it this belongs to you?"

"Y-yes!" Rory cried.

"I know this was what you went back to your father's house to get that day, Rory. You wouldn't have otherwise, had this not been so important to you. You hid it under your bed, afraid your dad would tear it to shreds. I know you feel Jason in your heart, flowing through your blood when you sleep in his shirt at night. I know it's Jason's, because he used to wear it all the time, and this was the one thing he left behind. Also...it's two sizes too big for you."

Rory scoffed less than half-heartedly. He slowly reached out for it.

"But you need to PROMISE to stop beating yourself up."

Rory frowned. "Alright," he finally said, for the first time with some conviction. "I promise. I promise." He clutched the shirt like a child clutches a teddy bear, like it was his last shred of life. Then he sank down into his pillows in a heap of sleepiness.

"Well, I'll just let Sleeping Beauty here get some rest," Todd said, getting up. I could tell by the twitch in Rory's eye at that comment that he wasn't really asleep. And I think Todd knew that too.

When it was just Rory and I, I bent down to him and whispered, "Merry Christmas, Rory."

He lifted his head slightly and brushed his lips against mine.

19

Epilogue—mid-February 1997

Rory

Sometimes I thought that there was nothing worse than when no matter how many times you tried, the zipper to your hoodie still ended up getting stuck. It could potentially ruin your whole day.

I was in my hospital room trying to zip up my hoodie when Todd entered, looking at his watch. "Rory, come on," he demanded. "They won't excuse you for being late just because you're in a wheelchair."

"I know, I know," I mumbled. I decided to hell with the zipper.

He pushed me out into the corridor where Gabriella was waiting, holding and flipping through a scrapbook. Behind her the window was set with the curtains wide open to overcast sky. Despite the dark skies, my mood felt bright.

My mother and Gideon were both waiting by the front doors. She was wearing a winter coat that she'd technically had for a year now, but I never saw her in it before so it looked new. She smiled at me, and I knew her and Gideon had gotten the last of everything we'd want or need out of our old house. In a weird way I was going to miss that house. And not even just the oldest memories in it of me and Jason (though those would definitely always be in my mind), but even the bad memories too. The last time I'd been in that house was the first time Jeremiah, Renee, and Sidney had been there.

We would leave when I was released, which would be a few more weeks.

They were all silent. Weren't adults supposed to know what to say?

I thought about my dad some more, in that house. I thought about the photo I'd kept. I wondered if he ever knew I'd seen it or taken it in the first place. Or if he'd been still aware of its existence in the first place.

"Wait, Rory, can I just show you a few pictures before we go out to meet the others?" Gabriella asked excitedly, jumping over with the scrapbook, keeping her place in it.

"Sure," I said, looking up at Todd. He nodded, as we still had a few minutes before we had to go.

We went into the cafeteria, and Gabriella spread the scrapbook out in front of me on the table. It was open to the picture that we'd taken yesterday: me, mom, Gabriella, Gideon, and Todd. It was the closest to smiling I'd ever seen Todd do. But for him, the minor rise in the corners of his mouth in this photo was like a wide beaming sun. I smiled in spite of myself.

There were also older pictures of us. Myself, Jason, mom and dad...even one of Jason and Todd. Or Mr. Zimmerman, as Jason would call him back then. Me and Jason and some neighborhood kids, when we'd all hung out together. When we were young. And somewhat free. It was a good thing Gabriella spoke up again, because I would've sat there staring at those photos forever.

"But these pictures are already in your memory," she said, bending down and hugging me gently. Gabriella aspired to be a counselor and already, she was well on her way to becoming one of the best ones I'd ever known. Not that I'd known many.

"Okay," Todd said, "let's go meet the others. Gabriella and I might have to leave a little early." He coughed. "In case of snow."

It wasn't in case of snow and I knew that, and he knew I knew that. It was Todd and Gabriella's anniversary. I grinned at Todd as he looked away, pretending to not know what I was grinning about. I had a strange idea in my head that he might even finally propose to her, but it was only an idea. I could only imagine the night they had planned, and it gave me a weird mix of amused disgust and adoration. Growing up I never really knew what it felt like when the other kids in the class would talk about how "nasty" it was whenever they saw their parents kissing. It'd made me feel like there was something wrong with me. But now, I thought I knew just what they meant.

Sidney and Renee were already sitting outside on the bench waiting for us. Sonny and Jeremiah stood beside them, Sonny attempting to do a trick with a yo-yo and Jeremiah on his Gameboy. Sidney, I noticed, had her nails exquisitely done. "Nail art" I think is what girls called it. They were white with blue snowflake prints on each one. Usually the only other nail colors I saw on her were black or dark red. This was a cheery change for her.

The girls got up and headed over toward me, warm greetings all around. Sonny came over, still trying for success with the yo-yo. Jeremiah smiled but hung back a little. He still looked a tad uncomfortable when he was around me. I nodded toward him. "I see you're sporting the Grunge look," I said, referring to his plaid shirt and ripped jeans.

Sonny was wearing a ridiculous shirt—it was a black T-shirt that said "I ♥ S'mores." I covered my mouth as I began cracking up.

Sonny looked down at his shirt and back at me. "This is no laughing matter," he said seriously.

"Wow," I said, impressed. "You're dedicated."

"I am," he said. "All of the s'mores in the world are going to me. You can't have any."

"That's okay," I shrugged, playing along. "S'mores are nasty."

The look of absolute rage on Sonny's face had us all bursting out in tear-inducing laughter. "I was just kidding, Sonny," I said.

"I'm hoping so," he replied.

"Look," Sidney said, taking a plastic container out of her bag and handing it to me. "I guess it's a late Christmas present. And a 'glad-you're-getting-better' present."

No wonder Sidney had pestered me so much earlier this year about what my favorite food was (until I finally answered and told her it was banana bread). *"Seriously?" she said. "Out of all the foods in the universe,* banana bread *is your favorite?"* It was freshly-baked, and there was a small container of butter in the corner. "It'll taste so much better when you put it in the microwave and spread the butter on it," she said.

"Thank you so much," I said, looking up at Sidney.

"We don't mean to be rude," she said, "but we actually can't stay for very long. Sonny and I have to get back and do some early Spring cleaning for our parents, and Jeremiah has some errands to run."

"That's alright," I said. I sensed some of these might not have been true and that they just wanted to leave me alone with Renee for a little while. Which was completely fine by me.

"Keep getting better," Sonny said. "Eat s'mores." Sidney giggled, and actually bent down to give me a hug. Something I hadn't thought she'd do in a million years.

Jeremiah stood there with his hands shoved in his pockets, gave a small smile, and nodded at me. "Good luck," he said. This was possibly the last time I would see any of them.

As soon as we said our goodbyes, Todd wheeled me out to the courtyard, Renee following. The place was green in the oncoming Spring, birds chirping in the trees, lots of shrubbery, and some benches. Only a few other people sat around. Todd placed me near a bench where Renee sat down.

Thankfully, the adults had the sense to realize we wanted to be alone.

Renee

Rory asked Todd if he could get his bag from his room. Todd brought it out and looked down at us. "I'll come back in about twenty minutes," he said, nodding at the both of us.

We sat there for a few seconds before he grabbed his bag and started rummaging through it. I'd thought it was just to have something to do, when his hand seemed to bump into something else, something he must not have known was there, from the surprised look on his face. He gasped, and I saw him pull out a collection of cassettes. Guns and Roses, Ratt, Poison, Warrant, WASP, Dokken, and Skid Row—bands he must've grown up watching and listening to with Jason, but had never owned any of their cassettes. *"Merry late Christmas, Rory,"* the sticky note on the top of the stack said. *"These are some of my old cassettes, and I know you'll love them. And here's my number again in case you lose it. Feel free to call whenever you start to feel bad or need anyone to talk to. –Todd"*

He stared at it in amazement.

"What's that?" I asked, peering over his shoulder.

"Oh," he replied showing me the wrapped stack of cassettes along with the note. I hadn't heard of most of these bands, but I could've sworn I'd seen Rory wearing T-shirts of some of them at certain points.

"Wow," I said, awed. "Todd really loves you."

"Yeah," was all he said. He was still so unreadable. I could only guess what kinds of thoughts were currently racing through his head. Was he thinking about how much he wished his father and Jason were still here? Was he wondering what it would be like, in another life, to have a family Christmas at his own house, with his own full family, everyone gathered around the table in full happiness and unity and gratitude? And most of all, was he scared to leave here? Was he afraid of what the future held, and was he afraid, like me, of going so far away from all of this?

"Luckily, we have a cassette player in the car," he said.

"I'm going to miss you so much," I suddenly said, my voice cracking.

I hadn't expected to do this, and neither had he. He frowned and beckoned me over. "Hey. Come here," he ordered.

"Oh no," I said, getting up. "Rory, I'm fine—"

"Just come here," he said, taking my arm. I bent down slightly, and he pulled me into his arms, making me sit on his lap. "You'll be okay," he said, patting and rubbing my back. "You'll be okay. I'm going to need to get help. Like...therapy maybe." He shuddered, as if he were going to have to go into a lion's lair. "But I'll be alright now. The doctors said I'll probably be able to walk again in the Fall."

"The Fall?" I groaned. That seemed like a long time. He'd miss all of Spring and Summer walking.

"I was really lucky," he said. "I didn't lose a lot of blood, and it missed my spine. I was also wearing heavy clothing, so that probably helped they said."

I shuddered. I really didn't even want to think about it ever again.

"But I think—and I know you and Todd don't like this but—even though in my head I know it's not me that really killed Jason, I still find myself in that mindset. So much of the time. It's the price I pay every day. Just because of how I treated him the last time I actually saw him, all those years ago." He squeezed my hand. "I'm...going to miss you too." He paused, gathering himself. "You've really helped me a lot, Renee." Rory let out a gentle, low, and warm chuckle. It made him sound much older than sixteen.

We sat there serenely for a few moments. After a while, Rory slapped his hand on his head. "You never met Patches. My pug."

"You have a pug?"

"I...sort of found him. I think he was a stray. He's so loveable. I never thought that a person like Todd would like the little guy so much."

"Todd?"

"Yeah. He doesn't know this, but Gabriella showed me a couple pictures of him cuddling Patches." We both burst out laughing. For some reason, the thought of Todd doing that was hilarious. He was usually just so stone-cold serious most of the time. Even on Christmas Eve. "Don't tell him I said that. Might ruin his reputation or something."

"I promise," I said, "cross my heart." I started to laugh again, and pretty soon his laughter followed mine.

I suddenly realized there were tears in his eyes. "I know," he said in a steady voice, "that Jason doesn't hate me." I saw him open his hand, and there lay the little piece of paper in tiny writing: *I love you.* Rory smiled. "My mom's with me again. Todd doesn't hate me. Hell...Sidney, Jeremiah, and Sonny don't hate me." He ran a hand through his curtained hair and looked at me again, and I knew it pained him that he would be moving soon. Separating himself from yet more people, but starting over fresh. There was nothing but pure love and friendship in his eyes. And to think that when I first saw him, he was laughing at me while I coughed.

"Renee!" my dad yelled. "It's time for us to go!"

My dad had stepped out the door with Todd in tow. I looked around at all the windowed walls bordering the courtyard. It was the only reminder that we were at a hospital, rather than just some park somewhere.

Todd wheeled Rory out front while my dad and I walked alongside. When we got to the front steps, Rory beckoned me forward, giving me one last hug. "Call me," he whispered.

Dad and I got in the car. I turned back and saw Rory and Todd at the front of the hospital as we pulled out. I waved to Rory from the car, and he waved back at me, smiling. He snuggled up in his hoodie and the wind blew his black hair in his face. He became smaller and smaller until he was nothing but a dot, and then disappeared completely. I didn't know when I would see him again after this.

Author bio:

Molly Ferguson wrote and completed the first draft of *Ren and Rory*, her first novel, when she was in high school. She was inspired by one of her favorite books, *The Outsiders* by S.E. Hinton, as well as the general nostalgia of the decade of the nineties (as well as the eighties). She hopes to complete several more novels in the future. Molly has a B.A. in English from George Mason University, with a concentration in Creative Writing. She loves to spend her time helping out cats and other animals, practicing art, reading, working on her writing, going on walks, and hanging out with her friends. She lives in Virginia with her older sister, and her cat, Clover.